WHERE IS THE BABY?

Charlotte Vale-Allen

This first world edition published 2012
in Great Britain and in the USA by
SEVERN HOUSE PUBLISHERS LTD of
9–15 High Street, Sutton, Surrey, England, SM1 1DF.
Trade paperback edition first published
in Great Britain and the USA 2012 by
SEVERN HOUSE PUBLISHERS LTD.

British Library Cataloguing in Publication Data

Allen, Charlotte Vale, 1941-
  Where is the baby?
  1. Rehabilitation--Fiction. 2. Connecticut--Fiction.
  I. Title
  813.5'4-dc23

ISBN-13: 978-0-7278-8135-9 (cased)
ISBN-13: 978-1-84751-432-5 (trade paper)

All Severn House titles are printed on acid-free paper.

Severn House Publishers support The Forest Stewardship Council [FSC],
the leading international forest certification organisation. All our titles that
are printed on Greenpeace-approved FSC-certified paper carry the FSC logo.

Typeset by Palimpsest Book Production Ltd.,
Falkirk, Stirlingshire, Scotland.
Printed and bound in Great Britain by
MPG Books Ltd., Bodmin, Cornwall.

For Kim & Tim and
Bodhi & Sloane
the present & the future.

*This book was
inspired by
two true stories.*

PART ONE
1970

ONE

Before they went, Wolf took off the door- and window-handles while Toadman put the pill in her mouth, the way he always did, and told her to swallow it. As soon as they were gone – she listened hard until she couldn't hear their voices anymore – she spat out the pill and crushed it between her fingers, then shook the dust away. It left a bitter taste in her mouth and she found her bottle of Coca-Cola and drank some. Then she sat and waited.

After a minute or two, she noticed something. The windows were painted black on the inside, but there was a crack at the top of one window where a thin strip of light showed. She looked at that strip for a time, thinking. If she could find something to push in there, between the top of the window and the frame, she might be able to get the window open.

Down on her knees in the back of the van, she pushed through pizza boxes and empty bottles, sticky straws and old newspapers, crumpled-up take-out bags and smelly clothes, groping in the dark for anything hard and thin she could push into that slit.

Then, just when she was ready to give up, her fingers found something and, near it, another something. A plastic knife and fork. She put them over by the window and searched some more, running her hands over everything until she was at the bottom, feeling the thin, gritty carpet that covered the floor of the van – and there was nothing else. Guided by that strip of light, she moved back to the window and examined her tools.

Deciding to risk the fork first, she fit the handle end into the crack, pulled down very carefully and the crack got a bit bigger. Encouraged, she pulled down some more and the window moved a tiny bit farther before the fork snapped and the handle end fell outside. Disappointed, the bitter taste of the pill still in her mouth, she sat for a moment then tried to put one of her fingers into the slightly enlarged opening. Not big enough. She reached for the plastic knife.

Its handle was thicker than the fork's but if she broke the knife, too, she'd have nothing left to work with. So she'd have to be very careful because she was determined now to get the window open far enough for her to climb out. She put just the edge of the handle end into the opening and used both hands to pull the blade down. The opening got bigger! Not yet big enough for her fingers, but almost. She tried again, pushing the handle a little bit farther outside before pulling down gently but firmly. It worked! The opening was wider. Still not wide enough, but almost. *Almost.*

It was getting very hot. The only fresh air was coming in through the small gap at the top of the window and she got up close to it, hoping to feel cooler air. But the air outside was hot, too. She was starting to feel as if she needed to pee, and the heat was making her sleepy. If she fell asleep, she might never have another chance like this. They might come back at any second, a thought that made her heart beat faster. It had to be now. So she put the knife handle back into the opening and this time, using both hands, she pulled down as hard as she could. The knife snapped and the part she was holding cut her hand. But she'd done it! Her fingertips fit into the opening. She was going to get out! Her heart was beating even faster now, and a voice in her head was whispering, Hurry, *hurry!*

With both hands, she pulled down on the glass as hard as she could and it started moving. Her arms began to tremble from the effort and she had to rest. But now she could get her hands almost all the way out. They might be coming. She had to be quick. So, her eyes fixed on that widened band of daylight, she put her palms over the top of the window and pulled down again, and again, and again. And little by little the window lowered, until both her arms fit through.

Wolf and Toadman could be on their way back, so even though her hand was stinging from the cut and her arms were aching, she pulled on the window with all her strength. Then, resting for another moment, she looked out. Straight ahead were rows of cars, and to the left were empty parking spaces.

And with a burst of excitement she saw a big store on the far right. She went back to pulling on the glass, which had become slippery with sweat and smears of blood. She wasn't sleepy anymore, but she really needed to pee. When she got to that store, she'd go find a bathroom first thing. Then she'd find someone to help her.

Moving quickly, able now to see the whole ugly interior of the van, she found a T-shirt Toadman wore all the time. He loved that T-shirt. If Wolf even touched it, Toadman had a fit. She didn't care. She grabbed it, and draped it over the top of the glass, then tried pulling on the window again. This time, the glass came down far enough for her to get her head outside. A bit more and she'd be able to crawl through. It didn't matter whether or not she could reach the outside door handle because Wolf always locked the doors and checked them before he and Toadman went anywhere. So she needed enough space to be able to climb out. Just a little bit more . . .

At last, scared they'd appear any moment, she pushed her head and shoulders through the window. Wriggling back and forth and from side to side, she was able to get more and more of herself outside. Then, suddenly, when she was slightly more than halfway out, she realized there was nothing to hold onto and she was going to fall. She couldn't stop herself. She tipped upside down. Her foot caught briefly on the top of the window and then she fell, throwing her hands out to try to break her fall. She landed on the ground. It hurt. But she was out, in a heap on the hot pavement.

Her eyes on the store, breathing hard, she stood up and began to run between the rows of cars, making her way to the wide entrance where people were coming and going. Heart thudding, her cut hand burning, both hands and knees skinned from the fall and her foot starting to hurt from catching and twisting on the window, she hurried toward the doors. The heat was awful, the sun-glare stung her eyes and she had to keep blinking because everything was shimmery and hot.

She followed a woman and her two children through the doors, at once feeling wonderful cool air as she stopped and looked around. Lots of people. Any second Wolf and Toadman would see her and . . . No! She headed away from the entrance and moved between racks of clothing, came to an aisle and looked both ways, hoping to see signs for the toilets. They'd be at either side or at the back, so she kept moving, making her way toward the far end.

Finally, struggling to hold it in, she saw a woman poking at dresses on a rack, and went up to her.

'I need to pee.'

The woman turned slowly, her gaze moving from the top to the bottom of her in a way that made her feel bad. Then, making a face, the woman turned away.

An ache in her chest and the need getting worse and worse, she hurried on, making her way through the massive store.

At last, desperate, she approached an old woman who was holding a pair of socks in each hand and looking first at one pair, then at the other.

'Lady, I need to pee, please.'

The old woman's head lifted. She stared for several seconds with a look that was almost as bad as the first woman's, then she suddenly dropped the socks and shuffled away, without saying a single word.

'Shitshitshit!' The women were no help. They looked at her as if she was one of Toadman's smelly T-shirts with the horrible pictures. Arriving at the end of the aisle, she went up to a very dark man in a suit, who had a kind face, and said, 'Mister, I *really* need to pee, *please!*'

He looked at her for what seemed a long time and then said, 'Are you all alone?'

She nodded her head and he said, 'Wait a second, okay?' and called out across the aisle. 'Lillian, come on over here, would you, please?'

When Lillian came, he said, 'Take her to the ladies' room, will you, please?' He and Lillian exchanged a look, then she smiled and said, 'Sure. Come on, hon. I'll show you where it is.'

Lillian had bright red hair and very white skin with freckles; she smelled wonderful.

'You smell good, Miss.' All grown-up ladies were 'Miss.' That's what they were called on the cowboy shows Wolf liked to watch on the TV when they stayed sometimes in mow-tels.

'Thanks, hon.' Another smile, then, 'Here you go,' she said. 'I'll wait for you right here by the door.'

'Thank you, Miss.'

She barely made it to the toilet in time. It was as if she'd had gallons of Coca-Cola to drink.

When she came out, Lillian was where she'd said she'd be.

'Better?' she asked.

'Yes, thank you, Miss. I really had to go.'

'Good. I'm just gonna take you back over here. Okay?'

'Okay.' She went along, breathing in Lillian's flowery perfume, until they got to an office where the dark man was talking to another man in a suit.

'Everything okay?' the dark man asked Lillian

'Yes.'

'Thanks, Lillian. You can go on back to work now.'

'Bye, hon,' Lillian said.

'Thank you, Miss.'

'You're welcome, hon.'

'Why don't you sit down,' the man in the suit said, indicating a chair beside his desk. 'Did you come with someone?'

'Wolf and Toadman,' she answered warily, staying upright.

The two men glanced at each other.

'Is one of them your daddy?'

She just frowned.

'What's your name, dear?' the dark man asked her.

'Humaby,' she told him.

'Pardon?'

'Humaby,' she repeated.

'How old are you?' the suited man asked quietly.

She shrugged.

'You don't know?' he said.

She shrugged again.

'Wolf and Toadman,' he said slowly. 'Are they related to you?'

She shook her head, and shrugged again, and said, 'I don't know.'

'Do you know where you live?'

'I stay in the van,' she answered. 'But I got out. The baby's still there.'

'The baby?'

'They just got her. She's sleepin'. I'm ascared they're gonna hurt her.'

'I see,' the man in the suit said, then turned to the dark man. 'Good you made the call, Aaron.' To her, he said, 'Do you think Wolf and the other man are in the store?'

'Yeah. They said they had to get some stuff for the baby. But maybe they went back to the van already. I'll be in bad trouble if they did.'

Three policemen came into the office and stood staring at her. One of them said something under his breath. He looked very angry and she wondered if he was mad at her. Wolf and Toadman always said to stay away from policemen. She didn't know why.

'Would you go with these officers and see if you can find those men?'

'Okay.' She got up, saying, 'But it's a big place.'

One of the policemen took hold of her hand and said, 'It is, but let's go try to find them anyway, and get the baby. Okay?'

'Yeah, we gotta get her.'

To the man in the suit and the one called Aaron, the other policeman said, 'Make sure the service exits are covered by staff. We've got the front. And I'll cover the rear. If they're still in the store, they won't be going anywhere.'

'I spitted out the pill,' she told the one holding her hand.

'What pill?' he asked as they left the office and started through the store.

'Toadman puts a pill in my mouth and makes me eat it if they're goin' somewhere and they're gonna leave me. Tastes bad. I don't like it, so I started spitting them out. I can't amember how long since I beginned to spit them out. When they come back, I pretend to be asleepin', so they don't know I didn't eat it.'

'Good for you. That was smart.'

His shoes made a squeaky sound as they went up and down the aisles. She looked down at his feet, then turned to look back and saw two more policemen following them, looking around.

'I think they gived one to the baby.'

'The baby?'

'Unh-hunh.' She was asleepin' when I got out the window. They gonna be in trouble, Wolf and Toadman?' she asked, shaky and scared inside her chest.

'Maybe so,' the officer told her. 'Did they hurt you?'

She just looked at him, not knowing how to answer. After thinking for a moment, she said, 'I'm ascared they're gonna hurt the baby. She kicked and screamed a really lot so Toadman crunched up a pill and put it in her mouth, made her drink some Coke. She went asleep right away. When she woked up and screamed again, he gived her some more. She's just little,' she said. 'She cries and screams "mama." I tried to make her stop but she kept on. I holded her after he gived her the pill and she went asleep on me. She's only little.' She was amazed by how small the baby was, and she liked holding her, even when she was crying.

'What's your name?' he asked, and she told him. 'That's kind of a strange name,' he said, his eyes moving over the faces of customers who stood frozen, watching their progress.

'It's what they call me,' she said and looked around, liking the cool feel of the shiny floor on her bare feet.

'What do they call the baby?' he asked.

'Nothin'. I don't think she's got a name,' she said thoughtfully. 'They only just got her.'

'Got her?' His eyebrows pulled together.

'They tooked her. She was in a push thing outside.'

'A stroller?'

'I don't know what it's called. It was outside, so Toadman jumped out and tooked her up from the push thing. Then we drove away *really* fast.'

'When was this?'

'Maybe yestermornin'?' She tried to think how long the baby had been in the back of the van with her. One night, for sure. 'I don't amember,' she said.

They were in a part of the store that sold baby stuff. She saw high chairs and the push things. '*There they are!*' she whispered, tugging on the policeman's hand, and shifting quickly to hide behind him. If they were in the store, they weren't in the van. And if they weren't in the van, the baby was okay.

Toadman and Wolf were looking at something, arguing and Toadman was calling Wolf names, the way he always did. The policeman with her had stopped and turned to the pair behind him, tilting his head in the direction of the two men up ahead.

'Got it!' one of the officers murmured, as they went on to approach the arguing pair.

'I'm ascared,' she said, clutching the policeman's hand. 'They're gonna be so mad at me. It's bad when they get mad at me.'

'Don't be scared,' he told her. 'You're going to be all right now. I'll look after you.'

'Yeah?'

'That's a promise,' he said, his face all tight and angry, even though he smiled at her. 'Think you could show me that van and the baby?'

'Maybe. There's lots of cars out there.'

'Tell you what,' he said. 'We'll drive around and see if you see it. How would that be?'

'Drive around in a van?' she asked, pulling back a bit.

'No, no. It's a police cruiser.'

'Is that like a car?'

'Yup.'

'You won't lock me up, make me stay inside?'

'Nope. Let's go see if we can find the van and get the baby. Then I'll take you to a place where some nice folks will look after those cuts and scrapes and make sure you feel all right, while me and my buddies try to sort things out.'

'Okay.' She watched the two policemen put Wolf and Toadman's hands behind their backs, then put shiny silver things on their wrists. 'What's gonna happen to them?' she asked.

'That depends on a lot of things,' the officer told her. As they were passing down an aisle with towels and sheets, he took a big towel from a pile on a table and wrapped it around her. Then he picked her up and carried her towards the entrance.

The towel was soft, and feeling sleepy all at once, she put her head on his shoulder. 'What's your name, Mister?' she asked him.

'Brian,' he answered, his voice sounding funny. His arm held her secure as he took her through the store and outside into the heat to a blue and white car. 'This is the cruiser,' he explained. 'You're going to sit right up front with me while we see if we can find the van. Okay?'

'Okay.'

He set her down on the seat, then closed the door and went around to the driver's side. She looked at all the buttons and dials while he started the engine, hearing little voices coming from somewhere.

'What's that?' she asked, leaning forward.

'What's what?'

'It sounds like tiny little people talking inside here.' She put out a hand and touched the dashboard.

He laughed and said, 'That's the police radio. You're a sharp little cookie.'

'What's that mean, Mister Brian?'

'It means that you're very smart.'

'Oh!'

'I have a daughter about your age.'

'Yeah?'

'She's almost five and her name is Lucia.'

'That's a nice name. I never heard it before.' She looked out at the rows of cars. 'I think it's way at the back. When I looked out the window, there weren't any other cars close by. Do you think maybe I'm almost five, like your girl?' she asked.

'You might be a little more, or a little less.'

She gazed out the window, considering the information. 'Maybe that's how old I am. Nobody never told me. Oh look, Mister Brian!' she exclaimed. 'There it is! Over there!' She pointed to the far end of the lot. 'I see it!' she said excitedly, her pointing finger jabbing at the air. 'It's the one with all the black windows.'

'Good girl!' He picked up his microphone and spoke into it, saying he wanted some uniforms to check for a baby in the back and put in a call to DCF, and a tow to load up the van.

As he put the microphone down, he looked over at her, asking, 'How did you get out of there?'

'With a knife and fork.'

His eyebrows drawing together, he said, '*What?*'

As they parked across the way from the van, she explained to him how she'd got the window open.

'And that's how you hurt yourself?' he asked.

'I cutted my hand with the knife when it broke. And I hurted my foot 'cuz it got caught in the window when I climbed out. I fell down on my hands and knees. See!' She held her hands palm outwards to show him.

'And how did you get these?' he asked, indicating the insides of her elbows.

'Toadman does those with his cigrets when I'm bad. I got more, if you wanna see,' she offered, reaching to raise the bottom of Wolf's T-shirt to show him.

'No, that's all right.' He stopped her hand. '*Bastard!*' he whispered fiercely, his face going tight again.

'Toadman calls everybody bastard, 'specially when people piss him off. Did I piss you off?'

'Not one bit. You're doing great, and nobody's going to hurt you anymore. You're going to be looked after now.'

'Unh-hunh,' she said disbelievingly, looking at him thoughtfully, as if trying to make a decision. 'Mister Brian,' she said cautiously, 'I'm very hungry. Nobody gave me any food today 'cuz they said I was bad yesterday when I holded the baby until she went asleep. They telled me to put her down but I wouldn't. But I'll be good now. I promise.'

'I'll get you something to eat as soon as the officers get here for the baby.'

'Okay,' she said, gazing at the partially open window of the van. The baby. Even when she cried and screamed, it felt good holding her, especially when the baby was all heavy, asleep. She liked the baby better than anything, ever. But she didn't want Toadman and Wolf to hurt the baby . . . no cigrets or other bad stuff. She gave her head a little shake, thinking about that.

'What would you like to eat?' the officer asked, drawing her eyes back to him.

'A cheese burgler an' fries,' she said in a rush. 'An' a chocolate shake?'

'Whatever you want, honey. Anything at all.'

'Thank you very much, Mister Brian,' she said softly, keeping her eyes on the van, wondering if he'd get on top of her after he gave her the food.

TWO

On his way back from a quick trip to the men's room, Brian Kirlane heard one ER nurse telling another that she planned to give that revoltingly filthy child in cubicle two a bath before she was examined. Overhearing this, Brian marched over to the woman and said, 'Hey! You *do not touch* that kid! The chief wants photos and someone's on the way. So until the photographer gets here nobody goes *near* that little girl.' He paused to draw in an uneven breath – the anger was like some weird kind of animal, crawling around under his skin – then he said, 'You're *supposed* to *know* that. Is this your first day on the job or are you just generally clueless?'

'Well, excuse me all to hell!' the young woman snapped.

'There's a protocol,' he said, brimming with anger. 'Or did you wake up today and decide to ignore all the rules?'

'What's biting *your* ass?' the young woman shot back, her round flat face now red.

'Right now, it's you. You don't *ever* clean up a victim. It's SOP.' Insults crowded into his mouth and it took every bit of his self-control not to let them out. At that moment he wanted to annihilate her, rid the world of her.

'I was just about to tell her that,' the second nurse interjected quietly.

'Oh, screw you both! I don't need this shit!' The flat-faced nurse whirled around and flounced off. Brian watched her bustle away, then turned to look at the second woman.

'She's down from pedes 'cause we're short-staffed. There was no one on to handle the kid. I'll call up and get them to send somebody else. Sorry about that,' she said, reaching for the phone.

'She's an *idiot*,' Brian said, unwilling to let go of his anger. It was keeping his attention off more dangerous emotions roiling in his chest: violent feelings he'd never had before.

Altogether he felt barely in control, as if the smallest thing would send him over the edge.

'Let's bring it down to room temperature now. Okay, Officer? I wouldn't have let her get that far. So she's not the sharpest knife in the drawer, but cut her some slack. She's from another world. Upstairs, if they need it, the kids get washed on admit.' 'It's her goddamn attitude I can't take. Nobody can tell her anything. I wouldn't want her around a kid of mine, pedes or wherever.'

'Have to agree with you on that,' the nurse said, starting to dial. 'Wouldn't let her touch one of my kids either.'

Mollified somewhat but still in a temper he knew was unreasonable, Brian went back to the curtained-off cubicle. The young candy striper he'd asked to babysit while he was gone was staring disconsolately at the child on the gurney who sat, still wrapped in the beach towel he'd grabbed at the Kmart, grinding grimy fists into her eyes. For some reason the blackened soles of her little feet touched him terribly, almost as much as her greenish teeth that had obviously never encountered a toothbrush, and her dark, depthless eyes.

'You can go now,' he told the teenager. 'Thanks a lot.'

The girl at last lifted her eyes from the child, and said softly, 'You're welcome,' then hurried away, visibly relieved to be going.

'You okay, honey?' Brian asked.

'I'm sleepy, Mister Brian. Where's the baby?'

'Someone's coming to take pictures of you, and then the nurses will give you a bath before you see the doctor. After that, you'll be able to have a good, long sleep.'

'But where's the baby?'

'They're taking care of her. I think she'll be going home soon with her parents.'

'She wanted her mama. She cried for her all the time.'

'I'm sure she did.'

A pause, and then, 'What's a bath, Mister Brian?' she asked apprehensively.

Jesus! Brian thought. 'You'll get washed up nice and clean. The nurses will probably find something for you to wear, too, instead of that T-shirt.' She was naked under the stained oversized shirt, and she reeked. Obviously it had been a very long time since anyone had taken real care of her. Dirt circled her neck, was crusted in the bends of her arms and legs. She was filthy from top to bottom. The visual evidence of how neglected she was revived his anger, made his teeth clench. She yawned hugely, her whole body shuddering with it. 'Please, can I see the baby?' she asked, looking past him at the doorway. 'She liked me,' she said almost inaudibly. 'She letted me hold her.'

'I'll find out about that soon as I can. Meanwhile, you go ahead and rest until the photographer gets here. I can see you're very sleepy.'

'I won't get in trouble? Toadman gets mad if I go asleep when he didn't say I could.'

'You won't get in trouble. Just lie down. Go on now.' He reached for the cotton blanket on the shelf and unfolded it as she curled up on her side on the gurney. Covering her, he couldn't resist running a hand over her greasy chopped-off hair, noticing as he did that the roots were fair. The bastards had not only hacked off her hair, they'd been dying it dark – maybe to keep her from being recognized.

She lay gazing at him so intently that he found it unnerving. He gave her a smile he hoped was encouraging, and whispered, 'It's okay, honey. Sleep.'

'Okay, Mister Brian.' But her gaze remained on him.

'Sleep,' he whispered. 'It's okay. Just close your eyes.'

At last, as her eyes fluttered closed, he sat down on the one chair in the cubicle and breathed slowly and deeply, reluctant – as the candy striper had been, but no doubt for entirely different reasons – to take his eyes off her. Having given his promise to keep her safe, he had the arbitrary idea that if he looked away, even for a moment, she'd be back in harm's way. So he sat and watched her tuck her small soiled hands under her cheek and almost instantly fall asleep. He watched, promising himself he'd go check on the baby's status once the photographer arrived.

Stricken by her deplorable condition but filled with admiration for her ingenuity, he told himself that if her family couldn't be found, he'd tell DCF that he'd take her in. He couldn't imagine that he and Janet wouldn't qualify as foster parents. He knew Janet would be okay with it. When it came to kids, they were on the same wavelength. And Lucia would probably be thrilled to have a live-in playmate. Okay, it was a fantasy, but he hated the idea of this kid getting put into the system, maybe winding up in a situation as bad or even worse than the one she'd just escaped from. Granted there were some decent foster parents out there. But some of the people were pure scum, taking in kids just to get the monthly checks. Some of them did things that kept him up at night, sitting in the dark in the living room, trying to get the images out of his head and battling the urge to drink himself into oblivion.

His second month as a cop almost seven years earlier, he and Chuck took a call from one of the worst downtown areas. 'Anonymous female caller says there's a kid screaming at this address,' the dispatcher told them. 'Caller said there's always a kid screaming in there.' Brian remembered what they had found as if it was yesterday.

The battered and bloodied body of a skeletal seven-year-old on the front hall floor, limbs twisted in ways they were never meant to go. The skinny, ferret-faced, forty-something woman – whiskey voice and an aggrieved attitude – standing over the child, sucking on a cigarette, while Brian checked for a pulse he knew wasn't there.

'Clumsy kid fell down the goddamn stairs again,' the whiskey voice said conversationally.

With open disgust, Chuck looked at the woman, saying, 'Yeah, I can picture it. He fell. Sure. That's what happened. You didn't starve him or beat him or toss him down the fuckin' stairs. You didn't do any of that, no.' Without taking his eyes from her, he said, 'Bri, check see if there's anyone else in this shithole while I give the homicide boys a buzz.'

'What're you talking, homicide? What homicide? I told you. Goddamn kid fell. Was always falling, for chrissake.'

'Lady, you don't want me tossing you down the stairs, shut the fuck up and sit your ass over there where I can keep an eye on you.'

'You can't talk to me that way!'

'I am talking to you that way, you evil piece of shit. Sit the hell down there and shut your face!'

She sat as told on an armchair just inside the dark, crowded living room, glaring at him: close-set eyes, hate-filled shiny beads.

Upstairs, two more emaciated little boys in stinking underwear huddled together on the stained mattress in a tiny bedroom like a cell: no sheets, a torn blanket, peeling wallpaper, bare floor, some ratty, reeking clothes heaped on the floor. 'Two more up here,' Brian called down.

'I'll get DCF in!' Chuck called back. Moments later Brian could hear him on the phone.

Then, as Brian brought the gaunt, trembling pair down the stairs – maybe five or six years old – Chuck squeezed the cuffs on the woman's scrawny wrists, tight as they'd go. The smaller boy whispered, 'She killed Paulie. Always kickin' and punchin' him. Him screamin', beggin' her to stop but she wouldn't never, ever.'

The other boy suddenly shouted, 'I HOPE YOU GET BEAT AND BEAT AND DIE LIKE PAULIE! I HOPE THEY MAKE YOU DEAD!' Then he broke into noisy sobs. Two tiny, fleshless bodies shaking, hands clinging. Victims of an indoor atrocity.

Later, after two women from DCF wrapped the pair in blankets and took the kids away, after the body was removed, the homicide guys were doing the scene. Brian and Chuck were ready to transport her for booking, and the woman complained about the cuffs. 'Loosen these things! They're too goddamn tight!'

In a voice thick with feigned concern, Chuck said, 'Oh, poor you! Does that hurt?' and shoved her so hard her head smashed into the door frame. 'Ooops!' Grabbing her by the hair, pushing her head down, he tossed her into the back. 'Gotta be careful there, Missus, watch what you're doing. Next thing ya know, being so clumsy, you could fall down the stairs and hurt yourself.'

Sliding behind the wheel, in a low voice, Chuck said, 'Hate these evil fuckin' people, hate these fuckin' dead kid calls.'

Six months later, Chuck got himself promoted to a desk. 'Can't take the ugly anymore, Bri,' he said apologetically.

'Come see me now 'n' then, 'kay? Lemme know how you're doing.'
Brian kept handling the calls with his new partner, Hal. He couldn't have said why, until today when dispatch sent them to the Kmart to see this grimy tyke, with intelligence just shining off her, as if she was lit from inside. So much fear, yet such courage. And, underneath it all, whimsy.

So maybe the seven years had been preparation for today, for dealing with this little girl who belonged to some family that might come rushing to claim her. He sure as hell hoped so. But if not . . . if not . . .

Determined to handle the case with the greatest care, the chief put out a call to Connie Miller. With the advent of mandatory sensitivity training in the department some months earlier, she'd been called upon to do the photography for new cases with increasing regularity, primarily in instances of aggravated rape or assault involving young females or children and, only sometimes, adult women. As far as the department was concerned, her greatest asset was that no matter how traumatized the victim might be, Connie managed to get the shots. Her congenial kindness enabled her to deal with the subjects without adding to their pain. She'd even been known to make some of them laugh. How she did it was a source of wonder to the men in the department. The few women on the force understood her magic from the start.

Connie had inherited her mother's clear deep-set blue eyes and her father's wide nose and heavy jaw. She was less than five feet tall, a plain-looking woman – until she smiled and became lovely in a singularly compelling fashion. Her smile was like an unexpected gift, containing great heart and gentle humor. When she came to the ER to document their injuries on film, she treated every female with quiet respect. She took a moment to lift the hair away from a girl's eyes, or made funny, self-deprecating remarks – about the difficulty of buying size five shoes, or about her forays into children's departments to buy clothes, or about her mad mop of black curly hair. 'Imagine trying to persuade someone to cut this.' She'd smile and tug at a handful of glossy curls. 'About as easy as finding a sweater in the kids' department that doesn't have ABCs or teddy bears on it.'

Keeping up a constant, distracting patter in a low voice that had a melodic, slightly foreign cadence, she got the pictures taken before the subject had a chance to feel ashamed or embarrassed. Connie swept around the woman or child like a small whirlwind, chatting and clicking away, the speed-winder zizzing as she shot thirty-six exposures which, without exception, were sufficient. Finished, she'd tenderly wrap her subject in the hospital gown, or sheet or blanket – whatever the nursing staff had given them – and with an affectionate smile, or squeeze of the hand or pat on the arm, she'd say, 'You're just wonderful. Thank you so much for helping me.' Then she'd leave, go directly to the nearest rest room, close herself into a stall, and either throw up or weep. Minutes later, her emotions once more rigidly under control, she'd be headed to the police darkroom or to her studio to process the film.

She was preparing to go shoot a golden wedding anniversary cocktails-and-canapés bash when she got the call to photograph the Kmart child. Although she was habitually early for assignments, she took a couple of minutes to phone and let the hosts know she might be a little late. Then she grabbed her camera bag, threw in extra film, and went downstairs to the car. As she headed off to the hospital, gearing up for the coming encounter, she was reminding herself as always that she was doing her small part to help right a terrible wrong.

The only child of holocaust survivors, she'd grown up not only translating her parents' native Polish into English but also interpreting their fraught silences and sudden fear-filled starts. She'd spent countless hours of her childhood at the library, reading what survivors had written about their experiences, and studying large-format compilations of black-and-white photographs: heaps of bodies tossed into pits, warehouses filled with mountains of suitcases, bins brimming with jewelry or with hair. The worst images were of the hollow-eyed skeletons covered with skin, living corpses in the last stage of starvation: the Musselmen (a corruption of the German word for Moslem, *Musselmannen*, so-called because their weakness caused them to sway from side to side, or back and forth, giving the impression they were bowing in prayer), staring out from behind wire enclosures; cattle cars disgorging hundreds of terror-stricken men, women and children; ominous bathing rooms where poison gas, not water, emerged from the shower heads; the open doors of massive ovens where bones could be seen in the ashes. She studied the photographs obsessively. Then she returned home and used her expanding comprehension to deal with her parents who, in the early immigrant years, were fearful and uneasy, prepared to take flight at the merest hint of perceived danger: a car door slamming in the night, heavy footsteps on the stairs, voices in the hallway outside their apartment, unexpected knocking at their door. So many things aroused the sleeping fear.

With time, though their fear diminished, her mother and father almost never spoke of what they'd endured, and eventually Connie gave up asking. She knew that for them to speak of their time in hiding and then in the camp was to relive the horror in every minutely recalled detail. They could scarcely bear the scenes recreated during their sleeping hours that caused them to awaken abruptly, crying out, hearts pounding with dread in the night-time urban stillness.

Gradually, the effects of the past seeped beyond their consciousness to penetrate their daughter's, endowing her with a substantial measure of survivor's guilt that seemed only to be briefly assuaged by confronting modern horrors. So when a detective she'd dated for a time had asked if she'd come photograph a young rape victim, she had, after the briefest consideration, said she would. It was an excruciating experience, but strangely rewarding.

What she saw on the face of that first twelve-year-old was identical to what she'd seen in photographs from the camps: horror and disbelief combined with physical pain to round and glaze the eyes so that they stared inward at the violation, while simultaneously looking blankly outward, focusless, in shock. Her heart, her very being seem to expand in order to absorb and share the trauma, in some small way making it a little bit less by offering kindness and consideration as balm for the unseeable injuries.

Subsequently, Connie never refused the work, regardless of

prior commitments, because it became an ongoing repayment of a debt of gratitude for the lives of her parents and for her personal freedom, a continuing effort to be among the Righteous. But nothing she'd read or seen or experienced prepared her for the child asleep in the ER cubicle, watched over by a young cop she hadn't met before. Putting down her bag, she offered her hand, whispering, 'Hi, I'm Connie, the photographer.'

'Hi. I'm Brian Kirlane. You'll take it easy with her, huh?'

'Absolutely,' she assured him, studying the girl. 'I hate to wake her. But the sooner we get this done, the better. I'll just get set up while you do the honors.'

'Okay.'

The kid came awake with an alarmed jolt, shrinking away from Brian's hand. 'It's okay, okay,' he crooned, stroking her arm. 'This is Connie. She's going to take some pictures and then you'll have that bath I was telling you about.'

'You're so lucky,' Connie said with a smile. 'I'd love to have a bath right now. It would be so nice.'

Connie plugged in her flash attachment, then lifted the camera. At the sight of it, the child squatted on the gurney and spread her knees, a lurid smile transforming her face. Connie felt as if her lungs had been punctured and all the air rushed out, leaving her breathless.

His stomach lurching, Brian said, 'No, no. Don't do that, honey. You don't have to do that.' His hand on her shoulder brought her back to a sitting position. 'Connie isn't going to take those kind of pictures. Are you, Connie?'

'Oh, no!' Connie managed, her pulse thudding in her fingertips.

'I'll just wait outside,' Brian said, prepared to give the two some privacy.

'Can Mister Brian stay?' the child asked uncertainly, looking from one adult to the other.

'Sure, if you want him to.'

'I want him to.'

'Okay. I'll stay over here, out of your way.'

Without looking at him, Connie said, 'Thanks,' as she put her camera down on the end of the gurney. 'What we're going to do,' she told the girl, 'is take off this T-shirt' – she got it off in one deft move and let it fall to the floor – 'and if you'll just stand here' – she lifted the tiny, malnourished child to her feet on the gurney, then grabbed up the camera – 'I'm going to take a bunch of pictures really, really fast. You don't have to do a thing but stand there for me.' Moving in a circle, automatically dividing the girl into quadrants that required nine shots each from head to toe, especially capturing the insides of her elbows and the concave belly, all covered with circular burns of varying ages, she kept talking. 'You are going to love your bath,' she said, the flash strobing in the small cubicle. 'I bet they'll even let you have some Mister Bubbles. It's the best. You can make big soap bubbles if you do a circle with your thumb and forefinger, and then blow very carefully into the circle.'

Mesmerized, the child stood listening, blinking at the repeating flashes, her head turning to follow Connie's progress. Brian, too, was awed by the woman's balletic sweep around the child and lulled by her low, calming voice. In what seemed like only seconds, Connie was putting the camera down and wrapping the girl in the blanket.

Then, to the surprise of them all, Connie took the child into her arms and hugged her. Stiff as a sculpture, the girl didn't respond but sat, plainly enduring the embrace. Pierced by sorrow she refused to show, Connie released her as a pair of nurses came in, the more senior one cheerily asking, 'All done?'

'All done,' Connie told them, looking into the deep brown depths of the little girl's eyes. 'Thank you, sweetie,' she said softly.

Looking dazed, the girl said, 'I forgotted your name.'

'It's Connie. What's yours?'

'Humaby.'

Connie blinked slowly, then said, 'Well, I'm going to call you sweetie. Okay?'

'Okay.'

'You're going to have your bath now,' Connie said merrily. 'With Mister Bubbles, right?' She looked meaningfully over at the older nurse.

'Definitely! You ready, dearie?' the woman asked.

The child shrugged.

'Okey-dokey, then. Let's do it.' She scooped up the girl, who at once asked, 'Can Mister Brian come too?'

'I have to go back to work now,' Brian told her. 'But I'll come see you tonight, if you like.'

'Yeah?'

'Yeah,' he said, then impulsively added, 'Connie will come back, too. Won't you?'

'Yes,' she said, her voice even lower than usual. 'I'll come back.'

The child said, 'Okay,' and the two nurses went off with her.

'I shouldn't have done that,' Brian said, 'volunteering you to visit. I was way out of line.'

'No,' Connie said slowly, at last taking a good look at the man. He was perfectly beautiful, with Nordic blond-white hair, dark blue eyes and features so flawless in their symmetry that his emotional availability was a bit shocking. In Connie's experience, beautiful people rarely had any emotional depth or a significant interest in anyone but themselves. 'I'm glad you did it.' She glanced at the time, then said, 'I've got to shoot a big party downtown. But I'll come back when it's over, bring her some treats. I'm glad you did that,' she repeated. 'I have to go have a little breakdown now, Brian.' She held out her hand. 'You want to take her home, too, don't you?'

He nodded. Then, as if there'd been a time delay, said, 'You, too?'

'Never wanted anything more in my life. Maybe I'll see you later.' She slung the camera bag over her shoulder and headed briskly away.

Standing alone in the cubicle, Brian battled a very childlike desire to break into tears. His brain felt big and hot and swollen inside his skull as if it had been boiled. He couldn't seem to move or think, stuck in place, staring at the grubby T-shirt on the floor. At last, taking a deep breath, he routinely patted his walkie, his cuffs and holster, straightened his shoulders and headed out to the cruiser.

THREE

The ladies in the white dresses worried her because they talked to each other but not to her. When Toadman and Wolf did that, bad things usually happened. So maybe a bad thing would happen now, even though Mister Brian and Miss Connie said she was lucky to have a bath. Maybe that was a lie. Big people lied all the time, saying one thing would happen and then something else happened instead.

The room they took her to was all white and the older lady held on to her while the other one started running water into what looked like a big sink. She'd seen those before, when Wolf took her to places where men would lay down on top of her. She remembered a few times when the men said Wolf had to clean her up or they wouldn't touch her. Then Wolf took her into the room that had that kind of big sink and also a little one, and he'd get a cloth and water from the little sink and scrub her bottom, hard so it hurt, then leave her with the men. When he came back, the men would always give him money. Then he'd say she did good, and he'd come back to the van with a burgler and fries for her.

'Don't forget the Mister Bubbles, Liz,' the old lady said to the young one, but smiling at Humaby.

She watched as the one called Liz picked up a bottle and squeezed it over the water.

'Lots of bubbles for you,' the young one said, smiling, too, as she put the bottle down. 'Don't be scared,' she said, her smile going away. 'It's nice. You'll like it.' She looked at Humaby for several moments, then her face went funny and she said, 'Ruth, I need a break. I'll be back in a minute,' and she ran out and closed the door.

The old lady jiggled her up and down on her lap while the water ran and ran. At last, Humaby tapped on the woman's arm and said, 'Please, Miss. I'm getting dizzy.'

'Oh, sorry, dearie.' She stopped the jiggling. 'I wasn't

thinking. I'm just going to sit you down here for one little minute while I turn off the water. Okay?'

'Okay.' Even though it was hot in the room, her teeth were chattering and she tried hard to make them stop, but she couldn't. Wolf and Toadman got mad if she showed she was scared. Toadman would say, 'I'll give you something to be scared about, if you don't stop that shit!' So she tried never to let anybody see when she was scared.

'There's nothing to be afraid of, honestly,' the old lady said. 'I'm going to lift you into the tub now.'

When her feet touched the water, she couldn't help herself. She shrieked. Then, instantly, she was afraid, her heart jumping fast.

At once, the old lady lifted her out. 'Too hot?' she asked.

'Don't like hot! Please, Miss!'

'Okay, dearie. I'll make it cooler.' The lady ran some more water, then said, 'Let's try it again.'

Humaby shook her head, but the lady said, 'You have my promise. I will *not* hurt you.' She looked right into Humaby's eyes. 'Please believe me. I would never, ever hurt a child. I have three of my own. I'd kill anybody who touched a hair on their heads.'

Maybe it was true, 'cuz when Wolf or Toadman lied they never looked at her, especially not in the eyes. ''Kay,' she said.

The old lady put her slowly, slowly into the water, then let her sit there for a while to get used to it. With an encouraging smile, the lady scooped up some bubbles and held them out on her hand, saying, 'Blow!'

Obediently, she blew, and the bubbles floated away. It made no sense.

'I'm going to wash you now,' the lady said, taking a white cloth and putting soap on it. 'Will you stand up for me?'

Humaby stood up, and the lady started to wash her bottom.

'Hurts, Miss!'

'It does?'

'Burns.'

'Oh, dear. I'll be extra careful, but we really need to get you clean. I'm sorry, dearie. Almost done, just another moment.' She kept going while Humaby chewed hard on her lower lip, then said,

'Good girl. We're all done with that part. You can sit down now.' After that, the lady scrubbed at her feet and in between her toes, then cleaned each leg. It felt all right. The heat was making her sleepy, and she could hardly keep her eyes open as first one arm and then the other got washed. Then her neck and inside her ears, down her back and, finally, the lady said, 'Close your eyes now, dearie,' and her face got washed. It did feel nice, although her bottom burned and burned.

'Now I'm going to wash your hair,' the lady told her. 'Just lean back against my arm. That's right. Good.' She put nice-smelling soap on Humaby's head, then rubbed her hair. With a big cup she washed off the soap then poured on some more and rubbed again. She hummed music while she did it, then said, 'One more rinse and we're all done,' and used the big cup to wash off the soap again.

The other lady came back then and held out a towel that she wrapped around Humaby when the older lady lifted her out of the water.

'Doesn't that feel better?' the young one said.

'Burns a lot, Miss,' Humaby told her. 'I'm sorry.'

'Don't be sorry, dearie. It's not your fault. The doctor will give you something to make it feel better,' the old one said, as the dirty water went glugging and whooshing away. 'She's a mess,' she whispered to the young one as she dried her hands on a towel, then said, 'Be right back,' and went away.

After she was dry, the young one put a kind of dress on her and tied it up in the back.

'That wasn't so awful, was it?' the young one asked her.

Humaby shrugged. Her skin felt funny and her head did, too, as if something big and heavy had been taken away. She breathed in deeply, then said, 'I smell good.'

'Yes, you do!' the young one said happily. 'You smell wonderful! And you look very pretty, too. Want to see?' She held her up in front of a mirror.

Humaby blinked, trying to understand what she saw. 'That's me?' She pointed.

'That's you!'

'That's *me*,' she repeated, frowning as she took in the details of the picture. 'I never saw me before. And I'm a girl?'

'Yes, you're a girl.'

'They said I was a boy sometimes. I don't know. The baby is a girl.'

'Ah, God,' the young one said sadly, and held Humaby so tightly she could hardly breathe.

Feeling the child squirming, the nurse eased her grip, and said, 'I'm going to cut your fingernails and toenails, then brush your teeth before I take you to see the doctor.'

'And then can I sleep, Miss?'

'After you see the doctor, you can sleep.'

She took each of Humaby's hands and snipped the nails on each, then did the same thing to all of her toes. After that, she got Humaby to stand on a stool in front of the sink and used a little brush with minty goo to scrub inside her mouth.

'Isn't that better?'

'Yes, Miss.'

The old lady came back, and said, 'This is for you, dearie,' and held out a fuzzy thing.

'What is it?'

'It's a teddy bear.'

'What's it for, Miss?'

'It's a toy. He's a very soft teddy. Would you like to hold him?'

'Why?'

'Because he feels nice.'

She could tell the lady wanted her to, so Humaby accepted the bear and looked it over, puzzled, as the nurses took her to a room where there was another table with wheels, lots of shiny metal things, bright lights that hurt her eyes, and a lady in a white coat with a funny thing around her neck. It was the scariest place yet and Mister Brian and Miss Connie had gone away, so she closed her eyes very tightly, the way she did when Wolf and Toadman took her to the rooms with men, and she didn't make a sound.

Brian was so distracted, so angry he could barely get through the rest of his shift which, mercifully, consisted of starting the paperwork for the file they'd opened on the child. He was hyper-aware that the two goons were being questioned separately just fifty or sixty feet away, and all he could think about was crashing into each of the interview rooms in turn and shooting first one of the sick bastards, then the other. He could see himself doing it, could feel the satisfaction it would give him. When he thought beyond that to the resulting life sentence he'd get, which would end his family life and, very likely, his own, he knew there wasn't a thing he could do. That didn't stop his revenge fantasy, though. It kept cycling through his brain like an annoying tune.

Without looking up from his labored poking at the keys as he dealt with his share of the reports, Hal said, 'I know where your head's at, buddy, and you need to get it together. Those two are going *a-way* for a hundred lifetimes. ''Course, bein' pervs, they'll be lucky to survive a week inside – cons loving child molesters the way they do – which won't break anybody's heart. Just do your job, man, and stop picturing yourself takin' them out. Mother Justice is gonna take care of those two sick fucks.'

'Hope you're right,' Brian said, wanting to take something, anything – a pill, a rye and ginger, a voodoo potion – that would untie the knot in his gut.

When he finally got home, his relief and the surge of emotion he felt at the sight of his wife and daughter made him tearful again. Twice in one day. Maybe he was starting to lose it, and it was time to do a Chuck, take the sergeant's exam and ride a promotion indoors to a desk.

'What's the matter?' Janet asked after Lucia had been put to bed. He was a sensitive guy, which was why she adored him, but she'd never seen him in such a state. Then, suddenly, the dots connected and she said, 'Were you and Hal the responding unit at the Kmart today?'

'Yeah. It was—' He shook his head and then it came out in a rush. 'In all my time on the force, I've never . . . That little girl, Jan. Maybe six years old, tops. I asked her, "What's your name?" and she said, "Humaby." I'm so damn dense, I didn't get it. I just thought it was some kind of foreign name. Hal had to clue me in later. Those two evil pervs called her Hump Baby.'

'God!' Janet's expression perfectly matched his feelings.

She was a civilian worker in dispatch and had heard a lot of rotten stuff in her time at the job, but this was horrific. She thought of Lucia, asleep upstairs, thought of anyone harming her, selling her body to grown men, and at once had to push it away – a mother's worst nightmare.

'I promised her I'd go back to see her tonight, Jan. She's all alone and probably scared, even though she does a good job of hiding how she's feeling. I mean, God knows how long she was kept in that van. Her teeth have never been brushed and she didn't even know what a bath is. You don't mind, do you?'

'Be serious, Bri. Of course I don't mind.' She looked at her watch, and said, 'You should probably head out or she'll be asleep. Wait one, okay?'

'Sure.' He watched her take the stairs two at a time, loving the fact that she talked the talk. Stupid maybe, but he felt closer to her because of it – as if she was one of them, another cop. In more ways than one, she was. And in other, deeply important ways, she wasn't. He'd managed to find someone who was a perfect fit.

She came back with a floppy rabbit that had been a gift from one of her aunts, but Lucia never played with it. 'Take her this, Bri. It's only going to sit here on the shelf until we give it to the Goodwill or something.'

'Jan, I was thinking. If they can't find her family—'

'We should offer to take her.'

'God, I hoped you'd say that!' he said fervently. 'She's so . . . it's . . .'

'I understand. Get going now.'

She'd been put in a private room, with a rookie who looked about twelve sitting guard in the hall. His chair tilted back against the wall, he was reading an old *Newsweek*. Brian said hi and badged him, then paused in the doorway.

Propped up by a couple of pillows, lit from above by the bed lamp, the child was alternately gazing at the wall-mounted TV that was tuned to *Let's Make a Deal*, of all things, and turning a teddy bear this way and that, as if she couldn't figure out what it was.

Now that she'd been cleaned up and her injuries bandaged,

aside from the chopped-off hair that was half a dozen different lengths and far lighter in color after being washed, she looked like an ordinary kid, maybe here to have her tonsils out – something minor like that. Yet she was about as far removed from ordinary as it was possible to get.

Finding a smile, he walked into the room, saying, 'Hiya, honey. How're you doing?'

'Mister Brian!' she said, her thoughtful expression brightening. 'You comed back.'

'I said I would. D'you mind if I turn off the TV?' he asked, reaching for the remote.

'Okay,' she said. 'I don't like it.'

'This is kind of a silly show for grown-ups, but there are some terrific TV shows for kids, like *Sesame Street* and *The Electric Company, Mister Rogers*. Those're good, but they're not on at this time of day. So what've you got there?'

'The old lady said it's a teddy bear.'

'That's what it is, all right.'

'I don't know what to do with it.'

He pulled over a chair and sat down. 'It's like a friend, kind of; something you can keep with you. I brought you this guy,' he said, giving her the floppy rabbit.

'Thank you, Mister Brian,' she said politely. 'What is it?'

'It's a bunny rabbit.'

'Another friend?'

'Yup.'

She placed it on her lap next to the teddy bear. 'They're different.'

'Right. One's a bear, the other one's a rabbit. Bears and rabbits are animals.'

'Like dogs and cats?'

'Yup. There are all different kinds of animals.'

'Oh!'

Watching her soberly study the toys, he realized he'd yet to see her smile or hear her laugh. Things that were everyday to Lucia were completely unknown to this kid. 'The thing about stuffed toys,' he elaborated, 'is they make you feel good when you hold them. They don't *do* or *mean* anything. They're just cute and soft and nice to hold.'

'I never had one before.'

'You'll probably be getting lots of them.'

'Why?'

He bit back the comment he was going to make about her family. There was no guarantee they'd be found. Instead, he said, 'Because you did something important today. You saved the baby.'

'I did?'

'You sure did. Lots of people, not just the parents, are very happy about that and want to do nice things for you. When people want to do nice things for a child they usually give you toys and stuff. Because most kids like those things.'

She nodded thoughtfully and went back to inspecting the rabbit and teddy bear. Taking advantage of her distraction, he walked to the foot of the bed to have a look at her chart. He started reading it, but had to stop and sit down with it, taking deep, measured breaths for a minute before he was able to continue.

Poor kid had suspected gonorrhea everywhere, including the throat, suspected trichomoniasis (whatever that was), seriously damaged and/or perforated internal organs that warranted surgery. She'd been prescribed a whole list of drugs and ointments. Surgery would be scheduled pending results of blood work, and a psych consult had been recommended for the next day. Feeling queasy, he got up, put the chart back – her eyes now tracking him – then resumed his seat.

'You look diff'rent, Mister Brian.'

'Yeah, I changed out of my uniform when I went home.'

'Oh! Did you see Lucia?'

He had to smile. 'Yeah, me and her mom gave her a bath and put her to bed before I came over.'

'I had a bath.'

'I can see that.'

'The white lady put bubbles in her hand and told me to blow them. Why did she do that?'

'Most people like bubbles. I guess 'cause they're pretty. What'd you have for dinner?' he asked, then saw by her blank look that this was another word she didn't know, so he rephrased. 'What did they give you to eat?'

Her hands holding the bear and rabbit steady on her lap, she said, 'Things I didn't never have before. One of the white ladies—'

'Do you mean the nurses, honey?'

'That's what you call them? The ladies with the white dresses?'

'Yup.'

'Oh! Okay. One of the nurse ladies said it was smashed toes and middle oaf and grinbins.'

He burst out laughing, and for the first time he saw a hint of a smile curl the corners of her mouth.

'What's funny, Mister Brian?'

He leaned closer to her and, enunciating with care, said, 'You had mashed potatoes, meat loaf and green beans.'

'I was funny, what I said, wasn't I?'

'Yeah, you were, but in a good way. Did you have anything else?'

'Yeah.' She paused, that hinting smile returning. 'Cusperd.'

He laughed again, then corrected her. 'Custard.'

'It was shit!' She made a face. 'Do I have to have that all the time?'

Forcing himself not to laugh again, he said, 'I doubt it. Listen, honey, little children aren't supposed to say words like "shit."'

Sober at once, shrinking back a bit, she said, 'I'm sorry. I'll be good. I'm sorry.'

'No, no. It's okay, it's okay. Nobody around here's going to get mad at you for making mistakes or for not knowing what things are. You're a smart girl and you'll learn lots of new things.'

'Like what?'

'Well, let's see. How to read and to write, and about games and toys. Lots of things.' How to have fun, he thought. How to stop being so afraid, how to laugh out loud. Maybe how to cry, too.

'Wolf and Toadman read paper books with pictures.'

'I think you mean magazines. Those're bigger and thinner than books and usually have pictures.'

'Yeah, magozeens. Pictures are like what Miss Connie did, right?'

'In a way. There are all different kinds of magazines. Some are called fashion magazines and usually women and girls like those. Men and boys usually like the ones that have cars and boats and hobbies, stuff like that.'

'And nekkid fuck pictures.'

'Those are not good pictures,' he said carefully, shocked. 'And that's another word little children aren't supposed to say.'

'Fuck?'

'Yeah. That's not a good word at all, honey.'

'I won't say it anymore, Mister Brian.'

'Good girl.' He noticed that her hand was now tightly clutching the stuffed rabbit and worry had put a crease between her brows. 'You'll learn which words are good and which ones are not all right.'

'Okay,' she said with apparent doubt.

'You're gonna do fine. You're a smart girl, like I said.'

'Mister Brian, when'm I gonna see the baby?'

'Maybe tomorrow. I know the parents want to meet you.'

'Why?'

'Because you rescued their baby, honey. They want to thank you.'

'I really want to see the baby . . . Maybe she misses me . . .'

It was killing him. He had no idea what to say, no idea if she'd get to see the baby. As he was fumbling for some kind of answer, a young nurse came in carrying a small tray with a paper cup of water, a saucer, a tiny cupful of meds, two spoons and a piece of banana.

'Time for your medicine, kiddo,' she announced. Setting the tray on the bedside table, she said, 'I know you don't like the pills, so I'm going to smoosh 'em up with some banana. Okay?'

''Kay.'

'I should go now,' Brian said. 'It's past your bedtime.'

'No, it isn't, Mister Brian.'

'Yeah, honey. I think it is.'

'What's gonna happen to me?' she asked, grabbing hold of his sleeve.

'The doctors and nurses are going to make you better while we try to find your family.'

'Toadman and Wolf said *they* was my family.'

'I don't believe that's true. But if it is, then we'll find you a nice *new* family, a better one.'

'How long do I have to stay here?'

'I honestly don't know.' He looked at the nurse, who was mashing up several tablets. 'As long as it takes to make you healthy.'

'Will you come see me again, please, Mister Brian?'

'Yes, I will.' He stroked the back of her hand, then eased his sleeve free from her grip. 'That's a promise. Have a good sleep, honey, and I'll see you soon.'

'Okay, now,' the young nurse said, drawing the child's eyes to her and giving Brian a chance to slip out of the room. 'You won't taste this at all.'

'It won't be bitter?'

'Nope. Bananas are yummy.'

The child was asking, 'What's that mean, yummy?' as Brian went out the door.

FOUR

During her drive to the hotel, Connie had an idea. Upon arriving, she made a quick call from the house phone in the lobby, explained what she wanted, then left money with the doorman to pay for the package. Throughout the anniversary party she was so anxious to get back to the hospital it was all she could do to focus on the job. As a result, she knew she'd have a hard time finding enough good shots to satisfy the client if she didn't shoot a couple of extra rolls. Finished at last, she collected her package from the doorman, gave him a good tip, then hurried out to the car.

It was almost nine when she got to the hospital and made her way to the pediatric floor. As the elevator heaved its way upward, in the unconscionably slow fashion typical of hospital elevators, she again reviewed her time with Officer Kirlane and the little girl in the ER. She knew without question that he had returned to see the child. He was a man of his word, a good man.

She showed her ID to the policeman on duty in the hall, who looked like a high school student not old enough for the job. 'I won't wake her if she's asleep, but I promised her I'd come back.'

'Sure, no problem. Officer Kirlane told me you might be coming. Go on in,' he said, returning his attention to a tattered copy of *National Geographic* he'd found in one of the waiting rooms. It was all he could do to stay awake and he was counting down the hours until his replacement came on at midnight.

Connie saw that the staff had had the wits to leave a night light burning, and as she approached the bed she saw that the child was curled up facing the door, wide awake.

Slipping into the chair next to the bed, Connie said, 'Hi, sweetie.'

'I thought you wasn't coming, Miss Connie.'

'If I say I'm going to do something, I always do it. Okay?'

'Okay.'

'I thought you'd be asleep by now.'

'I don't like it here. Too many strange noises, and it's so big in here.'

'It is a pretty big room,' Connie agreed, looking around the room that was barely large enough to contain the bed, chair and bedside stand.

'You smell like cigrets, Miss Connie.'

'I was at a party, taking pictures. A lot of people were smoking. The smoke got into my clothes and my hair. I'm sorry.'

'You don't smoke cigrets, Miss Connie?'

'Now and then I'll have one but, no, not really.'

'You drink beer?'

'God, no! It's disgusting,' Connie said truthfully. 'It tastes like a mistake, as if they meant to make something else but got it wrong.'

'That's funny,' the child said, without the trace of a smile.

'I have an idea,' Connie said, opening the package. 'Why don't I read to you until you fall asleep?'

'Read what?'

'A story. I brought some story books for you. This' – she held up an oversized volume – 'was one of my favorite books when I was little. It's called *The Stories of Beatrix Potter*. Since you have a bunny there, I thought we'd do *The Tale of Peter Rabbit*. Would you like me to read to you?'

'Okay.'

Connie turned on the bedside light and pulled it over toward her, positioning it so the light didn't fall into the child's eyes. 'I'll show you the pictures when I come to them,' she said, then began. '"Once upon a time . . ."'

'Rabbits have names, Miss Connie?' Humaby asked after a minute or so.

'Well, some children give their toys names. But these are pretend rabbits. The lady who wrote the stories and painted the pictures gave all the animals names. These are very special stories, from a long, long time ago.'

Confused, Humaby said, 'Oh. Okay.'

Connie continued reading.

'The rabbits live in trees and they talk?' Humaby asked after another minute.

Connie smiled. 'Only in stories. In stories, anything can happen. This one is about a mother and her children who happen to be rabbits.'

'So in stories animals pretend to be people?'

'In a way,' Connie answered. 'It's about pretending, really. Shall I continue reading?'

'Okay.'

'Are you sure? I don't want to make you too confused.'

'I've never heard a story before, but I think I like it.'

'All right. I'll go on.' She paused a moment, then picked up where she'd left off.

Captivated, the child listened intently, now and then lifting her bunny to take a closer look at it, as if expecting it to start moving or speaking. She managed to stay awake to the end of the story, her eyelids at last slowly closing.

Moving quietly, Connie turned off the light. Leaving the three books she'd brought on the bedside table, she tenderly adjusted the covers over the girl, then tiptoed away.

Driving home, she felt better.

When Humaby awakened in the morning she didn't know where she was. She had to look around, remembering all the things that had happened. Sitting up, she rubbed at the bandages on the insides of her elbows. She was itchy underneath, and itchy under the bandage on her stomach, too. Her bottom still hurt but not as badly as before.

A new white lady – a nurse – came in, saw her, and said, 'Don't do that, cupcake. If you're itchy, it means you're healing, you're getting better.' She put a glass stick in Humaby's mouth, then held her wrist and looked out the window for a while. Then she said, 'Good,' and took the glass stick and looked at it, before writing something down. 'Hungry?' she asked with a smile.

'Yes, Miss.'

'Need to use the potty?'

'What's a potty?

'The toilet. Do you need to go?'

'Yes, please, Miss.'

The nurse lifted her down off the high bed, then took her by the hand to a room by the door that had a toilet and a sink and behind a curtain was a standing-up place for washing in.

'Can you manage by yourself?'

'Yes, Miss.'

'Good. If you have any trouble, just pull this string. Okay?'

'What'll happen if I do that?'

'One of us will come back and help you.'

'Oh!'

After helping Humaby back into the bed, the nurse went away. Right after that a blue lady came with food on a tray and left it on the table with wheels that fit all the way across the bed. Humaby was hungry but nobody said she could touch the tray, so she sat and waited for someone to come say she could eat. She waited a very long time, her stomach making noises.

When the nurse came back, she said, 'I thought you were hungry.'

'I am, but nobody said I could eat.'

'Oh, cupcake, you don't need permission. It's probably cold now.' She lifted the lid off the plate with a sad look on her face.

'That's okay. I can eat cold.' Humaby picked up the spoon and started eating the scrambled eggs and toast.

The nurse leaned against the window sill, watching for a while, then she said, 'We're going to find you some clothes to wear, and maybe fix your hair, cut it some so it looks better. How would that be?'

'Cut with a razor?' Humaby asked worriedly.

'Scissors,' the nurse said. 'Do you know what they are?'

Humaby shook her head.

'Scissors are a tool. We use them to cut all kinds of things, not just hair. Paper and cloth, lots of things.'

'They don't hurt?'

'Not at all.'

'Okay.' Humaby put down the spoon, picked up the glass of apple juice with both hands, tasted the juice, then drank it all. 'What's this?' she asked, touching the bowl on the tray with the tip of her finger.

'Oatmeal cereal.' Pushing away from the window, the nurse sprinkled some sugar in the bowl, opened the milk container and poured it into the bowl too. 'It's good. Try it.'

Humaby took a bite, chewed experimentally, and decided she liked it.

'Told you it was good,' the nurse said, as Humaby began spooning the cereal into her mouth. 'I'll be back in a couple of minutes. Eat as much as you like.'

''Kay,' Humaby said, around a mouthful of soft sweet oatmeal.

When the nurse came back, she taught Humaby how to brush her teeth, watching with interest as Humaby switched the brush to her left hand. Then the nurse washed Humaby's face and hands, being careful of the hand with the bandaged cut, and dried her with a towel, saying, 'It's still early. Want to watch TV for a while?'

Remembering what Mr Brian had told her, Humaby said, '*Sesame Street, 'Lectric Company, Mister Rogers*?'

'Those shows don't come on until later. How about some cartoons?

Humaby shrugged. 'What's a ka-toon?'

The nurse turned on the set, then used a little black thing to go through the channels until she stopped, and said, 'This is a cartoon.'

A skinny rabbit was chewing on an orange stick and talking to a little man with no hair. It didn't make sense. But the nurse seemed happy, so Humaby sat with the bear and the bunny on her lap and watched intently, trying to figure out what was going on.

Everything felt strange: the underwear, the dress, the shoes and socks, even her hair, which she kept touching. It was very short and when the nurse put her in front of the mirror, saying, 'See! You look great!' Humaby thought maybe she was a boy-girl after all, because her hair looked the same as the hair on all the men she'd ever seen.

Her feet felt as if they'd been put in narrow little packages and tied up tight. And even though the nurses said the dress was pretty, and she said, 'Thank you,' so they wouldn't be mad, it felt stiff and uncomfortable. She'd never had on so many things at one time and she couldn't move right. All the bandaged parts of her were itching and she wanted to rub them but was afraid the nurse ladies would get mad. So she kept her fingers curled into her palms and tried not to think about it.

After a long, long time sitting in the chair by the bed, trying to watch the cartoons but not liking them, an old lady who had on regular clothes came and said, 'Come with me, dear,' and held out her hand. Not knowing what else to do, and afraid, Humaby took the lady's hand and they started walking. The dress and the shoes made noise and the underpants felt funny on her bottom.

They went down a big long hall that had lots of doors – some open, some closed. Voices came out of the ceiling, white ladies and men in white coats were hurrying here and there, and sad people were crying in the hallway. She'd never seen big people cry before and kept looking back at them.

They walked far and her feet hurt from the shoes. At the end of the hall, the lady pushed open some big doors and they were in another hallway. There were no more voices coming from the ceiling here, and lots more doors, but a different kind. At last, the lady opened one of the doors and said, 'Here we are,' and took her inside.

There was carpet on the floor, little tiny chairs and tables, and a big bright red wooden box of toys. 'Just wait here now,' the lady said. 'The doctor will be in shortly,' and she went away, closing the door.

Really scared now, Humaby studied the little chairs for a time, then turned and looked at the great big mirror on the wall where she could see a picture of herself like the one in the room with the bed where she slept. She walked over and pointed. The mirror-girl pointed back. 'That's me,' she said and the mirror-girl said it, too. Forgetting, she scratched at the bandage on her arm. So did the mirror-girl. She wasn't supposed to do that. 'Not s'posed to scratch,' she told the mirror-girl. And they both stopped.

The dress had a great big bottom. If she held each side of it in her hands she could lift it way up. Like wings. Birds had wings. Wolf told her that one time, not even getting pissed off the way he usually did when she asked questions. 'Those're birds. They can fly 'cuz they got wings. The wings flap up 'n' down and that's how they get up in the air and zoom around.'

'Maybe I'm a bird-girl,' she told the mirror. 'I got wings. You do, too.' She lifted the sides of the dress one more time, then let them drop and looked around again, wondering what this place was. She'd never seen a room like this before, or tiny chairs and tables. She went back to the middle of the room, curled her fingers into her palms so she wouldn't scratch, and waited, looking down at the horrible shoes. Brown with a strap and a buckle. Too tight. She wriggled her toes but they were trapped and hardly moved at all. She sniffed several times. She could still smell the hair soap. She kept sniffing. The nice way she smelled kept her from getting really scared. She looked around the room, wondering if maybe today she was going to see the baby.

Behind the two-way mirror were Brian and his captain, Jim Garvey; Dr Stefan Lazarus, the surprisingly young-looking child psychiatrist who'd been brought in by Margery Briggs, the rigid, unfriendly social worker from DCF, and two cameramen. One film was for the department, the other was for Dr Lazarus. This child's case was so unique that both the police and Dr Lazarus wanted the interview documented. The police believed it would have evidentiary value. Lazarus thought the film would allow him to pick up later on things he might not notice in the course of the interview.

He was anxious to take advantage of such a unique opportunity. Very few abducted children ever came under therapeutic scrutiny and he considered himself highly fortunate to have an opportunity to meet a stolen child.

Watching the girl, he felt very confident and was making mental notes, already working up his evaluation: dissociation, if her interaction with her mirror image was anything to go by, a level of fear that was off the charts, and yet a certain whimsy in her play with the skirt and her talk of wings. He thought this was going to be a relatively simple summation with some interesting particulars which, with luck, could find its way into one of the journals. He didn't foresee any problems evaluating her, and it could very possibly lead to his first professional publication.

Captain Garvey murmured, 'Cute kid,' and Brian said, 'Yeah.' He didn't want to talk. Watching her cut at him like repeated jabs from a scalpel: quick, sharp slices of pain; starbursts of shock that made him dizzy. Given an unguarded minute he'd tuck her under his arm and ferry her away to his home. He and Jan would get her out of those clothes that so obviously made her uncomfortable, stick her in some shorts and a top, soft moccasins maybe, or a pair of sneakers. Let her run through the sprinkler with Lucia, feed her up while all the injuries healed, teach her how to laugh, help her get past her fear. He longed to rescue her.

'Okay,' Stefan Lazarus said, startling Brian out of his imaginings. 'Time for me to get in there.'

He made it sound as if getting in there was a chore, and Brian wanted to beg the guy to go easy. But he was a doctor, a headshrinker who specialized in kids; he had to know his stuff. He didn't throw off a smartass vibe, he just seemed like a decent, kind of overly uptight academic type. Brian watched him leave the room, then he turned again to the mirror, anxiety bringing back the knots in his stomach.

Instead of his usual gray flannels and navy blazer, shirt and tie, Stefan had intentionally dressed down for the occasion in jeans, an open-necked button-down long-sleeved shirt, and loafers. He wanted to appear as non-threatening as possible. As his hand reached toward the doorknob, he was excited by the challenge and suddenly deeply apprehensive. The apprehension was unexpected. The calm demeanor he'd perfected in the course of his schooling tended to ease the often anxious children with whom he'd worked during his training; he was confident of that. But this child was presenting with problems and behaviors far beyond his experience. He doubted, in fact, if more than a handful of people anywhere had ever worked with a child whose circumstances were even remotely like this one's. He wanted to believe that he could help her; he also couldn't stop thinking about the paper he might be able to present on her case and the acclaim it would bring him.

He'd met Margery Briggs during his Child and Adolescent

Psychiatry Residency Training Program. It had been an incredible stroke of luck that he'd run into her on an errand at City Hall and she'd at once asked him to consult on this case. Flattered and intrigued, he'd accepted immediately without thinking it through. He didn't want to screw it up.

Wiping his hands dry on his jeans, he again reached for the doorknob. Taking a deep breath, he opened the door and walked in with a smile, saying, 'Hi. I'm Stefan.' Reaching for one of the small chairs, he sat down, saying, 'These are little chairs for little people. You can sit down, too, if you like.'

Her curled hands held tight at her sides, she watched him without the amusement the majority of children displayed when he folded his long, lanky frame into one of these chairs. She was, he could see, very suspicious. Ironically, she probably trusted her captors more than she trusted strangers; at least she had a frame of reference for how those two might behave. Strangers represented completely unknown, potentially dangerous, territory.

'If you don't care to sit down, that's fine,' he said, smiling again.

Nothing. She just kept on staring at him.

'Well, okay,' he said. 'Let's get started.'

''Kay.' As if he'd given a key signal, she yanked off the underpants, lay down on her back, flipped the dress up over her face and spread her legs.

'Oh, no!' he said, dismayed. 'That's not what I meant at all.'

''Kay.' She turned and positioned herself on her hands and knees, reaching back to raise the dress over her exposed bottom.

'No! Please,' he said. Something inside his chest tore away, like tape ripped off a raw wound. 'Don't do that.' *This was terrible!!!* Why had he imagined this would be simple or that he was sufficiently schooled for the job?

'No?' She sat up on her knees, looking at him over her shoulder, then turned and knee-walked toward him.

He thought she'd stop but she kept on coming until she was at his knees, trying to push them apart and reaching for his zipper. That raw place inside his chest was exposed and stinging as he took hold of her hand – so soft and scarcely formed; the dimpled hand of a child scarcely beyond being a toddler.

Sitting back on her knees, she studied his face as he struggled to speak.

Like the storied sin eater who for a small gratuity ate a piece of bread laid on the chest of a dead person, thereby taking the sins of that dead person upon himself, he had in just moments swallowed this little girl's metaphoric sins. He was muted and hamstrung by the process, left fairly grief-stricken. How could he possibly help this child? She'd been so thoroughly brainwashed that she interpreted most behaviors as having a sexual subtext. Aware of the arrogance he'd carried with him into the room and ashamed of it, aware too of the humbling realization that he knew far less of the world than he'd imagined. He understood with sudden, staggering clarity that he was too young and too inexperienced to be of use to this child. Just moments and much of what he'd believed he knew about himself had been invalidated.

That internal rending had been the peeling away of the hubris that had led him to say yes to the dislikeable Margery Briggs. He'd agreed to consult on this case knowing almost nothing of the facts. Top grades and high honors didn't magically endow anyone with wisdom or special insights and just now he was lamentably short on both. He was all at once choked with sadness for the losses suffered by this misleadingly dainty little girl. Only the housing was a child's. What was inside her was much used and mistrustful, perhaps irreparably broken. He felt, immediately and thoroughly, heartsick for her.

'I'm sorry,' he said, just then feeling scarcely older than the girl as, embarrassingly, tears welled up in his eyes and he released her hand to rummage in his pocket for a tissue.

'What'sa matter, Mister Stefan?' she asked, appearing fascinated by his distress. Getting to her feet, she put a hand on his arm. 'You cryin', Mister Stefan? It's okay. I won't get mad. You can cry. I sawed some other grown-ups cryin' when the lady was bringin' me here. Are you sad?' Her small hand patted him consolingly as he wiped his face with the tissue. Her features had softened and lost their suspicious tightness. An old, sympathetic soul gazed out at him through the dark windows of her eyes. And as he gazed back at her, he realized that if he was allowed to work with her it could be the greatest learning experience of his life. Her effort to comfort him derived from an innate sensitivity that had not been blunted by her young life's experiences. She was not beyond hope. He prayed he wasn't, either.

At last, having dried his face, he took hold of her hand again and said, 'Thank you. You're very kind. I was feeling a little sad.'

'You're not sad anymore?'

'No. I feel better now, thanks to you. Shall we see what's in the toy box?'

'Okay. Toys are like friends,' she said. 'They don't *do* anythin' or *mean* anythin'. But they make you feel good when you hold them.'

Hearing her paraphrase what he'd told her the night before, Brian emitted a sound that was half laugh and half sob.

'That's right,' Stefan said in surprise. 'Did someone tell you that?'

'Yeah. Mister Brian told me.'

'Mister Brian is quite right. There are other toys, too,' Stefan said, getting down on his knees and lifting the lid on the toy box. 'Some you can use to build things. Others are like games. Would you like to try one of the games, or play with some toys?'

'Mister Stefan?'

'Yes?'

'Please, could I take off the shoes? I don't like them.'

'If you could put the underpants back on, I see no reason why you shouldn't take off the shoes.'

She gazed at him for a few seconds, then sat down on the floor, reaching for the pants. She managed to get them back on, dragging them over the shoes, then rocking her way back into the underpants.

'Could you help me now, Mister Stefan? I don't know how to do shoes. I never had them before. I had rain boots in the winter but they didn't have these do-up things.'

He smiled, and said, 'You bet,' and bent to undo the buckles.

'C'n I take off the sock things, too?'

'If you like. Do you need help with those as well?'

'I can do those. I had some before when there was snow.'
She pulled off the socks, then wriggled her toes. 'I never had
shoes like that. They don't feel good.'

'Then you don't have to wear them,' Stefan declared. 'Now,'
he said, sitting cross-legged in front of her on the carpet, 'let's
try this game.'

''Kay. You gonna tell me how it works?'

'I am going to tell you.'

'What just happened in there?' Captain Garvey said quietly,
gazing through the glass and shaking his head. 'That was one
hell of a thing. I don't know if that young fella's crazy as a
loon or some kind of genius.'

'I think he's way out of his depth and she just threw him
a life buoy,' Brian said, deciding Stefan Lazarus was like a
kid playing dress-up, not someone he'd trust entirely to look
out for Humaby.

FIVE

'It's time to call in the press,' Garvey told Brian on the way back to headquarters. 'I've got as many men as I can spare going through missing persons reports but since we don't know how far back to go it's pretty much impossible. The media people are all over us, wanting to see the little girl who saved the baby. The baby's parents want to meet her, thank her, and give her some kind of gift. Thing is, we get her face out on the wire services and TV, maybe someone'll recognize her. I've got a call in for Connie Mason to come back ASAP and do some head shots, get them printed right up and aim to have them on hand for the press conference this afternoon. That way we're in time for the networks and the late editions of the national and local papers.'

'Sounds like a plan,' Brian said quietly, concentrating on his driving.

'Meanwhile, DCF wants to place the kid while she waits for her surgery.'

'When?' Brian was suddenly fully alert.

'When what?'

'When do they want to place her?'

'Soon as possible, I'd imagine. I get the distinct impression you've taken a big interest in this little girl.'

'Kind of, I guess.' It was hard for Brian to sound non-committal when he was anxious now to get back to the office and put his and Jan's names up for consideration as temporary foster parents.

'Did you ever in your life see anything like what happened in there?' Garvey asked, firing up a Camel and then rolling down the window. 'The guy completely fell to pieces and the kid put him back together. Never saw such a thing.'

'Me, neither,' Brian said. 'But she's got a pretty powerful effect on people . . . maybe because of the age and size of her. She's about the smartest kid I've ever encountered. You read my report on how she got out of that van?' Brian glanced over.

'Unbelievable!' Garvey shook his head, then took a hard drag on his cigarette. 'A plastic knife and fork. Just *unbelievable*.'

'Did they find any photographs or film in the van?' Brian asked. 'She seems to know about porn, went into a pose when Connie went to shoot her. I figure those animals took pictures, maybe even used her in a movie or two. What I'm hoping is they didn't sell any of it. It'd be a terrible thing for her, years from now, if that stuff surfaced.'

'The forensic guys are cataloguing the contents of the van. Seems there's a ton of stuff. It'll take time to sort through it all. Meanwhile, those two ratfucks don't even have the smarts to ask for a lawyer. The DA's gonna charge them with kidnapping, rape, unlawful confinement, and a bunch of other things. If there's a God, the court'll appoint a PD who's got about a week's experience and graduated at the bottom of his class.'

Brian had to laugh. 'It's what they deserve.'

'They don't deserve even someone that good,' Garvey said with disgust, and flicked his half-smoked cigarette out the window. 'With any luck, those two are going away forever. Too bad it's not a death-penalty situation.'

It was a relatively quiet day for Connie. She'd processed the previous day's party film and was drying the prints of the girl – the sight of her filthy, injured little body painful to see – when she got the call to go back and do some shots for the media. Having a legitimate reason to see the child again felt like a gift. Restocking her camera bag, she headed right out to the car. She wanted to get in a bit of shopping before returning to the hospital.

The too-young-looking guard was on duty again. Remembering her, he said, 'Go on in,' and went back to the paperback he was reading.

The child was sitting cross-legged on the bed, frowning at the TV set. As if possessed of radar, she turned the instant Connie walked into the room and said, 'Miss Connie! You comed again.'

'I told you I would. How are you, sweetie?'

'They gave me shoes 'n' socks but Mister Stefan said I didn't have to wear them, 'cuz I didn't like them.'

'You shouldn't wear things you don't like,' Connie said, putting her camera bag on the chair before approaching the bed. 'Your hair looks very nice.'

'I look like a boy.'

'No.' Connie smiled at her. 'You look like a pretty girl.'

'Is that good?'

'Very, very good. How do you feel about the dress?'

'Too many clothes, on top and under, too.' Humaby lifted the sides of the fussy dress as if they were unbearably heavy.

'I brought you some clothes I think you might like better,' Connie said, setting the shopping bag down on the bed.

'Mister Brian says when people like a child they bring you toys and stuff.'

'That's true. But I decided you need clothes more than toys.' Reaching into the bag, Connie laid out her purchases one by one. 'This is what people call a sweat suit, which is kind of a silly name. But it's made out of something called velour and it's very soft. Touch it and you'll see.'

Tentatively, Humaby put out a finger, as if the offering might be electric and give her a nasty shock.

'Go ahead and really touch it,' Connie encouraged her.

'It *is* soft! What color is this?'

'It's yellow. Do you like it?'

'Yeah.'

'And I got you some sneakers. I think you'll like these. They're soft, too. Not the way the sweat suit is, but they'll feel good on your feet.'

'Thank you, Miss Connie.'

'Would you like me to help you change into your new clothes?'

'I can wear them?'

'Yes, you can.'

'Okay.' Lowering her voice and glancing at the doorway as if fearful of someone overhearing, she said, 'I don't like this dress.'

'I know,' Connie whispered. 'And if you don't like these

new things, I won't mind one bit. We'll just find you something else that you do like. Okay?'

'Yeah?'

'Absolutely. We'll keep your socks on so the sneakers don't rub your sore foot when you walk,' Connie told her, getting the ugly shoes and then the starchy, oversized dress off. 'First we'll put on the bottoms. You can hold my arm while we get these on. Good. Now, the top. There! How does it feel?'

Humaby took her hands over her arms and legs, examining the sensation, then said, 'I like it, Miss Connie! It feels *nice*.'

'I'm glad. We'll try the sneakers on later. Okay?'

''Kay.'

'Could I give you a kiss?' Connie asked.

Humaby's brow furrowed. 'In my mouth?'

'No, sweetie. On the cheek.'

'Why?' she asked worriedly.

'Because I like you and care about you. Giving a kiss is a way to show how you feel about someone.'

A tide of doubt washed over the child's face.

Guilt, thick and gluey, collected in Connie's throat. The child had no comprehension of gentle gestures. 'It's all right, sweetie,' she said quietly. 'It was wrong of me to ask you. We'll forget about it.'

Not sure how it worked, but wanting to please her, Humaby leaned over and pressed her lips to Connie's cheek, then asked, 'That okay?'

'That was lovely, the nicest kiss I've ever had. Thank you so much.'

In a relieved rush, the child said, 'You're welkin, Miss Connie.' Searching Connie's eyes, she asked, 'You gonna read for me again?'

'I'd love to. But first I have to take a few pictures – just of your face, to show how pretty you look. Would that be all right?'

'I guess. But why?'

'Mister Brian and the other policemen are going to show your picture to lots of people and try to find your family.'

'What if I don't *have* a family?'

'Then arrangements will be made to find you a new one.'

'That's what Mister Brian said.' Humaby looked over at the window, wondering if a new family would live in a van, too.

'And he was right. This'll only take a minute.'

'Miss Connie, one of the nurse ladies said children like ka-toons.' She pointed at the TV. 'But bunnies and animals get hurted and there's lots of big noises that're scary.'

'Would you like me to turn it off?'

'Yeah. Why would children like those?'

'I really don't know. I never liked them when I was a kid.' Connie found the remote and switched off the set. 'I was born in another country where there wasn't any TV. It wasn't until we came here, when I was little like you, that I saw a cartoon. It scared me.'

Blinking at the now dark screen, Humaby said, 'You got ascared?'

'Yes, I did.'

'And you was little like me?'

'Yes, I was.'

'But now you're growed up and don't get scared anymore, right?'

'Sometimes, I do. Grown-ups get scared the same as little kids do, sweetie.'

'I didn't know that.'

'Well, we do.' Connie offered one of her big smiles, then said, 'If it's okay with you, I'll take the pictures now and we'll be done with it.' Connie got her camera from the case before adjusting the curtains to brighten the room. She sat the girl at an angle on the side of the bed so that the available light lent a lovely glow to her features, and quickly took a dozen close-ups from different angles. 'All done,' she announced. 'Thank you very much. You made my job so easy. You are *such* a good girl. Now we can read until your lunch comes.' She glanced at her watch. She'd have plenty of time to process the negs, print the film, then rush the best full-face and profile shots to the repro place to get copies made.

'Lunch is food?'

'That's right. Breakfast is what you eat when you wake up, lunch is what you have in the middle of the day, and dinner is what you have near the end of the day a little before it's time for you to go to bed. Are you hungry?'

'They gived me juice and cookies before. I didn't even have to ask.'

'That's great. Why don't you sit back against the pillows, get comfy, and we'll read.'

Humaby settled with the teddy bear and stuffed bunny on either side of her, every few moments rubbing a hand over her sleeve or her leg, savoring the plush feel of the velour. 'Are you old, Miss Connie?'

Connie laughed as she picked up the Beatrix Potter book from the bedside table. 'I'm twenty-five.'

'Is that old?

'Not very.'

'Is Mister Brian old?'

'I think he's probably a few years older than I am.'

'Could you and Mister Brian be my family?'

Profoundly touched, Connie chose her words with care. 'Mister Brian already has a family, sweetie. And they don't let women who aren't married take care of small children like you. But I'll be your friend always. Sometimes, friends can be just as good as family.'

'Oh!' Disappointed, Humaby looked down and stroked her sleeve.

Reaching to take hold of the child's free hand, Connie said, 'No matter what happens, you will *always* be important to me. I will come to see you, wherever you are, and you'll be able to call me on the telephone.'

'I don't know how to use the telephone.'

Giving the small hand a gentle squeeze, Connie said, 'Don't worry. I'll teach you how. Are you ready for a story now?'

'Yes, please, Miss Connie.'

Finding her place, Connie said. 'Today we're going to read *The Tale of Jeremy Fisher.*'

Early that afternoon, Margery Briggs, the social worker in charge of the case received four calls, each one an offer to provide foster care for the Kmart child.

The first call came in from Officer Brian Kirlane.

The second was from Connie Mason.

The third, at the urging of his wife, was from Dr Stefan Lazarus, who made the call because he didn't think there was any chance of the child being placed in their care.

And the fourth was from Captain James Garvey.

'Would I be breaking any rules if I picked her up at the hospital and brought her to the house for an hour?' Brian asked the captain. 'I just think it would do her good to be with ordinary people, meet another little girl. Maybe play a bit.'

'Let me make a call to that Lazarus guy. If he says it's okay then I can't see a problem. They're still waiting for test results so far as I know, and the poor kid's probably bored to death stuck in that room all alone.'

'Thanks, Cap.'

'Where we goin', Mister Brian?'

'I'm taking you to my house to meet my daughter, Lucia, and her mother.'

'Why?'

'I thought you might like to get out of that room for a while, meet some new people. I like your sweat suit. It's sharp. And so're the sneakers.'

'Miss Connie gave them to me. It's soft.' She held out her arm. 'Feel!'

He did and emitted a soft whistle. 'Wow! Is that *ever* soft!'

'Yeah,' she said, pleased.

As they pulled in to the driveway, the front door opened and Jan stepped out with Lucia at her side.

Brian went around and opened the passenger door, helping Humaby out, then took her hand to lead her up the walk.

'This is sweetie,' he told his wife and daughter.

At once, Jan dropped to her haunches and smiled, saying, 'Hi! I'm so happy to meet you. I'm Jan and this is Lucia.'

Humaby didn't speak. Her gaze was fixed on the girl with the long white-blonde hair and bright blue eyes, porcelain skin, exquisite features. She'd never been this close to someone her own age and size. It felt funny but good in a strange way.

'Pretty,' she murmured at last, not sure if that was the right word for what she wanted to say.

Lucia said, 'I like your hair. I wanna get mine cut but my mom says not yet. I don't know why. Wanna see my room? I got a new Barbie.'

'What's a Barbie?' Humaby asked, as if in a trance.

'It's a doll,' Jan explained as Humaby continued to study Lucia, taking in every detail of her appearance.

'A doll is another kind of toy,' Brian put in, as intrigued as his wife was by Humaby's reaction to Lucia.

'Miss Connie said giving a kiss is a way to show how you feel about someone,' Humaby said and kissed Lucia's cheek, then leaned away to resume staring in awestruck fascination at the first child she'd ever met.

'That's right,' Brian said, gripping Jan's hand as Lucia, with typical equanimity, kissed Humaby back, then took hold of her hand and said, 'Come on. Let's go play!' and towed Humaby off into the house. As they went, Lucia was saying, 'We made chocolate chip cookies and lemonade and everything. Like a party . . .'

'Did you get that?' Jan asked quietly.

'Yeah,' Brian answered. 'Lucia's her first friend.'

'How long have you got?'

'An hour. I have to get her back to the hospital before the press conference. It'll hit the airwaves and the papers, and then the calls'll start coming in. Every crackpot from here to hell 'n' gone'll be phoning to say they know who she is, and all the parents with missing kids will insist she's their little Jen or Sarah or Em. It's gonna be brutal.'

'Maybe they'll let her stay with us until something breaks.'

'Maybe,' he said, with a gut hunch that it wasn't going to happen.

SIX

A tall lady came to the room and looked at the clothes and said Humaby had to wear the scratchy dress and the tight shoes, and then she made Humaby stand still while she pulled off the nice soft sweat suit Miss Connie gave her and put all the other stuff on her, bending down to do up the tight shoes. After that she had to go with her to a big room and stand with the tall lady holding her hand too hard – it was the cut one with the bandage – where people shouted at her, hurting her ears, and lights kept going off and on, making her eyes sting. It was very loud and bright, then very loud and dark, over and over. She kept looking for Mister Brian or Miss Connie, but didn't see them or the baby anywhere.

With the lights and the yelling and so many people, she felt scared and had to work hard not to cry. The tall lady leaned down to her and said, 'It'll be over soon. Just try to stand still,' then she gave Humaby a tiny little smile that was angry underneath. Why was she mad? And why were there so many people, all yelling and making the lights go on and off? None of it made sense. She only hoped she'd get to see the baby, the way Mister Brian said she might.

Then it got quiet and a man and lady came in. The old policeman from before said they were the mama and daddy of the baby. They held hands and started talking into a whole big bunch of what looked like gray ice-cream cones or big lollipops all pushed together on big stands, saying how happy they were to have their daughter back and it was all because of this special little girl. Humaby looked around to see the special little girl. Maybe the baby was there and she just couldn't see her because of all the lights. People laughed and more lights flashed off and on, off and on. Then the mama and daddy came over and the mama bent down to her, taking hold of Humaby's hand.

'We're so grateful to you,' the mama said in a very quiet voice, holding Humaby's hand to her cheek. 'I will *never* forget what you've done for us.' Her voice got all choky and Humaby could tell she was going to cry, so she pulled her hand free from the tall lady and patted the baby's mama on the shoulder. That made the mama start to cry really hard and all the lights started going off and on again. The mama stood up, then the daddy leaned down and spoke softly to Humaby, as if he didn't want anyone else to hear, and he was all choky too. 'We're going to see that you're rewarded for making it possible for us to get Gracie back.'

Humaby asked, 'Please, can I see the baby?'

He looked at the mama who was holding a cloth to her eyes now and shaking her head back and forth, saying, 'I have to get out of here, Ben. Please get me out of here.' Then he looked again at Humaby and said, 'We'll work something out. Thank you, dear heart, thank you so very much. You are a brave and clever girl, and we are forever in your debt.' Then he took the mama by the arm and some men in suits hurried away with them.

The old policeman got in front of the gray ice-cream cones and said, 'Okay, folks. That's it. You, print people, we'd appreciate your convincing your editors to put this remarkable child's picture above the fold, so people see it first thing. And if you TV folks could persuade your producers to make this tonight's lead story maybe we'll get lucky and find her family. Thanks everyone. That's it for today.'

As the old policeman and some others held the yelling people back, the tall lady grabbed her by the arm and hurried Humaby toward a door, away from everybody. 'But how come I couldn't see the baby?' she asked, craning to look back as the door closed behind them and the tall lady yanked so hard at her arm that Humaby stumbled and nearly fell. It was familiar treatment. Under her breath, she whispered, '*Hate you!*'

As predicted, the calls started coming in before the local TV segment was finished that evening. 'The network news hasn't even aired and the lines're lit up like Christmas,' Captain Garvey observed to no one in particular as he paused in the squad room. How the hell they were ever going to sort it out was beyond him. All he could do was recruit more of the civilian staff for overtime, to help man the phones that were ringing nonstop, calls on hold on every phone on every desk. God forbid there was an emergency – nobody would get through. Meanwhile, they'd dismiss all the obvious whackos, log the information on those calls that seemed remotely legitimate then, from those, they would filter out the ones that might be a fit. A massive job.

The next morning the applicants got the news from Margery Briggs, Humaby's social worker, who'd had a brief meeting with her overbooked superior to state her case. Her decision-making as to who might be best suited to provide temporary foster care for the child both before and after her surgical procedures was based on her hour-long exposure to the little girl when she got her ready and then accompanied her to and from the press conference, and on her prior acquaintanceship with Stefan Lazarus.

Brian and Jan were turned down as possibilities because Miss Briggs (who had made no home visits or – so far as Brian knew – interviewed any of those who'd volunteered to take in the child) declared that in her professional opinion Humaby would be a negative, possibly dangerous influence on Lucia.

'Are you *kidding* with this crap?' Brian snapped, deeply offended.

'I assure you, sir, that I am not kidding,' Briggs said, and put down the phone before Brian could argue with her decision.

In Brian's view the reverse of her so-called professional opinion was true. Lucia's effect on the other child was evident after mere minutes. She did her special voice, a startling baritone rasp, saying, 'I'll be Ken and you be Barbie,' and Humaby had actually laughed at the big, gruff voice that emerged from the girl's mouth. Just a small, abruptly cut-off sound. But she'd *laughed*. And when they were leaving to head back to the hospital, she'd climbed into the squad car, exclaiming, 'Look what Lucia gived me!' showing him a somewhat worse-for-wear Barbie. 'She said I could *keep* it.'

'That's great, honey.'

'Lucia says we're *friends*!' she said wonderingly. 'Can I come to play again amorrow, Mister Brian?'

'I hope so. But I can't promise. We'll try, though.'

As she'd expected, Connie was rejected as a viable foster parent because she was unmarried. The social worker was abrupt and cold, saying only, 'In the agency's view we don't consider you a suitable match.' And that was that, end of call, no room for protest. And what argument could Connie have offered? That she had an intimate understanding of the lifelong effects of pain and fear? That she already loved the child? None of that mattered. She had no husband; therefore she was not fit for parenthood.

Despite its being expected, it felt as if she'd lost something very precious. Her mood remained dark throughout the morning, the persistent ache of the icy rejection like an internal injury. She sat in the kitchen drinking coffee and staring at the wall, trying to get herself moving. There were prints to be delivered, a pair of back-to-back bookings scheduled for late morning. But for a time all she could do was sit staring into space, benumbed by disappointment.

Captain Garvey and his wife were deemed to be too old to take on the burden of a very young, very damaged child. Indignant, Garvey slammed down the receiver, emitting a disgusted bark of laughter. Since when was forty-one too old to handle one more kid in a house that already had three of them and plenty of room for more? DCF didn't know his Angie or what a great mother, what a fine person she was; they didn't know that to be close to this woman was a privilege. '*Assholes*,' he muttered, and slammed his fist on the desk. What was the big hurry? Why couldn't they take the time to do their homework properly, make sure the kid was placed with the right people?

Stefan Lazarus topped the list despite his being only recently married and lacking any experience in raising a child. He was a newly licensed doctor, a child psychiatrist. What more experience did he need? Plus being the son of prominent doctors

– his father and mother also both psychiatrists – cinched the placement as far as Margery Briggs was concerned.

Stefan was shocked by the decision, and immediately doubt-filled. Was he really the proper choice? Monica had been excited when he phoned to tell her they'd been awarded temporary custody, but she hadn't yet met the child. She had no idea of the level of abuse the child had suffered. His hand kept wanting to go to the phone, to call back the woman at DCF to tell her it was a mistake to entrust the girl to him and Monica. Monica's degree was in botany, for God's sake. She knew more about fern fronds than she did about people.

Yet he couldn't help thinking that there was something to this: there was significant information to be gleaned from living with the little girl, observing her on a day-to-day basis; there was knowledge to be gained that he could share professionally, knowledge that would provide great insight into the long-term effects of prolonged abuse on the heart and mind of a small child. And if he were to be entirely honest with himself, working with her, publishing articles or even a book about her, would establish him as someone to be taken very seriously in the world of child psychiatry.

So, despite his personal misgivings, his professional ambition won the day. He didn't make the call back to the coldly elitist Briggs at DCF, one of the least-appropriate people performing as a social worker that he'd ever encountered.

When he finally learned who'd been chosen to foster the child, Brian couldn't help thinking the poor kid would feel like some kind of lab specimen, lodged in the midst of a family of doctors. But he kept remembering how Lazarus had cracked during that session with Humaby, how he'd wept so brokenly. If the rest of his family was anything like him, maybe they'd treat the child with sensitivity.

'I truly hope so,' Connie said fervently when they ran into each other at the station later that morning. She was dropping off the photos she'd shot the night before of a nine-year-old, so severely battered that it was doubtful that she'd survive the day. She repeated to Brian what Captain Garvey had told her of DCF's decision to place Humaby with the Doctors Lazarus.

'The last thing she needs is to be put under a microscope,' Connie said.

'Especially if it turns out to be for any length of time,' Brian said. 'She needs some pretty major surgery, and she's already suspicious of most people and things. Every new person is a potential threat. You know?' Connie nodded, and he said, 'I'm hoping Lazarus will let us come see her.'

'If you talk to him, please ask for me, too.' She gave Brian her card, then said, 'Keep me posted?'

'Count on it. Wait one and I'll give you our home number.'

When the social worker told her she'd be going home with Mister Stefan, Humaby was upset but tried hard not to show it. 'Please, Miss, can I stay with Mister Brian and Jan and Lucia?' she asked, rubbing her velour-covered knee. 'Or Miss Connie?'

'That's out of the question. You're a very lucky girl to be going to the Lazarus family. They have a lovely big house and you'll have your own room. Dr Lazarus's parents' house even has a swimming pool,' the woman told her, irked by the child's reluctance. To be fostered by a family of this caliber was unprecedented.

'But I don't know how to swim.'

'Well, maybe you'll learn.' She wanted to grab the child and shake her.

'But if I stay with Mister Brian, I could play with Lucia. She's got *Barbie dolls*. She even *gived* me one. See!' She held up the doll to show the angry-looking woman. 'And she's got a *bicycle*, a pink one! Miss Jan said she'd teach me to ride it and let me make cookies and I could stay with Lucia in her room.'

Stymied, more annoyed by the moment, Margery Briggs said, 'Dr Lazarus and his wife are top-rate people and his sister's very nice. I happen to know her myself.'

'Is she a little girl?' Humaby asked hopefully.

'No, she's a grown-up, a doctor.'

'Don't *like* doctors,' Humaby said under her breath, gazing at her sneaker-clad feet.

'There are arrangements to make, paperwork to be done. I have to go now,' the woman said, looking at her watch. 'You'll be fine with Dr Lazarus. But if for some bizarre reason it doesn't work out, we'll find another placement for you.'

'What's a placeman?' Humaby asked.

Fighting to contain her impatience, the woman said curtly, 'Another family. I'll be back tomorrow to take you to the Lazarus home. Do as you're told and be a good girl now.'

'I *am* a good girl!' Humaby whispered at the woman's back as she marched away. She was a mean lady, like the ones in the big store – people who didn't like little children.

Scared and sad, she sat on the side of the bed, looking at the doorway, seeing people going by in the hall and hearing the voices come out of the ceiling. The TV set was showing cartoons again and she didn't want to look at them. *I* am *a good girl*, she thought, stroking her soft sleeve. But it didn't matter. No matter how good she tried to be, bad things always happened. She wanted to cry – her chest all tight with it – but she wouldn't let herself give in. Crying made people mad, and she'd learned a long time ago not to do things that made people mad. So she tried not to let anything show. Sometimes, it was very hard.

Connie's mood just wouldn't lift and, finally, after leaving the station house, she drove to the hospital.

There was a different cop sitting outside the door; he looked scarcely older than the previous one. She showed him her ID, explained who she was and the youthful officer in an unexpectedly low, mellifluous voice said, 'Poor kid's just been sitting there for hours, since that pickle-puss babe from DCF left. Kid didn't even eat her lunch. I tried to keep her company a while ago but I could see I was making her nervous, so I backed off. She's been watching the door like she's waiting for somebody. Could be you're the one. Her lunch tray's still at the nurses' station. I asked them to hang on to it. Maybe you could get her to eat something.'

'That was smart. Thank you. I'll go get it.'

Carrying the tray, Connie returned to the room, brightly saying, 'Hi, sweetie. I've got your lunch.'

'Hi, Miss Connie,' Humaby said dully. 'I'm not hungry, thank you very much.'

Putting down the tray, Connie sat beside her on the bed, asking, 'What've you got there?'

'It's a Barbie. Lucia gave it to me.'

'Who's Lucia, sweetie?'

'She's Mister Brian's little girl.'

'That was very kind of her.'

'She's my *friend*. We played with the Barbies and we had lemonade and cookies. I want to go stay with them, Miss Connie. Or with you. But the mean lady's making me go with Mister Stefan to his house.'

'I'm sure it'll be very nice. And Mister Stefan must like you a lot or he wouldn't have asked to have you stay with him.'

For the first time, the child looked up at her. 'People asked to have me?'

'A lot of us did.'

'I didn't know that.' Lowering her voice to a confiding tone, she said, 'When we were in the room with the little chairs and all the toys, Mister Stefan was very sad. He cried.'

'He did?'

'Yeah. I never saw big people cry before I was in here.' She made a gesture meant to include the entire hospital. 'But today the mama cried when she said to me they were happy to have the baby back. And the daddy, he cried too.'

'Sometimes people cry when they're actually happy, not sad.'

'I never knew that either.'

'It's true,' Connie told her. 'I felt like crying this morning when I found out you weren't going to be staying with me.'

'But you didn't cry?'

'No. I wanted to, but I didn't.'

'Why not?'

'I'm not really sure why. Sometimes, it makes me angry with myself if I cry . . . as if I'm being weak instead of strong and I don't like the idea of being weak.' She could scarcely believe she was confiding something like this to a small child, but her instinct told her it was the right way to go.

'So you don't let yourself cry?'

'No,' Connie admitted. 'Sometimes I don't.'

'Me, too,' Humaby whispered. 'If I cried, Wolf and Toadman got very mad . . . So I teached myself not to cry anymore. But . . . Miss Connie, I don't *want* to go with Mister Stefan. I'm ascared to go with him.'

'Oh, you don't need to be afraid.'

'But I *am*! I'm *ascared*! He's . . .' She groped for the right word to describe him. 'He's all sad, Miss Connie. I want to be with Lucia and her mama and daddy, or with you. I'm not ascared when I'm with you.'

Aware of how hard she was struggling to hold on to herself, Connie longed to comfort her but didn't dare risk touching the child. 'I know, sweetie,' she said. 'I know.'

Humaby told herself she wasn't going to cry. But she couldn't keep it in. Her head came to rest against Connie's arm and she felt so worried and so tired that the tears just came out by themselves. And that made her even more afraid, because you could never be sure about people.

'Don't be mad at me, please, Miss Connie,' she begged, wiping her face with her hand.

'I could never be mad at you,' Connie said and, surrendering to instinct, she lifted Humaby onto her lap, where the child settled without protest. 'That's better,' she murmured. 'That's much better.'

Sitting on Miss Connie's lap was like something she almost remembered; something from a long, long time ago. But she couldn't remember what it was; it was just somehow okay.

Connie silently rocked her until she actually fell asleep, her chest shaken by residual sobs. Holding her, feeling the warmth of the child's slight weight, finally eased the day-long ache of disappointment.

PART TWO
1983

SEVEN

'For what it's worth, I've always believed you were innocent.'

Soberly, Tally said, 'Thank you,' and turned to look at the stocky middle-aged woman in the boxy gray suit with a white blouse buttoned to the neck. To all outward appearance an unremarkable person: plain-faced, with gray-threaded black hair blunt-cut to her square jawline. But to study the warden's sadly intelligent brown eyes quickly erased the impression of plainness. She was a woman who'd seen and heard it all but, incredibly, still had an open heart. And it lent depth and humor to her deep-set eyes. So, in spite of the severe clothes and ugly shoes, the thick body and unmade-up face, she was a singularly appealing person.

'I wish you well,' the older woman said, and offered Tally her hand.

For a moment Tally was bewildered by the gesture. Then long-ago training kicked in and she took hold, absorbing the details of the woman's firm grip.

Behind her the door clicked open and Tally felt the sound travel through her entire body. She hadn't expected to have any reaction, but the sound of that door opening dried her mouth and accelerated her heartbeat.

'God bless, Tally,' the warden said as she withdrew her hand, 'and good luck. Let me hear from you.'

'I will. Thank you.' Tally turned slowly to look at the door. She could see sunlight and moved toward it, then stopped and looked back.

'Go on now,' the woman said quietly. 'Don't look back.'

Tally put the flat of her free hand against the door and pushed. Near-blinded by the sunlight, she stepped over the threshold. The door closed heavily behind her with another click, and she stood shielding her eyes with her hand.

Warren Berman was standing next to a gleaming black

Mercedes, waiting for her. As she stepped outside, he came toward her with a smile and a hello, automatically reaching to take hold of the small cardboard box she carried.

Leading the way to the car, he held open the passenger door and waited until she was inside before closing it. Then he stowed the box behind the driver's seat and slid behind the wheel.

'How are you?' he asked.

'Older,' she said. 'Do you happen to have a spare pair of sunglasses, Warren?'

'As a matter of fact, I do.' Reaching past her, he opened the glove compartment and pulled out a pair of aviator-style Ray-Bans. 'There you go.'

She thanked him and put them on, at once eased, and turned to look at the structure that had contained her for the past fifteen years. *I'm outside*, she thought. *Out. Free.* After five thousand three hundred and seventy-two days. She had on clothes that were, surprisingly, too large, and in the back of the car she had a small carton containing the few items of any significance to her: a thin eight-by-ten-inch envelope of photographs, some photocopied articles from various journals, and the diary she'd kept during her first two years of incarceration before the point-lessness of the exercise had struck her and she'd stopped.

'There's a not-bad-looking diner about ten miles up the road,' Warren said. 'How does that sound?'

'Fine,' she answered quietly as he put the car into drive. 'You look very well, Warren,' she said, studying his profile.

He glanced over with a smile. 'So do you, Tally.'

She didn't respond to this but looked for a time at her hands, at her just-returned wedding ring and wristwatch – items that felt more substantial than she remembered. Then she turned to look out the window at the scrubby, featureless land flying past. She wanted to get as far from Nevada as possible, to be somewhere with trees and seasons and snow. And that, for the moment, was all she knew. Simply being outside the walls was a shock to her system, as if the top layer of her flesh had been sheared away. She felt shaky inside and hollow, as if a good shove would cause her to collapse in a heap of discon-nected bones.

The car flew noiselessly along the highway – a sleek steel capsule with a console that she thought would have looked appropriate on a space ship. So many panels and controls: mobile luxury. There had been a time when a car like this would have seemed perfectly ordinary; a time when life had been so filled with promise that nothing had seemed impossible. And then, everything changed irrevocably. The suddenness of those past events still shocked her; the way the world could tilt without warning and send things sideways. The details would probably always sit in her head, like exposed wiring, capable of shocking her. Nothing else would, though. All these years later, she'd been disabused of the old notion of women as the gentler of the species, of the belief in family as an indissoluble unit, and of personal safety as something ordained. She had, in fact, lost her faith in pretty much everything. Thirty-seven years old and she felt at least twice that, like someone edging toward the end of her life, not someone moving back out into what was, purportedly, the middle.

The middle of nowhere. That's where they were. And in the middle of this nowhere was an unlikely oasis, complete with neon sign (D-I-N-E-R, ALWAYS OPEN) and half-a-dozen cars, including a state police cruiser, in the parking lot.

'I saw this place on my way to get you and thought it looked decent enough,' Warren said. 'But if you'd rather go somewhere else . . .'

'No, this is fine,' she said, looking for the door handle, briefly wondering if the door would actually open. It did. And heat gushed into the car's cool interior with the heft of a gigantic hand that wanted to hold her in place on the leather seat. She fought past it and climbed out of the car to stand looking down at her feet, at the black leather high-heeled pumps she'd worn at her sentencing. Long-accustomed to sneakers, the shoes struck her as ridiculous. She'd once been someone who actually paid hundreds of dollars for footwear that made her feet feel as if they were being crushed.

Mental note: buy some sane shoes.

Another mental note: buy some clothes that fit and dump the Chanel suit.

Everyone looked up when they walked through the door.

The two state troopers at the counter stared at her as Warren took her arm and led her to a booth at the far end.

As she sat down she could still feel the troopers' eyes, and wondered if they knew she'd just been released. The out-of-date clothes were probably a giveaway. But it didn't matter. She'd served the full sentence. She was free. She did not have to return after this outing, did not have to report to a parole officer. Free of all obligations.

Warren had brought his attaché case in with him and laid it with care on the seat beside him, saying, 'I'm actually hungry. I drove up last night and' – he looked at his wristwatch – 'my flight home is in a couple of hours. I was hoping you wouldn't mind dropping me at the airport.'

Frowning, she tried to make sense of what he was saying.

'The car's yours,' he explained, 'but for a technicality. I've got a folder of documents that need to be signed.'

'Mine? Did they imagine I'd want a car like that, Warren?'

'I guess they did. Your mother's instructions were explicit. I was to deliver the car to you here, along with . . .' He stopped and reached for the menu. 'I really have to eat. My blood sugar's plummeting. The last thing I need is a hypoglycemic attack. I won't be able to get on the plane and I've got meetings all day tomorrow.'

'Of course,' she said, and out of curiosity reached for the other menu, thinking this was alarmingly typical, familiar in a hateful, well-remembered way. The family lawyer sent to deal with the malfeasant child. 'I don't have a valid driver's license,' she said, thinking about the car outside, now hers.

'Yes, you do,' he told her. 'You've got a temporary that's good for sixty days. Plenty of time for you to settle somewhere and get a permanent license.'

'How do you do things like that?' she asked wonderingly.

Warren smiled at her over the top of his menu. 'Magic,' he said, eliciting a small smile from her.

The waitress was high school age, slim and pretty, and smiled when she came over, pencil poised above her order pad.

Warren asked for coffee and a BLT with crisp bacon.

Tally ordered the first thing that came to mind: a grilled

cheese and coffee. It was an extraordinary luxury to be able to eat whatever she wanted, even something so mundane.

The young waitress smiled again and went off.

'So,' Warren said, flipping open the catches on his attaché case, 'let's get this out of the way while we wait. Then we can talk.'

'Of course,' Tally said again.

Warren brought out a good-sized manila folder and placed it on the tabletop, then momentously opened it. He withdrew a legal-size brown envelope and slid it over to her, saying, 'Your temporary license, the title to the Benz, and the insurance policy. The registration is in the glove compartment.' Next came a larger clasp envelope. 'Check book, cash, credit card, and the current bank and trust statements. Look everything over. If you have questions, you can call me any time.' He looked up at her. 'You do know that, don't you, Tally? *Any time.*'

'Yes.'

'Okay. Now for the signatures.' He took a fountain pen from his inside jacket pocket and placed it carefully on the tabletop before picking up several documents. 'This top one acknowledges that you've received the items.' He handed her the pen and indicated the line at the bottom. 'If you'll just sign there, and the copies as well.'

The pen was a black Mont Blanc with a gold nib, and it sailed smoothly across the pages.

Mental note: buy a Mont Blanc fountain pen.

'Good, thank you.' He returned those documents to their folder and picked up the next. 'This is the letter of agreement we discussed last time I came up to see you.'

'I remember.'

'Once you sign this, Tally, any connection with the family is officially severed.'

As she signed, she said, 'I can't help wondering why they waited until now for this. They severed me long ago.'

'It makes no more sense to me than it does to you, dear,' he admitted. 'This is all your mother's doing, of course. She is a *cold* woman.' He seemed to shiver without any physical movement, and she was reminded of how much she liked his honesty. Always had.

'A couple more to sign and we're done. One is for the trust, stipulating that you are assuming control of the funds, and the other is for the bank account and the credit card. The last one is my surrender of your power of attorney.'

She signed everything, in triplicate. Warren placed copies in an eight-and-a-half-by-eleven envelope and passed it to her. 'Your copies,' he said. 'Once you're settled, stow them in a safe deposit box.'

'I will do that,' she assured him, trying to show some warmth. She knew her manner was distant; it was hard to switch from cool self-preserving to engaged and friendly. Fifteen years made for an ingrained habit that might never get broken.

'And that is that!' he declared, snapping closed the latches on the case and gazing at her. 'Now! Tell me. Have you some idea of what you're going to do?'

She shook her head. 'All I know is that I'm going to get as far away from here as I can.'

'Like where?' he asked with interest.

'I'm going east. When I find a place I like, I'll stop.'

He smiled, and she thought, not for the first time, of what a very kind man he was. And handsome, still. He had to be in his late fifties but didn't look it. Dark-haired, dark-eyed, fair-skinned with a smile that dimpled his cheeks; a good height, trim and well dressed. He'd been coming to see her two or three times a year for the past fifteen years – not on family business, but because he'd known her most of her life and cared about her. He'd been in the courtroom, her only outside support. And when the judge had pronounced sentence on her, Warren had covered his eyes with his hand and wept soundlessly. She'd been so completely dazed at that point that she'd studied him with something akin to fascination. The family lawyer who cared more about her than her own family – a fact to ponder for five thousand three hundred and seventy-two days.

'Will you let me know where you are when you stop?' he asked.

'I will,' she said. 'I definitely will.'

'This is my last . . . act, I guess, for the family.'

'Oh?'

'I've turned them over to one of the junior partners. I'm retiring.'

'Oh! Won't you be bored?'

'Tally, the last thing I will be is bored with three kids who view Alexis and me as unpaid babysitters. Four grandkids all under five keep us very not-bored. Luckily, we rarely have all of them at the same time. Ah, great! Here's our food.'

'I can't picture you as a grandfather.'

'I'll see that you get some snapshots to help you with that.' He smiled again as he lifted the top of his sandwich, making sure the bacon was well done.

Amazing, she thought, the things you don't forget – like driving a car. When they left the diner, Warren handed her the keys, then went to the passenger side. She got behind the wheel and studied the instrument panel while the air conditioner worked to dispel the accumulated heat inside the car.

The car was a big beast, yet responsive and quick. In seconds, she'd accelerated up to sixty miles an hour and her chest was a cage filled with fluttering birds. Her foot shook and she had to focus furiously to keep it firmly on the accelerator. God! She was *out*!

At the airport, she stood outside the terminal to say goodbye to Warren. He hugged her – a truly startling physical contact, the first she'd had with another person in thousands of days – then stood with his hands on her shoulders and said, 'If you need *anything*, call me. Alexis and I care about you, dear. Please remember that.'

'I will.'

'Try to find your life,' he said. 'It's still out there somewhere.'

'That was a long time ago, Warren. I have to find something else now.'

'You always did love to haggle over semantics,' he said with another smile, withdrawing his hands from her shoulders. 'Just, please, stay in touch. Otherwise, I'll worry.'

'I will. Thank you so much – for everything.'

'You're a good woman, Tally. Someday you'll be vindicated.'

'I never will be,' she said softly, 'but it doesn't matter.'

'It *matters*,' he insisted. 'Take good care. Okay?'

'I will. And I'll be in touch.'

He hugged her, kissed her cheek – leaving behind the scent of citrus cologne – then released her.

She watched him go into the terminal, then stood for a moment looking around at the people coming and going, porters and cab drivers; varicolored motion, tidal and dizzying.

'You'll have to move your car, Miss,' someone said, and she turned to see a police officer smiling at her across the roof of the Mercedes.

'Yes,' she said, 'sorry,' and hurried through the sickening heat back to the driver's side of the car.

She followed every sign that said 'Eastbound,' until she connected up with Interstate 80, a highway that she knew went all the way to the east coast. She was amazed at the volume of traffic and the size of the cars – smaller than they'd been in the sixties. And the truck drivers, those fellows who used to be referred to as 'the knights of the road,' now seemed remarkably aggressive, even hostile, getting almost on top of her rear bumper before swinging out to pass. Their intent seemed to be to instill fear. They didn't frighten her; they merely made her wonder what had transpired that had so enraged the truckers during the fifteen years she'd been locked away. She'd entered prison only months after the famous 'Summer of Love.' Her happiness had crescendoed that summer. Peace, love, and rock 'n' roll. And then came the fall.

Her foot still unsteady on the accelerator and the grilled cheese sandwich sitting in the pit of her stomach like a golf ball, she kept driving – awed by the depth of the sky, the lack of enclosing walls, the endlessly unfurling road that arrowed toward a horizon that kept receding, until the daylight was fading and she was suddenly very tired. She'd been behind the wheel for hours, only stopping once to refuel the car.

She took the Elko exit, pulled into the parking lot of a new-looking motel with an attached restaurant, paid cash, and let herself into a very clean, over-chilled room. After locking the door, she turned up the thermostat, then stood marveling at

the size of the room – at least fifteen by twenty – and the
luxury of her own TV set, a double bed, and a private bathroom. She would get something to eat, she decided, then come
back and sit on the bed and watch TV. And in the morning,
she'd buy some clothes.

She felt horribly conspicuous in the restaurant. Her hands
shook as she read the menu. There were too many choices
and the waitress, this one middle-aged, hefty and impatient,
stood tap-tapping her pencil on the edge of her order pad.
'What's good?' Tally finally asked her.

For some reason, the question generated a conspiratorial
smile. 'The restaurant a mile down the road,' the woman said
in an undertone.

Tally laughed, then marveled at the sound of it. She couldn't
remember when she'd last found anything funny. 'Okay, I'll
rephrase the question. What is acceptable?'

Grinning now, the woman said, 'You can't go wrong with
a cheeseburger. And the fries are fresh-cut, not frozen.'

'Then that's what I'll have.'

'How d'you want your burger done?

'Well done, please.'

'Good call. Something to drink?'

'A Coke, no ice, please.'

'You got it, hon.'

'Thank you.'

Tally wished she had a book to read while she waited, but
she'd left her books behind. They were all bestsellers in paperback, none especially good, but she'd read them several times
each.

Mental note: buy books.

Unaccustomed to the relative silence of the place, she went
to the cash register for some change and then fed a couple of
quarters into the jukebox, pushing in random selections and
hoping for the best.

A moment or two after returning to her seat, a voice started
growling about being born in the USA.

Mental note: buy some music to play in the car.

*   *   *

She sat on the bed in her slip and aimed the remote control at the TV set, changing channels until she found a PBS station. Then she tried to watch but her eyes kept sliding to the corners of the room. A car door slammed outside and she jumped, looking over at the tightly drawn curtains, then at the locked door, the security chain in place. As her heart settled into a more temperate rhythm, she looked back at the TV screen, turning and turning the wedding ring on her finger.

EIGHT

Tally slept badly, waking every half hour or so with a start, to look wildly at the shadowy corners of the room, then over at the reassuring spill of light from the bathroom. Perhaps it was the absence of the night sounds that had grown too familiar over the years – the weeping, the whispered prayers, the moans of illicit sexual activity, even, occasionally, a brief scream – that kept her on the rim of sleep. Listening hard, all she could hear was the rushing sound of traffic on the interstate a mile or so away. And listening to that muted rush lulled her back to sleep each time. Then, as dawn approached, she slipped at last below the surface, and slept for just over two hours.

Unaccustomed to being enclosed while she bathed, she kept the shower curtain halfway open while she stood under the weak spray of hot water. Her fingers, as always, briefly touched the raised scar from the knife wound just below her left shoulder, then the slightly puckered scar near her right hip and the third, a long but less prominent one on the outside of her right forearm. The scars were flesh memories, encoded with detail.

Just the two of them: herself and a small enraged woman in the shower room. Brandishing a teaspoon, its handle honed to razor sharpness, the small woman sidled near, whispering, 'La-di-da-ing your way around here, but you're no better than nobody else. I know all about you from the TV, Miss Murdering High-Society Bitch.'

When Tally said softly, 'If you want to kill me, go ahead,' the ratty-haired, shriveled little woman, who could've been any age between thirty and sixty, was thrown, a furrow forming between her brows. Tally turned, presenting her naked back. Several weighted moments of silence followed, when Tally could almost hear the woman thinking. Then the stabbing began. Half-hearted, it seemed. Tally didn't move, made no sound.

Then, in moments, it was over. The woman was gone, leaving the spoon embedded in Tally's hip.

Punishment, but not death. She was disappointed. Permission had defused the woman's rage, but prison form mandated that some injury be inflicted. Tally understood. Form dictated behavior, no matter where you were. If there were a next time, she'd vowed, she'd simply offer herself in silence. Go quietly.

Some weeks later in the food line, the woman had murmured, 'Why'd you do that: tell me to go ahead? And how come you didn't say it was me that did it?'

Turning to look at the woman, seeing the confusion in her faded eyes, Tally said in a very low voice, 'You can't kill someone who's already dead.'

Taking the remark almost literally, the woman was so frightened that she dropped her tray and fled. At the noise, everyone looked up to watch her go, then turned with speculative interest to look at Tally, who'd already moved along in the line and was paying no attention. But she could feel the eyes on her; they had weight, as if the combined gazes had actual density.

Amazing how superstitious, how literal some people could be; how fearful and angry. She later learned that the woman's name was Angie and, after years of being beaten and burned and raped, she'd stabbed her husband seventy-three times while he was sleeping off a three-day bender. She was given life, without parole; no death sentence because of the extenuating circumstances. After that day in the food line, she kept well away from Tally, never again coming anywhere near her. No one did. Newcomers were warned off soon after arriving. No point trying to scare or hurt someone who was, according to Angie, already dead – a ghost, a zombie, or maybe just plain crazy. And in a sense Tally was all those things. Unintentionally perpetuating the myth, she never spoke, unless one of the staff addressed her directly. There was nothing to say. Her fellow inmates eyed her warily and kept their distance. The warden found it amusing. 'You're either a brilliant strategist,' she said, 'or the saddest woman I've ever encountered. Probably both.'

In the years that followed, the warden summoned Tally to her office a few times a year. Initially, Tally thought the conversation was a preamble to some discussion pertaining to the institution, to a rule or regulation she might unknowingly have violated. But no. The conversation was for its own sake, and that seemed eminently reasonable. So they talked, with the warden always taking the lead, setting the topic. And those were the only occasions when the disused machinery in Tally's head got lubricated and began to function. Twenty or thirty minutes of conversation, about books, about music, about art, amounting to perhaps ninety or so minutes a year had fused her grip on reality, keeping it intact.

She wondered, suddenly, if that had been the woman's intent. An extraordinary notion, but one that now occurred to her as true. In the unlikeliest of places, someone had cared enough about her to make an effort to keep Tally's brain alive. Unrecognized kindness in an unlikely place.

Mental note: write to the warden with the new Mont Blanc pen – when she got it.

The motel's free shampoo left her hair feeling greasy; the small hard square of soap dried out her skin, and she added a stop at a drugstore to her growing shopping list. Shampoo and conditioner, face and body moisturizers, a decent hairbrush.

Dressed again in the old ill-fitting Chanel suit and the pantyhose she'd washed the night before depressed her as she sat on the end of the bed to open the folder Warren had given her. There was five thousand dollars in hundred-dollar bills, and a Visa card. The checks were on her old account at Wells Fargo. Warren had kept the account active with just a change of address, so that her statements were sent in care of his office. He'd slipped a new register into place in the check book, and she stared at the balance, thinking that compound interest, like rust, never slept. The income from her grandmother's trust kept on growing exponentially. Love, from beyond the grave. The sole member of the family who had cared for her unequivocally, without stipulations.

Closing her eyes, she could almost smell the clean fragrance of her grandmother's Blue Grass, could see her in one of her favorite Anne Fogarty shirtwaist dresses with the Capezio flats

she'd worn to minimize her height. Tall and narrow, her black
hair in a ponytail, her eyes very blue and her teeth very white
in her always suntanned face. Strong hands and long legs.
There wasn't a horse born that she couldn't ride. But there
was a skittish two-year-old who'd reared one morning when
a stray dog came from out of nowhere, barking and trying to
nip the filly's fetlocks. And the widowed fifty-three-year-old
Annalise Paxton had died of massive head injuries sustained
when she was thrown onto a rocky outcropping.

Her entire estate, including the Nevada ranch, was bequeathed
to her only grandchild, who looked so much like Annalise that
strangers had invariably taken them for mother and daughter.
She'd left fourteen-year-old Tally with a dry, aching sorrow
that failed to diminish with time, along with a place to stay
(now long gone) should she ever need refuge, an income for
life, and an understanding of love that Tally could never have
acquired from her carping, disinterested parents.

With a sigh, Tally put several of the hundred-dollar bills in
her absurdly dated black leather clutch bag, along with the
credit card and check book. After a quick look around the room
to make sure she'd left nothing behind – she didn't *have*
anything to leave behind, she chided herself – she went out
to put the folder in the trunk of the Benz. Annalise would
have sent Warren to meet Tally with a station wagon or a
pickup truck. But Annalise's son had married a woman who
dictated the terms and conditions of her family's life, and Tyler
Scott Paxton had never once gone against his wife's wishes,
had never voiced disagreement with any of her opinions, no
matter how ill-conceived, or foolish, or mean. Ivory Rowe
Paxton controlled everyone and everything within reach. She
said a Benz. Warren would merely ask, 'What model?' No
wonder he was retiring. For twenty-odd years of dealing with
Ivory, he deserved a Purple Heart.

It was only eight a.m. and the remnants of the cold night
air still lingered as Tally walked, shivering, to the restaurant,
pausing outside to buy a newspaper from the box – a useful
prop to ease her nervousness at being on view in a public
place.

The same hefty middle-aged waitress was on duty and came

over smiling with a menu tucked under her arm, a thick white mug in one hand and a coffee pot in the other.

'Have a good night, hon?' she asked. 'Coffee?'

'Yes, please.'

The woman poured the coffee, then put down the menu.

'I need to buy a few things,' Tally said. 'Are there stores nearby?'

'Just hang a left when you pull out of here, and go straight into town. You'll find everything you need.'

'Thank you.'

'Sure thing. Back in a minute to take your order.'

Eggs still hot from the griddle seemed a great luxury. She managed to eat half the food on her plate, and drank a second cup of coffee while she absorbed information from the newspaper. It all seemed alien, not quite real. The prices in the ads struck her as exceptionally high. But then, fifteen years later, London broil wasn't still going to be fifty-nine cents a pound. She knew, though, that the 1968 prices were always going to be her yardstick. That was the year her life had ended. No matter what happened now, she believed that her brain would remain snagged on that point in time.

She was halfway to her car when the waitress called out to her. Tally turned back.

'I think you made a mistake, hon,' the woman said, holding out the hundred-dollar bill Tally had left tucked under her empty coffee mug.

'No. No mistake. That's your tip.'

'On a three-dollar tab?' the woman said, her expression both amused and disbelieving.

'You've been very kind,' Tally said. 'I appreciate it.'

'You sure? It's a hell of a lot of money.'

'Positive.'

The woman shook her head, her grin reappearing. 'Well, I thank you. You take good care. Okay?'

'I will do my best.'

Tally turned away and again started toward the car.

'Just outta curiosity,' the woman called. 'Where're you headed? After you finish up shopping, I mean.'

'No idea. Just going east.'

'Wish *I* was. Good luck to you, hon, and thanks again.'
'You're most welcome.'

In jeans and a long-sleeved cotton shirt, a Shetland crew-neck
sweater tied around her neck by its sleeves, with short socks
and soft leather loafers, Tally felt more comfortable behind
the wheel. Her purchases were in the trunk, along with a new
Hartmann suitcase and a small backpack. When she stopped
for the night she'd organize the bags, and have her choice of
a dozen books to read.

She popped one of the new cassettes into the player and felt
a surge of genuine pleasure as the first notes of the Haydn *Cello
Concerto in C* emerged from the speakers. The music lifted her
mood, just as the clothes had done. Her foot no longer shook
on the accelerator. In less than twenty-four hours, driving had
become automatic, natural. With luck, she'd make it into mid-
Wyoming by nightfall. Hundreds of miles now lay behind her.
She wanted it to be thousands. Distance couldn't alter the past,
but at the very least she could be physically removed from it.
And perhaps at a great distance, she might be able to consider
everything that had happened fifteen years before – something
she did only involuntarily, in dreams. During all the waking
hours of her five thousand three hundred and seventy-two days
of being encaged, she'd focused only on the moment. Get through
one hour, then the next. Somehow, the hours accumulated into
days, weeks, months, years. And she'd withstood the tedium,
kept her mind engaged by reading anything available, by doing
crossword puzzles, and by conversations with Warden Hughes,
a woman with a surprisingly diverse range of interests.

For a moment, without knowing she was going to do it, she
tried to remember Anna's face, but all that appeared on her
mental screen was an amorphous outline. She had only a
handful of photographs of her. She had some of Clayton too,
but she hadn't looked at any of them since the day of her
allocution and sentencing. His face, too, refused to come into
focus. Someday she might look at the pictures – but not in
the foreseeable future. Just this brief, unanticipated bit of recall
created a pain similar to that first slash from Angie's teaspoon-
knife: a searing electric message. She pushed it away, returning

her attention to the music, Jacqueline du Pré dragging passion from her cello.

The place names struck her as odd, even funny. 'Deeth' she read as Death. The exit for Danger Cave was intriguing, and she was tempted to stop, but didn't. She crossed into Utah, taken with Wendover, an ambling, pleasant name. *Let me know when it's over*, she thought, glancing at the gas gauge.

She stopped outside Salt Lake City to fill the gas tank and use the restroom, deciding she'd eat once she was on the far side of the city, approaching the Wyoming border. She was now in a part of the country she'd only ever read about in history and geography textbooks. Studying the map she'd bought before leaving Elko, she thought she'd try to make it to either Green River or Rock Springs. And tomorrow she'd aim for Nebraska. There was no rush. She had no destination, except away. All she knew with certainty was that she would never go back to Nevada, or to her birthplace, San Francisco. The place once called home had been no more than an illusion, no more real than a child's fervid imagining.

Who was it who said that home is the place where, when you go there, they have to take you in? Frost, that was it. Robert Frost. Must have had an actual family, she thought. The same fellow who wrote about the lovely dark woods and promises to keep.

'Ah, Mr Frost,' she said aloud, 'I have no promises to keep. But I do have some miles to go.'

Mental note: buy a collection of Frost's poems.

The Wyoming license plates stated: Like No Place on Earth. It was true. Vast beneath a wide-open sky, the land stretched into the distance on all sides with scarcely a sign of habitation. She felt dwarfed by the great expanses, and genuinely free. Beyond the leathery-smelling confines of the car, there was nothing on the landscape to restrain her. She went rocketing along the highway, jittery with the knowledge that no one was monitoring her actions, that there was no one to whom she was obliged to answer for her decisions. Free in The Equality State, headed east toward Ever Upward, and Live Free or Die.

*   *   *

That evening, unwilling to face another diner where people would look her over and the waitress might not be as good-humored and accommodating as the woman in Elko, she opted for the drive-thru at McDonald's. It was her first experience of drive-thru service. Although she wasn't given sufficient time to decipher the menu, she very much liked the concept of being able to purchase a meal without having to leave the car. A bit rattled by the impatience of the young woman at the window, Tally said, 'Why don't you order for me?'

'O-kaaaaay!' the teenager said, mildly exasperated, eyes narrowed for a moment before she turned away. Seconds later, she held out a bag, stated a price, and Tally paid. She then returned to her motel with what she determined from the wrapper was a Big Mac, an enormous order of fries, and a large Coke. Actually, she decided, removing the plastic lid to look inside, it was a large cup of ice with Coke flavoring.

She watched television, switching channels every few minutes, as she worked on the food, preferring the fries to the immense burger, which she abandoned after only a few bites.

The offerings on TV fascinated her. Some of the prime-time shows had been popular inside – *That's Incredible* was a great favorite of the inmates. Tally had found it incredible that anyone would watch such crap. Years ago, she'd loved *The Avengers*, and Carol Burnett's show: Jonathan Winters made her howl with his edgy, half-mad humor. Best of all was Dick Cavett's morning interviews. There were things worth watching then. Now, as she ran through the channels, the offerings seemed shoddy. Mental popcorn: pleasant to eat, never filling.

Finished with the food, she sorted through her purchases, setting out fresh underwear and clean socks for the morning, and her new pajamas and slippers. Everything else went into the suitcase, except the Kurt Vonnegut novel she'd decided to read first, and her toiletries. Car doors slamming outside her door made her jump. Then came the voices of a couple, talking as they opened the door of the room next to hers.

God! She remained in place, eyes on the curtained windows, until her frenzied heart-rate began to ease. Then there was the sound of another car pulling to a stop, another car door slamming, and her common sense – *it's a motel, people are stopping for the night, pull yourself together* – did battle with old fear. *The pounding on the door will start any moment now. No, it's just people ready for a rest after a long day of driving But what if it's . . . NoNoNo it's over, over!*

Long minutes passed before she was able to move. But as she washed her face and cleaned her teeth before brushing her hair, she kept looking over at the windows, then at the door. She could tell herself over and over that history didn't repeat itself, but she couldn't quite buy into that – not with a history like hers.

Even settled in bed with the Vonnegut novel propped on her upraised knees, her eyes went repeatedly to the windows, then the door. And each time a car door slammed, her heart did, too.

NINE

For a second night she kept waking every half hour or so. She thought it might be because she no longer had the security of a set of locked bars across the entrance to the cell she shared with sixty-something Bertie, who was as silent as Tally. Bertie was lean in a constricted fashion, as if (like Tally) her primary goal was to keep everything within her closely contained. Clean and tidy, her hair surprisingly thick and lustrous, her features a time-dulled portrait of the pretty girl she'd once been, she spent her days working in the prison laundry and her nights reading. A small transistor radio, the volume low, was always tuned to an easy-listening station. She and Tally shared books without comment beyond a 'thank you' and 'you're welcome.' Despite the proximity that stirred so many of the other cell mates to acts ranging from petty spitefulness or sexual partnership to all-out violence, Tally and Bertie were virtual paragons of politeness. In a place that didn't allow for privacy, they managed to give it to each other. Despite their mutual silence, they respected and even liked each other. Tally always thought that had she been given a life sentence she would, eventually, have become very like Bertie. It was sheer good fortune to have been paired with one of the few other women in the institution with no inclination to bemoan her fate or to volunteer tidbits of her past.

Gazing at the spill of light from the partway closed bathroom door, Tally decided that the notion that she missed the cell bars was crazy. Still, she had to admit that anything that kept caged angry women away from her while she slept had to be construed as a good thing. Now, that particular safety was gone and she wondered how long, if ever, it would take to become accustomed to her newly recovered freedom. It seemed to be fraught with hazards she couldn't have imagined. Certainly, she could never again take for granted the things that had once been an elementary part of her life: the right to go where she wanted, when she wanted, and to do as she wished when she got there. It wasn't surprising that so many of the women wound up back inside again. The system robbed you of the skills needed to live an ordinary life. And the halfway houses she'd overheard the recidivist women speak of sounded worse than the prison, with thefts and fights and endless bitter criticism of everyone and everything.

Tally's refusal to go before a parole board and declare herself sorry for the crime of second-degree murder had kept her contained, like an artifact in the cornerstone of a new building, for the full term of her fifteen-year sentence. She was sorry for many things. But that? No. She preferred to endure the entire fifteen years of lockup rather than make a false declaration. She'd made up her mind at the outset that if she managed to live through the whole sentence, she wanted to leave completely free, answerable to no one. The fact that she didn't care whether or not she lived had made her prison existence tolerable. Interestingly, although they'd never come even close to discussing it, she knew that Bertie shared her attitude, even though Bertie was going to live out her life inside the barbed-wire-topped walls.

So here was Tally, supposedly free, startled by slamming car doors and unable to sleep and unable, too, to cry. She remembered clearly the last time she'd shed tears. It wasn't likely she'd ever forget. But if there was one lesson she'd learned in prison it was that tears were viewed as a sign of weakness. Weep, and the predators would be all over you.

There were broomstick rapes in the shower room, beatings and knifings and killings, too. Depending on your crime – and somehow the details were common knowledge the moment you set foot inside – you were marked. It was a strange and primal code, established so long ago that no one knew who'd first decided that certain crimes deserved additional punishment. After the justice system's penalty, came the penalty of your so-called peers. In many ways it was far worse than the loss of autonomy because it meant that there was almost nowhere inside the institution you'd be safe – unless you became someone's sweetheart or their slave.

She yawned, longing for sleep, and pushed away the ugly

memories. She pictured Annalise, strong hands holding the
reins, her face lit with pleasure as her stallion carried her away
at a gallop. Breathing deeply, contentedly, that long ago Tally
watched her grandmother ride out of sight. Then she looked
up at the vast, empty sky, feeling the heat of the desert sun.
The aroma of roasting meat drifted through the screen door
from the kitchen, where Alba was making dinner, humming
softly as she worked. Over by the barn, Joe was hosing dirty
soap off the pickup, which he washed faithfully every week.
'Preserves the paint,' he'd long-since explained to her. 'Take
care of your vee-hickle and it won't never let you down when
you most need it.' Moondust, the retriever bitch, kept jumping
at the spray, trying to get a mouthful of the sun-spangled water.
And a small lizard dashed down the side of the barn and
disappeared into the scrub.

So enamored was she of the drive-thru that she picked up her
breakfast at the McDonald's window. The food wasn't particularly good, the coffee was tasteless and far too hot, but she
was content to park in a corner of the lot and listen to the
radio while she ate her Egg McMuffin and scalded her mouth,
trying to wash the greasy food down with the coffee.

When she'd finished, she dumped the trash then studied the
map, deciding she'd try to make the Nebraska border by nightfall. She was, she knew, creating meaningless destinations. It
didn't matter if she went a hundred miles or four hundred. But
she'd always been someone who had to set goals, no matter
how minimal. So today she would aim for Nebraska.

After tucking the map into the door pocket, she reached for
another of the new cassettes and began removing the cellophane.
Ray Charles and Betty Carter, one of her all-time favorite
albums; music her mother had dismissed as mere noise.

'You have low tastes, Natalie,' her mother had declared from
the doorway of Tally's bedroom. Permed and girdled, tight and
judgmental and unsmiling, she stood fingering her pearls as if
drawing solace from their shape and feel. Heaven knew she
got no satisfaction, never mind comfort, from her intractable
daughter. She stated often and unhappily that if she'd known
how unrewarding it was to have such a disobedient daughter,

she'd never have had a child – a statement that, in its repetition, served to solidify Tally's dislike of her mother.

'Actually,' thirteen-year-old Tally had replied pleasantly, looking over her shoulder, 'I have very good taste. Granna's crazy about Ray Charles. This record's going to become a classic. Annalise would love this as much as I do, that is why I plan to buy a copy for her.'

Her mother had made a too-familiar noise that Tally had seen written in old-fashioned books as *harumph*. Close enough. Ivory Rowe Paxton dismissed anything she didn't like or understand, especially music created by people of color. Her deep-seated prejudices always made Tally cringe. Ivory had married above herself but expensive clothes, a wealthy husband and a lavish lifestyle couldn't wipe out the hateful predilections bred into her very genes. She was the worst kind of elitist: an ignorant, uneducated one who latched on to whatever was in vogue with her 'set' – those well-born, educated elitists whose experiences out in the world were carefully cushioned to keep life's grittier aspects at a safe remove, and the women who tolerated Ivory only because she was Tyler Scott Paxton's wife and who were (Tally had overheard their whispered comments when Ivory was out of earshot) privately amused and repelled by Ivory's extravagant efforts to fit in.

Tyler Scott Paxton was a force to be reckoned with in international banking, but was weak-willed and needy when it came to the icy, big-breasted blonde with the flawless milky complexion and flat blue eyes who held the keys to his psychosexual well-being. 'He's a disappointment,' Annalise had confided to her twelve-year-old granddaughter. 'But not a surprise, I'm sorry to say. He was a fearful little boy, and your grandfather was not a kind man. I should have heeded my instincts and told Scott to leave the boy alone. I was too young,' Annalise confessed. 'I was going by the book, and by the time I realized the so-called book was nonsense, Tyler was as set in his ways as a concrete patio.'

Tally had laughed appreciatively.

'No, really. It's as much my fault as it was Scott's. I should've intervened much earlier. By the time I began defending Tyler it was too late. Everything I said and did only seemed to make matters worse. Even after his father died, when Tyler was a teenager, nothing could change the established pattern. I love my son. He has a hidden vein of sweetness that gives me hope for him. But I can't honestly say I admire the man he's become. And that's a terrible thing for a mother to admit. It's like the worst sort of failure.'

'Dad's all right. At least he talks to me when Ivory's out of the way, and acts as if I mean something to him. Ivory doesn't love me *or* like me,' Tally had said quietly.

'I am sorrier than I can say about that. Your mother is an absolute horror,' Annalise had said, making a face. 'Just know that *I* love you and like you. I always have. I always will. You're a girl after my own heart and you're going to grow up to be a remarkable woman.'

Well, no. She had grown up to be notorious, a world away from remarkable. Still, she knew that Annalise would have understood what had happened, and would have stood staunchly by her. Annalise would have been by her side every step of the way. And everything would have played out very differently. There wasn't a day when Tally didn't feel the loss, longing for the sight and sound and smell of her grandmother. It was a wound that had never healed, as if one of Tally's limbs had been ripped from her body. The resulting damage to the muscles and nerve-endings was permanent.

Once she'd merged into the eastbound traffic on the interstate, she finally pushed the cassette into the player.

There was the hiss of leader tape for several seconds and then Ray Charles's voice seeped from the speakers.

He sang, and the smooth mellow clarity of his voice penetrated the immense structure inside her that had built itself day by day for more than fifteen years. Suddenly, painfully, it began developing fissures; parts started to fall away, becoming an avalanche. And all at once she was sobbing, blinded by tears that burned like acid. Years of control gone, just like that. *Gone.* She couldn't see the road and put on the windshield wipers. With a disgusted yelp, she turned them off, crying so hard that the car was lurching all over the road. Cars in the passing lane honked out their annoyance as they shot by.

Signaling, she pulled off onto the shoulder, threw the shift into Park, and clutched the steering wheel. Shaken by sorrow that seemed to rise from the lowest depths of her body to take flight from her throat, the interior of the car was filled with cries that might have come from some mortally wounded creature in its death throes. She screamed until her throat was raw and only a hoarse barking accompanied the tears, while Betty and Ray sang 'We'll Be Together Again,' and then 'People Will Say We're in Love.'

Cars flew past, mere blurs, as her hands pulled at the steering wheel as if she might rip it from its moorings. Everything that had been so carefully stored inside her was gushing out, tearing itself free from its forced containment. Emotions were swirling like invisible dervishes inside the expensive leather interior of this car she'd get rid of as soon as she could. Ivory's choice: it was tainted. Tally hated this goddamned car.

Growing wearied, her chest heaving in spasms, she let her forehead come to rest on the steering wheel, her hands still fastened to it so tightly that her fingernails were digging into the fleshy part of her palms.

There was a rapping at the window and she gasped, her body jolting upright as her eyes turned to look.

A young state trooper was gazing in at her, signaling to her to open the window.

With an effort, she freed her right hand from the steering wheel and reached to the control on the center console to open the window.

'Are you all right, Miss?' the trooper asked, his eyes doing a quick sweep of her, of the car's interior.

She shook her head, then mopped her face on her sleeve.

'Can I be of help?' he offered.

'Somebody died,' she said hoarsely, her voice ravaged. It was the truth, after all. Just rather late.

'Sorry to hear it. You might want to get off the highway 'til you've calmed down some. Parked on the shoulder the way you are, it's not exactly safe.'

His name badge read Brendon O'Neill. He was very young and had a sweetly earnest face.

'Yes, I'll get off,' she said, again wiping her face on her

sleeve. 'It just suddenly came over me.' Her lips were moving and words came out but she felt utterly removed from the conversation. She was aware primarily of her emptied interior, of feeling eviscerated.

'I know how that can be,' he said, with genuine-sounding sympathy. 'Next exit's just a few miles ahead. You might want to get off there, maybe get yourself some coffee at the truck stop. Maybe even sleep for a time. You don't want to be driving, the state you're in.'

'Maybe not,' she agreed robotically. 'Thank you.'

'My sympathies for your loss. You be careful now, okay? You're a long way from California and home. I'm sure your family wouldn't want anything to happen to you.'

'No,' she said, finding that exquisitely ironic. 'They wouldn't want that.' *They'd have preferred it if I'd been stillborn.*

He touched two fingers to the brim of his hat, then returned to his cruiser where he slid behind the wheel and sat waiting for her to pull back into the traffic.

She had no choice but to drive. And glancing into the rear-view mirror to see he was following her, she also had no choice but to take the next exit. Watching as she drove along the off-ramp, she saw him shoot past, heard his siren give a brief *wheeep*.

Maybe coffee was a good idea, she told herself. That pitiful brew at McDonald's had been undrinkable and a caffeine lift would help.

She parked at the service station, then went inside to buy a package of tissues and a newspaper. She ordered a coffee, doctored it with cream and sugar, and took a sip. It was good, strong coffee.

Thank you, young Trooper O'Neill, she thought as she felt the warmth soothing her raw throat. *Somebody died.* She was amazed that those words had come shooting out of her mouth of their own accord. *Somebody died.* In fact, everyone who mattered to her had died. The only person left for whom she had any feeling was Warren. And Warren was behind her now; not beyond the reach of the telephone, but behind nonetheless – of the past.

*   *   *

She drove just under two hundred miles that day, exhausted by her astonishing breakdown early that morning. By four thirty she was yawning so hard her eyes were watering. Her body wanted to shut down. Surrendering, she pulled off at the next exit and followed the signs to a row of motels, fast-food outlets and filling stations.

She checked into a Howard Johnson's, dropped her bag, pushed off her loafers and got into the bed fully dressed. When she awakened she had no idea where she was, and turned over to look at the clock-radio on the bedside table. It was coming up to five thirty a.m. She'd slept for more than eleven hours.

Switching on the light, she sat on the side of the bed staring at the carpet and thinking about that mad spasm that had overtaken her in the car the previous day. Had it been her psyche's way of responding to freedom? Was she now, finally, going to revert to the feeling, reactive person she'd been before?

Doubtful. Swimming in the now-shallow depths of her interior like a tiny fish was her death wish. Biding its time, fed on minuscule flakes of nourishment, it lived on. Like some mutated survivor of her personal holocaust, the little fish swam, and waited. Yes, it had been tossed about by the emotional storm, but it remained, active and unscathed.

She needed a shower, a change of clothes, and food. Then she'd continue on her way east in this altered world of hostile truck drivers, interchangeable strip malls with their McDonald's and Burger Kings, their Wendy's and Kentucky Fried Chicken outlets. What she also needed, she decided, was to get to a place without strip malls and franchise fast-food emporiums; a place with old-fashioned stores, and restaurants that advertised 'home cooking,' and tree-lined streets. She had in mind four-color print images of places she'd looked at in oversized picture books of New England. White churches surrounded by densely leaved trees, generous clapboard houses with black shutters, populated by families whose accents were as crisp as fresh autumn apples. Somewhere along a sinuous two-lane road, there was a house with a porch and an attic and big kitchen, with land enough for privacy and a vegetable garden. Maybe a lilac tree in the back and a sweeping view from the front porch. She'd know the place when she saw it.

Her ribs tender and her throat still raw, she showered and washed her hair, then pulled on fresh underwear and socks, clean Levi's, a pale blue cotton button-down shirt and a navy wool cardigan to shield her against the morning chill. After stowing her things in the trunk, she headed for the restaurant. Dismayed as she was by that emotional hurricane that had swept over her, she had to admit that she felt better than she had in a long, long time.

TEN

The traffic on Interstate 84 heading east was heavy. Until she'd crossed over into New York state, driving had, after four days on the road, become a mechanical exercise. With the cruise control set at four miles over the speed limit, she'd listened to her new cassettes, studied the changing landscape, and considered the way the behavior of the people she encountered had grown progressively cooler the farther east she got.

From the overt friendly warmth of the west, to the civil warmth of the Midwest, the interpersonal climate was positively chilly by the time she stopped to get fuel sixty-odd miles before the Connecticut line. No one smiled; people seemed unwilling to make eye contact. She was well accustomed to that. To keep your eyes forward in prison meant you were either crazy or looking for trouble. Since the majority of the inmates believed she was more than a little crazy, she'd never acquired the habit of averting her gaze. There were occasions when common sense dictated she turn away from some scene too ugly or upsetting to tolerate. Otherwise, she'd gone about her business, absorbing facts and details of faces but maintaining always a bland, non-judgmental expression.

Now it seemed to her as if easterners could well be inmates in some gateless prison. Contact was limited to a clipped please or thank-you from people seemingly bereft of curiosity or emotion. Perhaps the east wouldn't be right for her. But then it was possible no place on earth was right for her. The best she could hope for was to find some area that didn't have a prison-like feel to it. Vermont perhaps, or Maine. Somewhere remote but beautiful, with distinct seasons rather than the blurry sameness of a year in California or Nevada. And if she saw nothing that appealed to her in the northern New England states, she could keep on going into Canada, a country she'd always wanted to explore. The Canadian population was a tenth of the American but with a far greater land mass, and there were vast stretches of open, scarcely populated territory. Nova Scotia was appealing. So was New Brunswick, or Prince Edward Island. She would go as far east as it was possible to go, and then head north on secondary roads, eyes open for the place that would speak to her, that would invite her to stop, to settle in.

Once over the Connecticut state line, the traffic turned positively crazy, with cars darting from lane to lane without signaling, and traffic pouring incautiously onto the highway from the access lanes. The drivers all seemed to be in a state of blended rage and indignation, as if their rights were somehow being impugned. They all wore an infuriated how-dare-you expression and took extraordinary chances, ignoring the speed limit and cutting in and out of the traffic so recklessly that she held her breath as cars kept narrowly missing the rear-ends of slower-moving vehicles. Keeping close watch on the traffic, her hands grew damp on the steering wheel. She'd never encountered anything remotely like this form of vehicular madness.

On top of all that, she was stuck in the passing lane, and kept glancing over to her right, hoping for a gap that would let her shift out of the lane. But most of the cars and trucks were tailgating dangerously. A big sedan was riding her bumper. Were she to apply the brakes, the irate guy she could see in her rearview mirror would slam into her. She could see him swearing at her, his face twisted as he cursed her.

She tried to maintain a decent distance from the car ahead of her but other drivers kept zipping into whatever space she allowed. It was like a demented game and she wasn't enjoying being a participant. She had to hike up the air conditioning to compensate for her body's heat, and turn down the volume on the radio in order not to get distracted.

Then, just past the Danbury exits, her lane of traffic began peeling off at a left-hand exit and, unable to get out of the lane, she had to follow the line of cars onto what a roadside sign identified as Route 7 northbound. A quick look in the rearview mirror showed the car that had been tailgating her swerving out of the lane, barely missing the front fender of a vehicle that had to slam on its brakes to avoid a collision.

In the now considerably calmer flow of traffic, she debated taking the next exit and circling back to the interstate. But considering the lunacy she'd just left behind, she decided to keep going. It was early evening, and she was tired after seven hours of driving. Besides, the trees were old and lushly leaved, arching protectively over the road in spots; the grass looked thick and rich, and flowers adorned the gardens of most of the white clapboard houses she passed. They were old dwellings, with deep porches, multipaned windows and red-brick chimneys; houses she'd only ever seen and admired in books.

And all at once, just like that, she wanted to have one of them. They were the antithesis of the San Francisco houses where her childhood friends had lived – those narrow, improbable dwellings that clung like limpets to steeply pitched streets. Her parents' house had, from very early on, been a source of embarrassment to Tally. Once upon a time it had been some important family's home, set in imposing grandeur at the apex of a hill and commanding an extraordinary view. It had architectural niceties, like gingerbread trim and fine wood paneling, panes of stained-glass flanking the front door. But that was once upon a very long time ago.

Aside from it being far too large for a family of three, the house had been hideously fitted out by an interior decorator more anxious for her huge fee than for any cohesiveness in the design. The woman had taken Ivory's measure and run wild, knowing full well that Ivory would accept the word of a so-called expert and not question the style or the acquisitions required to accomplish what Tally came to think of as Gothic Noir.

The foyer was so crowded with Victorian pieces that the area looked half its actual size. There was a mirrored oak coat rack with pegs and a lift-up seat, an oriental rug completely at odds with the furniture, several murky pastoral oils on the walls and, to compound the horror, flocked wallpaper and swagged velvet draperies over the double doorway to the living room. All the downstairs rooms were similarly dark and crowded. But the library, created especially for her father, was the *pièce de résistance*, complete with hunting scenes in heavy frames, creaky leather armchairs, a vast Persian carpet, potted aspidistras, and more velvet draperies.

Ivory had adored it. Tally had pitied her, wishing there were some way she could tell her mother how truly awful it all was. But Tally couldn't tell her mother a thing; her opinions were of no consequence. 'What would *you* know?' was Ivory's inevitable scathing response to any comment Tally might make, about anything.

The house, like Ivory herself, was beautiful outside. And, inside, it was dark and chaotic, crowded with too many things all at odds with each other: bedlam.

So, Tally thought now, no matter how unfriendly the people might be here in the east, this was what she wanted to see every day: towering old trees and clapboard houses that had long-since finished settling and weren't entirely square but had innate charm. Perhaps, quite by accident, she was on the right road after all.

The traffic thinned and she drove on, with no idea where she was headed. She'd buy a local map when she next stopped to gas up the car.

A river appeared on the left-hand side of the road, dappled gold with the waning sun, and deep green fields were on her right. The scenery was enchanting, so lavishly beautiful that she was quite overwhelmed, with a feeling akin to happiness – something she hadn't felt in many, many years. The wealth of the landscape filled her senses, gave her an odd sense of privilege. It reminded her of the final scenes in *Soylent Green*, a film she'd watched back in the mid-seventies in the prison common area. Everyone had been stricken by the film. There'd been none of the usual asinine comments or inchoate shouting at the screen. In fact, there'd been no talking at all, not even when it was over and the screen went white. Everyone dispersed in rare, thoughtful silence. It wasn't a particularly good film, but Edward G. Robinson had given great depth to his final screen performance. And each woman watching understood his character's longing to see the verdant world of the past. Even if the inmates had lived their entire lives within the state of Nevada, that view of the wider world struck a powerful chord and set every one of them longing for an earthly beauty beyond their reach.

The farther north she got, the more splendid the scenery became. She passed through Gaylordsville, then little communities that were scarcely more than clusters of houses, yet the past seemed to come to life in the details glimpsed in passing: a weathered barn atilt in a field, lace curtains on a narrow window, hanging plants suspended from the beams of a porch, a low white-painted picket fence defining the perimeter of a house front. Tally stopped at last at a gas station at a place near Bull's Bridge, where she fueled the car and bought a regional map. Standing outside in the cooling end of the day breeze, she studied the map, trying to fix her position. She was in Litchfield County. The river that appeared intermittently was the Housatonic. And ahead on Route 7, according to the map's legend, there was a covered bridge. Beyond that was the town of Kent. And provided there was accommodation to be had, that's where she'd stop for the night. Finding it highly significant, she noted in the map's legend that the state motto was 'He who transplanted still sustains.' This did seem to be a nourishing area, where things grew with abandon.

Back inside the station, she asked the pleasant middle-aged attendant, 'Are there motels in Kent?'

'Nope. There's a couple over west t'wards Salisbury or north up to Canaan, if you want to go that far. But Mae Duffy's just opened some rooms she's renting, in that big old house of hers. Made it kind of like an inn. You might try there. Just stay on Seven here and it's on your right as you're heading outta Kent, about eight miles ahead. You want, I could give 'er a call, see if she's got a room.'

'Yes, please. That would be wonderful.'

'Sure thing. Lemme just check the number.' The fellow reached for a slim telephone book while Tally revised her opinion of easterners.

'You're in luck,' he told her a couple of minutes later. 'One room left. What's your name?' She told him. He spoke into the telephone again, then hung up. 'She'll hold it for you. Check in at her restaurant in town. Chez Mae, it's called. Can't miss it, on the right side as you're headin' north, smack in the middle of town. They'll get you squared away. Food's real good, too. Kind of on the pricey side, but worth the money. Don't know what they're askin' for the rooms but one thing for sure, it'll be nice. Mae's a stylish gal. New Yorker originally.'

'Thank you so much,' Tally said, offering the man a twenty-dollar bill.

'Oh, no!' Color rose into his face as he smiled sheepishly and held up his hands palms outward. 'Happy to help.'

'Please take it,' she said quietly. 'You didn't have to go to so much trouble.' Leaving the bill on the counter, she again said, 'Thank you,' and made her way back to the car. As she pulled away from the pump, she realized the attendant was in the doorway, watching her go. She waved. He waved back. Then she accelerated back onto Route 7.

She was foolishly disappointed to find that the covered bridge was not, as indicated by the map, actually on Route 7. It was very near to where she'd stopped and she slowed the car, trying to see the structure as she passed the sign for the turnoff, but it wasn't possible. Then, too soon, she was past it. She promised herself she'd return to have a look at the bridge up close. There was something immensely appealing about the very idea of a covered bridge; it typified what she expected of this part of the world.

Kent was a charming little town with a church at the cross-roads and a scattering of shops on either side of the street. And, as the fellow at the gas station had told her, in the middle of the shops on the right was Chez Mae. She pulled into the first available parking spot, then got out and looked around. To the north, Route 7 continued on into the countryside, heading up to Massachusetts and then Vermont.

The restaurant was busy and she had to wait a few minutes before the hostess could get to her. Tally didn't mind. There was low classical piano music emanating discreetly from hidden speakers and the volume of conversation among the diners was also low.

'How long will you be staying?' the hostess asked, as Tally signed the guest register.

'I'm not sure. Maybe a few weeks.'

'Mae'll have to let you know if that's do-able. I don't have time now to check the reservations. But it should be okay. The rooms've just opened so we don't have all that many advance bookings. Will you be having dinner?'

'Yes, please.'

The hostess looked around the room, then turned back. 'I'll have a table clear in about half an hour. We're short-staffed tonight, so if you don't mind I'll run your credit card when you come back. Okay?'

'Sure. Thank you.'

The woman handed her a ring with two keys and told her how to gain access to the house up the road. 'You'll want to park at the far end of the driveway, because you get to the rooms through the back door. It's the top-floor room on the right. By the time you get your bags in and come back, I'll have a table ready for you,' she told Tally, before hurrying off.

She found the house without difficulty and let herself in. The room was spacious and charming with a steeply vaulted, timbered ceiling from which a fan was suspended. The walls were covered in blue-and-white-patterned wallpaper. And there was actual furniture, constructed of actual wood – not a veneer in sight. A dozen or so books stood in a small bookcase to the left of the windows on the near wall; a TV set sat atop an old, well cared-for chest of drawers with a wall-hung mirror above it. By the windows on the wall facing the door a small wing chair was partnered with a side table upon which stood a ginger jar lamp. A canopied four-poster double bed with pretty linens was centered against the right-hand wall with night tables on either side, each bearing lamps with pleated shades. There was also, she noted with pleasure, a coffee maker, tea bags, packets of biscuits, and a bottle of sparkling water. The bathroom was big. It had an old-fashioned claw foot tub to which a shower extension had been added. There was a stack of fluffy towels on a stand next to the tub, and flowered curtains hung over the window.

It was the first place she'd stayed in that didn't feel like hastily constructed, inferior accommodation for transients who didn't care about their surroundings as long as there was a TV set and a bed. She opened a window, taking a deep breath of the grass-scented air, then went down to the car to bring in her bags. After a quick wash, she added the now-finished Vonnegut novel to the collection in the bookcase. She grabbed *White Mischief* to read over dinner, pocketed the room keys, and made her way back to the restaurant where red-headed Mae dropped by Tally's table to say hello. She was high-fashion model: tall and slim, an arresting woman who looked to be in her mid- to late forties, with a pale, flawless complexion, startling green eyes that glowed with intelligence and good humor, and a lovely smile. 'We'll get acquainted tomorrow at breakfast,' she promised. 'But be warned. My conversation consists mainly of little grunts and head-nods. I am not one of those sunny, morning people. Now, if you're not dieting and you're up for a fabulous meal, order the Lobster Newberg. The town council's talking about making it illegal.' And with a big laugh, she moved on.

A woman prone to frequent gusting laughter and stops at each table to chat for a moment with the guests as she traveled through her restaurant, Tally liked her at once and knew she'd landed in a good place.

That night she dreamed of Annalise. Her sleeping self knew it was a dream but it had such authenticity, contained such a wealth of emotion and such remarkable clarity of detail that she was desperate to know how it played out.

In the dream it was full night, and Tally and her grandmother sat side by side on the long bench on the veranda. Annalise was smoking one of the Gauloise cigarettes she had every evening after dinner. The pungent smell of the foreign tobacco hovered in the cooling night air, mingling with the fragrance of Blue Grass. The sky in the distance was dark as an inkwell, massed clouds moving in to block the starlight.

Tally gazed at her grandmother's face, fascinated as always by her features: the blue eyes clear in her darkly tanned face. She wanted, for a few moments, to *be* her grandmother: grown-up, competent and completely her own person.

'You're staring,' Annalise said, without turning her gaze from the horizon.

'Sorry. I was just thinking.'

Her grandmother turned and smiled. 'And what were you "just thinking?"'

A bit embarrassed, Tally confessed, 'That I want to be like you when I grow up.'

'I hope you'll be smarter than me and make wiser choices.' Annalise drew on her cigarette, then turned aside slightly to exhale the smoke away from Tally.

'Wiser how?

'In how you choose to give your heart. Don't mistake attraction for love.'

'Sex, you mean?

Her grandmother smiled. 'Wanting to make love to someone doesn't necessarily mean you love that person. Love is what remains after the heat dies down. If you still want to hear what he has to say, if you still like him in spite of his annoying habits, if he makes you laugh and is willing to listen to what you have to say, then what you've got might actually be love.' She paused to draw again on the cigarette before crushing it out in a small ceramic ashtray. 'Take the time to get to know the one who seems to be the man of your dreams. Don't give your heart away too quickly.'

'What if I never meet that person?' Tally asked.

'Then enjoy your own company. Make friends and work hard to keep them. Friends are sometimes more valuable than husbands.' She looked off again into the distance. 'We're in for quite a storm,' she observed. 'We'll have to stable the horses and put the truck in the barn. Time to take shelter, Tally.' She turned and looked meaningfully at her granddaughter. 'It's time.'

Tally chose to interpret the dream as a message. This was the place. The next morning, after a wonderful breakfast that included locally made jam, fresh-baked bread, eggs from cage-free chickens, and rich flavorful coffee, she decided she would stay here. She walked down the road toward the shops in the fresh and fragrant morning air, savoring the beauty of the trees

and shrubs that were thick and richly green – at their peak.
The town was a manageable size and had several restaurants
aside from Chez Mae, a supermarket, a drugstore, sundry shops
and, best of all, a book store. The houses on either side of the
road were well-tended and charming. And she would stay here
and find one that would suit her.

ELEVEN

The snow started falling just after eleven in the morning. Dense flakes filled the air, whipped around by the wind. Tally stood at the window watching for quite some time, awed by the sight of what was going to be, according to the radio, a major storm. The visibility decreased rapidly so that within less than an hour all she could see from the window was a shifting curtain of white. Gone altogether was her hilltop view of the countryside spread below.

After a spectacular autumn with the lush foliage aflame with colors that seemed to glow from within even when it rained, there was a new fullness in her chest that displaced a small measure of her long-time sorrow. And she began to anticipate the onset of winter.

A couple of weeks earlier there'd been two days with some snowfall that had failed to accumulate, and she'd been disappointed. This, now, was the real thing: her first snowstorm. As she worked at stripping the layers of wallpaper from the dining-room walls, the radio playing low, she paused every so often to listen to the sound of the wind buffeting her house. She'd had the chimneys cleaned and pointed, so the fire in the living room burned well, an occasional puff-back caused by the wind.

She'd taken possession of the decrepit, long-vacant Victorian in early September and, in accordance with the building inspector's recommendations, she'd had all the major jobs done immediately, relying on Mae's excellent recommendations for various contractors. So, while one team was at work outside redoing the roof and another was dealing with the badly neglected septic system, a third team was removing and replacing rotted sections of clapboard.

Inside, a trio of electricians were rewiring the entire place from cellar to attic, alongside the plumber and his two helpers who opened walls and floors to remove what seemed like miles

of lead piping before installing new copper pipe. After the
wiring and plumbing had been brought up to code, the tile
man and his assistant got to work redoing the two bathrooms.
Then in the solid and fortunately dry stone-walled basement
came the installation of the new furnace and hot water heater,
followed by new fittings for the two and a half bathrooms and
the kitchen. While this was going on, two more men pulled
out the kitchen floor and laid down a new subfloor, over which
went wide-board oak flooring to match the rest of the downstairs floors. Then a team of kitchen specialists tore out the
old cabinets and counters, stripping the room back to the walls
before installing new glass-fronted cabinets and butcher block
countertops. When that was completed there came the delivery
of the new kitchen appliances as well as the washer and dryer
which went into what had formerly been the pantry. A glazier
and his crew replaced the glass in most of the windows while
in his wake came yet another crew fitting new storm windows
and screens. Painters followed the carpenters and glaziers,
sanding and scraping away the old flaking exterior paint,
priming the window frames and new wood before applying a
coat of white paint to the entire house and a coat of black to
the repaired and rehung shutters. The painters would return in
a week's time to begin the interior painting.

From early morning until six or seven in the evening for
two and a half months, a dozen or more workmen had been
all over the house. Every morning after a night at Mae's bed-
and-breakfast, Tally stopped to pick up coffee and rolls in
town and then set off in the new Jeep Grand Cherokee (which
she'd acquired from the delighted, overawed dealer in Danbury
in an even swap for the Mercedes which he intended to keep
for his own use) to meet with the workmen at the house. Over
the coffee and rolls they discussed their schedule before she
set off to shop for more of the items on her very long list:
kitchenware, and small appliances, bedding, a new mattress
for Annalise's four-poster which, along with the rest of the
furniture was due to arrive in a week's time; towels and shower
curtains, a stereo system, a TV and VCR, groceries, and staples
to stock the kitchen.

Along with these things, Tally acquired more books and

music; she also ordered a Mont Blanc pen from a specialty shop in Manhattan along with some heavy-bond monogrammed note paper with matching envelopes. She bought more clothes, and a complete wardrobe of winter wear.

When, after seven weeks' work, the house was relatively habitable, she'd moved finally from the bed-and-breakfast. On her first night in the house (where she planned to spent her nights in an L.L. Bean sleeping bag on the floor of the master bedroom), she wrote to Warden Hughes and to Warren, letting them both know where she'd chosen to settle and providing her new address and telephone number. That done, she'd walked through the house, pausing to study each room's potential and planning where she would put Annalise's things.

Since moving into her new house in early November, she'd been stripping the walls. Now, in the first week of December, the second-floor walls were bare, ready for paint. She'd also finished the living room and downstairs half-bath and had just started on the dining room which had at least six layers of paper. The steamer she'd rented was some help but for the most part she had to resort to a scraper, working with care, trying not to damage the plaster that lay underneath.

As she scraped away now, her eyes went repeatedly to the windows and the white world beyond. The house felt as if it were wrapped in thick layers of cotton; all sound was muffled except for the wind causing puff-backs in the fireplace, and howling like something alive that wanted to push its way through any slight crevice and get inside.

Hayward struggled up the inclined driveway, near-blinded by the snow. Guided by the amber glow of light from the uncurtained windows, he made his way through the accumulating drifts toward the porch that extended across the front of the house. In the past couple of months, he'd noticed in his travels up and down the road that someone had, at last, had the sense to buy the battered old beauty. He'd long admired the house. He just hoped the new owners didn't ruin it with their efforts to renovate. He'd seen a lot of men at work on various parts of the house, their radios battling for ascendancy – a blaring level of discordant sound that made him wince as he'd gone past. Reaching the shelter of the front porch, he hoped now that he didn't scare the bejesus out of whoever was inside.

He knew the impression he made on first sight: a hefty, long-haired, bearded guy in old camouflage gear who might be the neighborhood weirdo or a visiting serial killer. Add the snow caked in his hair and beard and coating his down jacket and he'd probably have the door slammed in his face. He knocked, then waited, hearing footsteps approach.

The door opened and for several seconds Hayward couldn't speak. Standing there, gazing at him with no evidence of apprehension whatsoever, was the loveliest-looking woman he'd ever seen. Glossy black hair pulled into a loose ponytail, fine, fair skin and deeply sorrowful dark blue eyes; slim and medium height, she had on Levi's, a navy Shetland V-neck over a white T-shirt, and best of all, red high-tops. The high-tops made him want to smile, but he kept his expression neutral. One hand on the door, the woman waited calmly for him to explain his presence. The wonderful look of her made his knees want to buckle with pure pleasure. He'd felt this way a few times in his life about paintings he'd seen, or a spectacular view from a hilltop, or some exhilarating piece of music he'd heard. She was a living high-contrast work of art.

At last, realizing his silence could be construed as creepy in the extreme, he said, 'I'm sorry to trouble you but my truck went off the road at the bottom of the hill down there.' He looked over his shoulder as if he could see it through the wall of blowing snow, then turned back to her. 'The thing is, there's no chance of getting a tow in this.' He indicated the snow with a lift of his hand. 'So I was wondering if you'd mind me bunking down in your garage until morning when this blows by and I can get someone up here to tow me out of the ditch. I've got a sleeping bag back in the truck.'

'There's no heat in the garage. You'd freeze to death. Come in,' she said in a rich, low voice, stepping away from the door.

His brows drew together. 'Are you sure? Most people around here are scared to death of me.'

'Do they know you?' she asked seriously.

'Only by sight.'

'So they're scared by the look of you.'

'That's about it.'

'Should I be afraid of you?'

'No,' he said, amused, risking a smile. 'I'm utterly harmless.'

'Then come inside,' she said. 'I was about to put on coffee and make some lunch. Are you hungry?' she asked, going into a bathroom off the hall and returning with a towel.

'Thanks a lot. I'm sorry to trouble you,' he said again, accepting the towel as she went off toward the kitchen. He was having difficulty accepting the fact that he'd been invited in. He'd always wanted to see the inside of this house but could never have imagined this scenario, couldn't have conceived of this woman.

'I was going to break for lunch now anyway,' she said, without turning, on her way down the hall to the kitchen.

The towel was thick and soft and he glanced around as he dried his face and hair. Then, the towel draped over his arm, he unlaced his boots, pushed them off and placed them on the rubber mat by the door, before removing his parka and hanging it over the closet doorknob so that it dripped onto the mat.

Straightening, he looked at the woman in the kitchen, the sight of her like something that might heal the sick or produce stigmata in believers. She really wasn't the least bit frightened of him. Beautiful, plain-spoken, and unafraid. He didn't know what to make of her and wondered if maybe he was actually still in the truck, succumbing to hypothermia. But no, he could move and he could see, noting that the living room had a good fire going. There was a TV set and a stereo system, both on the floor, but no actual furniture except for a couple of over-sized pillows and a low table. None of the interior walls had been taken down, which was a good sign. The paneling, though, had been painted at some point in time, and he shook his head at the sight of it. There was probably beautiful wood under that yellowed, flaking paint. The idiotic things people did never failed to dismay him – destroying natural beauty, creating wars to boost a flagging economy . . . *Don't go there!* With another shake of his head he proceeded down the hall, pausing to return the towel to the rail in the bathroom.

In the kitchen doorway, he said, 'My name's Hayward

Baines. People call me Hay. This is very kind of you.' Very brave, too, he added silently.

'It's not kind, it's practical. How would I explain a frozen corpse in my garage?' she said without the hint of a smile.

'I can see how that would be a problem,' he said wryly, reminded of the children he'd seen in Viet Nam, their painful gravity. 'I'm used to the cold,' he explained, 'and my sleeping bag is down-filled, good up to twenty below zero. Anything I can do to help?' His hands were stinging as they thawed.

'Have a seat. The coffee won't take long and you look as if you could use some.'

'I could. You're kind of short on furniture,' he observed, easing into one of the two chairs at a table that could have come from the Goodwill or had maybe been picked up from the side of the road. In this part of the world, when people didn't want things, they left them out, and in no time at all they were gone. It was an efficient system, all things considered. He'd picked up some useful items that way.

'My things are due in another week,' she said. 'The moving van is en route.'

'I guess you'll be glad of that. Nice job on the kitchen,' he said, taking in the bright white appliances and near-empty glass-fronted cabinets, the new oak floor and butcher block counters.

'Yes,' she said vaguely, scooping aromatic coffee into a paper filter seated in a holder. 'This and the bathrooms are the only rooms that are finished. The interior painting still needs to be done but I wanted to get the major exterior work finished first, before winter set in: the roof and siding, the windows. And the interior necessities,' she added. 'Furnace, water heater, new plumbing, all that.' She slid the holder into place in the coffee maker, pressed the ON switch, then turned to look at him.

'Do you live nearby?' she asked, able to see why people would be frightened by him, with the wild red-brown hair to his shoulders and shapeless bushy beard, the shabby clothes. His eyes, though, were gray-green, clear and direct, not the eyes of someone intent on harm. She'd seen killer eyes in prison: they were flat and dull, bereft of curiosity, dead. This man's eyes reflected intelligence and curiosity. And his soft-spoken, apologetic manner spoke of education and a gentle nature.

'My place is about a half-mile past here,' he answered, 'at the top of the big hill.' He pointed at an upward angle and she pictured the hill that crested behind her property.

'Why were you out in the middle of a storm, Mr Baines?'

'Hay,' he corrected. 'Would it bother you if I smoke?'

'No, it wouldn't.' She turned and got a saucer from the cabinet, placing it on the battered table. Then she watched as he pulled a pouch from his pocket and efficiently rolled a cigarette. It took her back and, without thinking, she said, 'Joe Seven Moons used to roll his own.'

'Seven Moons?' Hayward asked.

'He was Paiute-Shoshone. He and his wife Alba managed my grandmother's ranch.'

'You're from out west?'

She nodded, her black hair gleaming with reflected light, then turned away to busy herself taking paper-wrapped packages of cold cuts from the refrigerator.

Hay lit his cigarette and looked over at the window, the view almost entirely obscured by the snow. 'I was on my way home from an emergency repair job,' he at last answered her question. 'Thought I could get back in time.'

'A repair job?'

'I'm what I guess people call a handyman.' He shrugged and took a drag on his cigarette. 'I get odd jobs here and there, and I work in the kitchen at The Farm.'

'The Farm?'

'It's a retreat just outside of town. Pretty famous in this part of the world.'

'A retreat,' she repeated. 'For what?'

'For people dealing with alcoholism.'

'Oh!' She nodded again as she began preparing sandwiches. 'What sort of handy work do you do?'

'Some carpentry, some electrical. This morning it was a plumbing problem: had to replace the ballcock valve on an overflowing toilet. Mind if I ask your name?'

She turned, saying, 'I'm sorry. My name is Tally,' and made a mental note: remember to introduce yourself.

'Interesting name. Short for something?' he asked, before taking another drag on his cigarette.

'Natalie.' With a slight frown, she said, 'I didn't think there were any houses at the top of the hill.'

'There aren't. I've got a campsite with a shed I put together from bits and pieces.'

'Are you a squatter, Mr Baines?'

He smiled. 'I might be,' he admitted. 'As far as I know, I'm on state land. But I could well be a squatter.' He thought about the track he'd created over time – undoubtedly illegal – that ran off the main road and took him to the top of the hill where a turnaround, worn into the ground from repeated use, allowed him to park and reverse back onto the track. A hundred years earlier he'd have been considered a homesteader; nothing illegal about his actions.

'Have you been up there long?' she asked.

'A few years, four or five.'

'I can see how appealing it might be for most of the year, but it must be rough in the winter.'

'It can be tricky but I've managed so far. I've picked up things here and there, so the shed's well insulated and I've got a kerosene heater.'

'What do you do if you get snowed in?' she asked, curious. 'And how do people reach you when they require your services?'

'I read, mainly,' he said. 'Oil lamps. And I've got a battery-operated radio-cassette player. As for reaching me, I've got a CB radio hooked up to a little generator that powers a few necessities in the shed, and another CB in the truck.'

'It sounds like an efficient set-up,' she said, reaching for two mugs. 'How do you take your coffee?'

'Cream or milk and two sugars. You sure I can't help?'

'No, thank you. Coffee and sandwiches are within my skill range. I plan to try my hand at a stew later.' She waved at an assortment of winter vegetables on the countertop as she brought a mug over to the table.

Again he was silenced for several seconds by the way she looked, and covered by busying himself putting out his cigarette. Then he took a sip of the best coffee he'd had in a very long time. 'Coffee is definitely within your skill range,' he said. 'This is a fine brew.'

'It is good,' she agreed. 'I've been trying out a lot of different blends but I think I'll stick with this one.' She finished assembling the sandwiches, sliced them diagonally and brought the plates and two napkins to the table. Sliding into the chair opposite, she looked briefly over at the window.

Seeing her wedding ring, he asked, 'Your husband caught in the storm?'

She looked at him blankly, then saw his gaze fixed on her hand and said, 'I'm a widow.'

'Oh, man, I'm sorry.'

'This is my first snowstorm,' she said, changing the subject. 'It's nothing like I imagined it would be.'

'What did you imagine?'

'Something more cinematic,' she said with the faintest of smiles, holding her mug with both hands, 'with better visibility.'

He smiled, showing good teeth, and she wondered how he could maintain any kind of hygiene living in a shack, even with a generator.

'The higher up you are in this part of the world, the less visibility you're going to have in a genuine nor'easter, which is what we're having right now,' he explained.

'A nor'easter?'

'This qualifies. We're in an Arctic high-pressure system with clockwise winds. Strong northeasterly winds pull the storm up the east coast and it meets with cold Arctic air blowing down from Canada. When the two systems collide, you've got yourself an honest-to-God nor'easter.'

'You sound like a schoolteacher,' she said, with that same faint smile.

'What I've got is a head full of useless facts.'

'That wasn't useless. It was most informative. Please eat.'

'This is very kind of you,' he said again.

'Mr Baines—'

'Hay,' he corrected.

'Have you eaten today, Hay?'

'No, I have not.'

'Are you hungry?'

'I am.'

'Then it is a practical measure, nothing to do with kindness.'

'Now *you're* sounding like a schoolteacher,' he said with humor in his expression.

'I, too, have a head full of useless facts.'

'I see you're stripping the wallpaper in the dining room. Maybe I could lend a hand.'

'That would be most appreciated,' she said, biting into the turkey and Swiss with dill mustard on pumpernickel bread.

'This is *good*,' he said appreciatively.

'It is, isn't it,' she agreed. 'I'm still not used to real-world food yet.'

He studied her, trying to interpret the meaning of the sentence. She didn't look as if she were recovering from some illness. And from the way she lowered her eyes, he had the impression she regretted having said what she had. He knew how that felt, so he let it pass. If she wanted to explain, she would. If she didn't, she wouldn't. Either way, he knew all too well that you couldn't make people do one damned thing if they didn't want to. You couldn't change people; couldn't force events; you just had to work the steps and try to live in the moment. And he was actually enjoying the moment.

TWELVE

It was something remembered: an activity or domestic chore performed with another person. Cohabitation had been such a brief part of her life that it was easily forgettable. But still, this time shared had a pleasant resonance, reminding her of when she was young and believed in possibility and the future. Fifteen years later, all but burnt-out synapses were sparking to life. She could no more control that process than she could the busy, swirling snow. She couldn't will herself back into the benumbed state that had helped her survive the years in prison.

She and this burly man worked in companionable silence but for the occasional comment about the job at hand, their efforts accompanied by Paganini, then by Mendelssohn, and the remaining wallpaper came down quickly. He was easy to be around, emitting no waves of tension or impatience; he seemed just to *be*, reminding her again of Joe Seven Moons. Some people were enviably contained, with no obviously frayed edges demanding attention, in need of mending. They finished the job in just over two hours.

'What do you plan to do about the paneling?' he asked, picking residual paper shreds from his scraper before depositing it in the bucket of thick, sticky water. 'There's probably fine wood under that nasty paint.'

She took a step back to scan the walls. 'It *is* nasty,' she agreed. 'I hadn't actually given it any thought. I just assumed it would be repainted.'

'These Victorian houses have good finishes. There could be maple or walnut or even cherry under there.'

'You're interested in old houses?'

'Only in passing, or historically. The historical part has to do with having grown up in a big Victorian.'

'So did I,' she said. 'Hundreds of years ago.'

'*Hundreds* of years,' he repeated, noting that she hadn't

asked him where his growing-up had taken place. Most people couldn't resist openings like that. 'Way back, when, as the song goes,' he said, 'the world was young.'

'Yes,' she said, her eyes on the near window which was entirely snowed over. Allowing herself a bit of free association, she continued: 'It's like being in an exotic cave.' She paused, gazing at the whitened expanse. Then, 'Are you proposing to strip the wood?' she asked, turning to look at him.

'I was just making an observation.'

'Would you be interested in doing the work?' she asked, somehow knowing as she asked that he didn't need money and wasn't soliciting her for a job.

He had to pause and take a slow breath. She watched with interest, seeing another dimension to him – one that was a little jittery, a little injured.

'Truthfully,' he said, 'I wouldn't be. You'd probably be just as happy going ahead with painting it.' He was suddenly feeling very uncomfortable. Just like that. It was crazy, the way he could without warning find himself on the verge of a chasm, like skydiving without a chute. He hated it, worked so hard to get it all under control.

'You don't like to say no, do you?' she observed cannily, quietly.

'It's a problem,' he acknowledged. 'I'm in the process of learning how.'

'It's a hard thing to learn. How about some fresh coffee?'

'That'd be good,' he answered, relieved to get off the topic. For a long, awful moment he'd feared finding himself stuck with a job he didn't want, simply because he had such difficulty saying no. And she'd sensed that, which surprised him. In his experience, most beautiful people – of either gender – didn't give a good goddamn how other people felt, what they cared about or feared. But this woman wasn't like anyone else he'd ever encountered. She seemed to be tuned to a wavelength unknown to the general population. Considering that notion, he decided she lacked guile. She was beautiful and forthright – he found it a rare combination. This was a first in his experience of people which, admittedly, didn't exactly set world records. He'd never been the life of the party. At best he was a reluctant attendee who instinctively tried to disappear into the first available corner where he was content simply to observe the goings-on, a fact that was a perpetual small sorrow to his ever-popular father, the truly charming and always elegant Hayward Baines the Second. There had been a time when Hay would have made any sort of Faustian deal in order to have his father's social assets. But he had ultimately conceded that it was never to be.

'I'd be like you if I could,' he told his father in a rare confessional moment during a visit home before his deployment. 'I hate to be a disappointment to you.'

And his father said, in that voice that drew people to lean close so as not to miss a word, 'You're never a disappointment, son. Never, no matter what. Your mother and I just want you to be happy, to enjoy life. That's all. You take good care and come home safely to us.'

Life was a jokester, loving nothing better than ironic turnabout – killing the father and saving the shambles that had once been the sober son so full of promise.

'I'll just wash my hands, if I may,' he said as she added her scraper to the bucket, then lifted it to take to the kitchen for emptying.

'Please help yourself. You can use the bathroom down here or one of the ones upstairs. I'm going to dump this and then get another pot of coffee going. I've got some wickedly good cookies I picked up yesterday at the bakery.'

'The pralines or the chunky chocolate?' he asked.

'Both. They're the best cookies I've ever had.'

'They are,' he agreed, and they exchanged a smile.

Curious to see the rest of the house, he elected to go up to the second floor, where the filtered snowlight lent the quartet of unfurnished bedrooms with their wide-beamed floors and naked patchy walls a dated quality – like old-fashioned sepiatinted prints. Struck by the effect, he lingered for a moment, studying each unfurnished room before stopping in the doorway to the large master bedroom. He took in the sleeping bag and pillow on the bare floor of the otherwise empty room. With paired windows on two walls and a fireplace centered on the wall to the right of the door, the snowlight and bareness gave the space an ascetic feel. He took a step back and continued on to the hall bathroom.

Everything about the bathroom was new and yet it had been done up in a way that was gratifyingly faithful to the heritage of the house. White wainscoting, a porcelain pedestal sink with a square basin and simple faucets, an oblong claw foot tub with a rolled rim. Above it, a chrome shower rail suspended from the high ceiling extended from one end of the tub to the other. It held a plain white curtain. Chrome towel rods held thick white towels. The walls awaited painting but he suspected they, too, would be white.

Considering that large master bedroom, monastic was the word that came to mind as he washed his hands. Not a word he'd initially have associated with this woman, based solely on her appearance. But it felt appropriate. He couldn't have said why. Impressions were stacking up, one atop another, fleshing out his mental image of her. He liked her ability to be silent, her obvious intelligence, her failure to ask typical questions. And of course he liked simply looking at her. She was a gift, in red high-tops.

'Would you like to use my phone to call about getting towed in the morning?' she asked when he returned downstairs.

'I would. Thank you.'

'Help yourself.' She pointed to the wall-phone situated just inside the kitchen door.

While he made his call, and the coffee was dripping, she went to the dining room and started gathering up the last of the wet wallpaper shreds from the tarp, pushing them into one of the huge garbage bags the general contractor had supplied.

Already the room looked bigger, cleaner. And Hay was right: the yellowing paint on the paneling was dreadful. Perhaps she'd investigate the specifics of paint removal; a project to work on during the winter. Save painting this room for later.

'You're going to try doing it yourself, aren't you?' Hay asked from the doorway.

It earned him a little smile. 'That's exactly what I was thinking,' she admitted. 'You read my thoughts.'

He nodded. 'You read my reaction to stripping the paneling a little while ago. And now I guessed your thoughts. Transparency seems to be the order of the day.'

'Sometimes it feels good not to have to explain things. My turn for hand washing,' she said, pushing the garbage bag into the corner. 'Coffee will be ready in a minute or two. You're probably dying for another cigarette. Feel free, please. And if you have the skill, you could relight the fire in the living room.'

'I have the skill,' he said. 'I've been known to start a fire or two. And I wouldn't mind a cigarette. Thank you.'

'Given that you work in a kitchen,' she said lightly, on her way to the stairs, 'you could help peel the vegetables for the stew.'

'Happy to. I have peeling skill, too.'

Amused, she continued on her way, thinking that this was the longest conversation and the most exposure she'd had to another person in more than five thousand days.

'I'm curious about the logistics,' she said. 'What do you do for water on your hill? And plumbing?'

'I have a jury-rigged composting situation for waste. I keep a rain barrel filled with water for cooking and washing up. When the water freezes I use an ice pick to fill a big pot with chunks that I melt and replenish every couple of days. Laundry I do at The Farm once a week or so, and I grab a shower there most mornings before work. Now and then, if the weather is really bad or I just need a break from the rustic life, I'll bunk there for a night or two.'

'And there's always room for you?'

'Worst-case scenario, I can bed down in my sleeping bag on somebody's floor. But that's only happened a couple of times in all the years I've been here.'

'How many years is that?' she asked.

'Six now. I came in July of seventy-seven as a client.'

'A client?' Her brows drew together slightly.

'I had a little drug problem courtesy of my stint in 'Nam . . . along with a few other issues.'

'I see,' she said, eyes on the carrot she was peeling over a stainless steel basin. 'A lot of the boys came home messed up in some way,' she said softly. 'It was a terrible time.'

'That it was,' he agreed. 'There were moments when I used to think the guys who didn't make it back were the lucky ones. Those of us who did come home . . . we weren't the same.'

'No,' she said. 'Not the same at all.'

'People you knew?'

'We should change the subject,' she said, 'for both our sakes.'

'Agreed.' He was quiet for a moment, then said, 'About this stew.'

'What about it?'

'Why don't I show you how it's done.'

'You actually cook at The Farm?'

'No.' He shook his head, emitting a low laugh. 'There's an honest-to-God chef. I'm a helper and a server. I do whatever needs doing in the kitchen. But I like cooking and I don't often get a chance to use *that* skill beyond prepping salad or veggies.'

'In that case,' she said, 'please teach me. I have no skill at all.'

After the vegetables were done and they'd carried everything to the kitchen, Hay said, 'I think I should go get my sleeping bag from the truck. From what I can see, the snow is really piling up out there. If I wait much longer, I may not be able to get to the truck.'

'You're going to need that sleeping bag,' she said, somewhat apologetically. 'A couple of weeks from now there will actually be furniture, so no one will have to sleep on the floor.'

Picking up on her tone, he said, 'Believe me, I'm glad to be indoors. As I said, I'm used to bedding down on the floor now and then. I even keep a change of clothes in the truck, just in case.' Was she saying he might be welcome to return? He hoped so. He didn't have many non-program friends. And though he was deeply grateful for the program and the support that was always there for him, while it was unlikely he'd ever admit this to any of his sober friends, every now and then he got tired of drunks and druggies, their drama and the sometime narcissism that so tediously placed them at the center of their personal universes.

It wasn't that he ever forgot he was one of them; it was just that there was a larger world he also belonged to. And sometimes he deeply missed that world: its casual chaos or calm, its risky so-called normalcy. Usually after a few days or even only a few hours in that world, he was glad to return to the patterned, predictable sanity of the program. Yet that longing for the other world was like the ache of grief that was never far from the surface. It pulled at him, a siren song trying to lure him back to a past that could never be resurrected. They were gone and so was the shyly optimistic young man he'd been.

A minute after he went out, she grabbed her down jacket, pulled on her boots and stepped out onto the porch, watching as he pushed his way through the drifts, moving down the driveway. The snow closed around him about halfway down and she stared into the gusting snow, trying to see where he'd gone.

Irrationally, she felt a surge of fear. It was, she reasoned, because she couldn't see more than a few feet in front of her, something she'd never before experienced. But what did she really fear? she wondered, reminding herself that she was the woman who believed her life or death was of no consequence. Had that changed? She didn't think so. Was she afraid of this man she didn't really know? Never. She knew with certainty that he was harmless, kind-hearted, good-humored. What then?

Such a strange, unsettling sensation, all because she was unable to see her surroundings. She pushed her hands deep into her pockets, making herself smaller inside the jacket, while the wind pushed the snow in at her, getting into her eyes and down her neck, robbing her body of its heat. The snow was piling up against the inside perimeter of the porch railing. The snow, she decided, was like her beautiful mother: soulless and cold. But unlike her lack of feeling for her mother, Tally actually liked the snow, respected its beauty, its power. And yet there was this inner shaking.

She was so startled when Hay suddenly appeared at the foot of the porch steps that she laughed – a surprised little yelp. And then she was embarrassed.

'What?' he asked with an automatic smile, sleeping bag under an arm that also held a backpack, a gloved hand wiping his eyes.

'I couldn't see anything,' she confessed. 'It gave me the willies. And then you suddenly appeared. I don't know . . .'

'Welcome to the northeast,' he said cheerfully. 'We get a lot of this in the winter.'

'I'm looking forward to it,' she said, as they returned inside to remove their boots and jackets in friendly silence. 'Now that I know what to expect, it won't give me the willies.'

She was glad he was there. He was good company. Perhaps they would become friends.

THIRTEEN

Faith walked slowly through the downstairs rooms, a nearly full glass of neat Scotch in one hand and a single-edged razor blade in the other. It was dark, past nine o'clock, but she hadn't bothered to turn on any lights down here. In the dark, the house seemed even larger, yet felt oddly less imposing. She hated this goddamned house.

She paused in the living room, carefully turning the razor blade over and over in her fingers as she took a sip of the Scotch. Maybe she'd do it in here, smack in the middle of the antique oriental carpet. That'd be good. She smiled briefly, more of a grimace really, feeling the shallow, worn-away nap of the pile beneath her bare feet. Upon consideration, it struck her as disrespectful to damage a carpet that had probably caused several young Chinese women to go blind as they worked the wool day after day in some unheated place with almost no light. So she moved on, into the front hall.

Here, for some reason, the cool marble floor made her think of the bathroom upstairs. She turned and looked up. The light from her bedroom cast a remote glow. Experimentally she tightened her hand around the blade. A bit more pressure and the slick metal would slice neatly into the cushion of flesh at the top of her palm. She relaxed her grip slightly, the blade resting almost weightlessly against her incurled fingers.

Another sip of Scotch while she considered doing it right here in the hall. Someone or other would open the front door and there she'd be: eighty-one pounds of unadorned flesh sprawled in a pool of blood on the perfectly polished black and white marble squares. Quite a statement that'd make. She smiled again and started up the stairs, taking her time because she wasn't sober and the last thing she wanted was to fall ass-over-teacup and break her neck. No. It couldn't be an accident. For once in her life she wanted to be the one in control.

She stood in the bedroom doorway for a time, looking in

objectively. It was inarguably a nice room, spacious, with graceful dimensions. There was a fireplace, a walk-in dressing room/closet, an en suite bathroom. The fabric of the curtains matched the custom-made bedspread, and the upholstery on the settee positioned at an angle in front of the fireplace matched exactly the bluish green that predominated in the curtains and spread. Antique-white finish with subtle gold trim on the headboard, night tables, and desk. Three expensively framed prints of pastoral scenes hung in a precise row over the mantel. The walls were covered in beige silk. Silk! A bedroom right out of a forty-year-old decorating magazine. 'House and goddamned Garden,' she said aloud.

Making a face, she went to sit on the side of the bed, looking down at herself. Her belly curved inward as if pushed in by the weight of the surgical tracks, her thighs were narrow blue-white cylinders of meat, her ribs were visible and she had no breasts. 'Jesus!' she whispered, despising herself. Half an inch over five feet tall, eighty-two pounds: the size and shape of a ten-year-old. She took a gulp of the Scotch, then put the glass down on the bedside table, pulled open the drawer and got out her Marlboros and the ashtray.

After a hard pull on the cigarette, she positioned the razor blade point-down just above her knee, applied a moderate degree of pressure, and drew it up the length of her thigh.

She gasped. It stung, and in the blade's wake a thin strand of blood welled up. Gazing at the cut, she took another drag on the cigarette, wondering what would happen if she just went to work and started cutting off her flesh in slabs. She could slice herself down to nothing. Too bad she'd bleed to death before she had a chance to see her skeleton.

Repositioning the blade, she concentrated on making another cut, exactly parallel to the first. It was slow, painful work. Tears built up in her eyes. Her nose started to run. She sniffed, paused to take another drag, propped the cigarette on the lip of the ashtray and swallowed half the remaining Scotch. She was starting to feel a bit sick. Little beads of blood dotted the length of the two cuts.

She wet a finger and rubbed at the blood, making sticky smears on her skin. Her leg was smarting now. She reached over and took a last puff of the cigarette, stubbed it out, then turned to look over her shoulder at the room, a sob taking her by surprise.

Gripped by despair, she thought how much she hated this room, this house, everything and everyone in it. She hated the tedious predictability of her existence in this house. But most of all she hated the loathsome body she had to drag around every day. She held up her left hand and looked at her long, blood-red-painted fingernails. What a joke! As if people would be so distracted by her fabulous nails that they wouldn't notice she was about fifteen pounds underweight and had a face that, in profile, looked like a wedge of cheese.

Closing her eyes, she could see him wearing his indulgent expression, could hear him saying, 'There's no need for you to have these problems. It's purely an issue of mind over matter.' He said it in a tone she knew was meant to be gentle, kind, concerned. But it came across as condescending, superior. He couldn't help himself. She knew that, too.

She rubbed her eyes with the back of her hand, anguish lodged like a brick in her chest as she directed her gaze at the open door to the bathroom. *Do it now*, she told herself. *Stop trying to make tricky plans. Just get it over with once and for all.* For years she'd been considering ways and means. Maybe now was as good a time as any.

Just walk in there, start the tub filling, then climb into the hot water with the razor blade and open the nice blue veins running upward from her wrists. Never mind the Oriental carpet or the marble floor in the hall. Dead was dead. Why not keep it tidy so that the poor overworked, undervalued housekeeper would only have to rinse out the tub.

Her thigh was stinging, itchy, irritated. The skin on either side of the twin lines was enflamed, starting to swell. She opened her hand and stared at the blade. There was an entire box of them on a shelf in the utility room in the basement. One hundred single-edged blades, each contained in a neat little protective paper casing. She could kill herself a hundred times.

She laughed, sobbed again, sniffed hard and reached for the glass. About an inch left. What a joke! She didn't even like Scotch. The taste usually made her gag. But there was a certain rightness that had appealed to her when she'd padded down-stairs to the liquor cabinet. If you were going to plot and plan and perhaps, ultimately, die, why drink something you liked? Pleasure was completely inappropriate to the occasion. You had to go for a taste that would reinforce all your misery and frustration. If you were going to parade naked through the house in the dark, planning your suicide, Scotch was just the ticket. She gulped down the last of it, returned the glass to the bedside table, opened the drawer and stowed the ashtray.

Time to get this show on the road, she told herself, the blade secure in her hand, eyes again on the bathroom door.

The phone rang. She jumped, heart jolting, automatically turning to look nervously at the phone. It rang again. Her under-arms were suddenly damp. She blinked, heart racing now. She couldn't ignore ringing telephones or save letters to read later. She intensely disliked leaving things unfinished. *He* considered this another of her many noteworthy quirks, forever analyzing every last thing she said and did. With a shaky hand, she lifted the receiver and got out a hello, her voice sounding old, crusty.

'Faith?' A pause. Then, 'You don't sound like yourself. Are you all right? Did something happen?'

'Nothing happened,' Faith said tiredly. 'It's just the same old crap.'

'Seriously, what's going on?' A worried tone attached itself to the familiar voice on the other end. 'Talk to me. Are you really okay?'

'Seriously?' She sat down on the toilet seat and gazed at the tile floor. 'I was just finishing a cigarette and a glass of Scotch, and making practice runs on sundry parts of my person with a razor blade.'

'Oh, of course that's it. Silly me for asking.' She was silent for a moment, then said, 'You're not kidding, are you?' Another pause. Then, 'You're scaring me. I think I should come over.'

'I'm *not* all right,' Faith admitted with a shuddery sigh. 'I haven't been *all right* for a long time, and you know it. You're really the only one who does know it. But please don't come here . . .' She paused for a moment, then said, 'Could I come to your house? I need to talk to someone who doesn't want anything from me, who doesn't treat me like I'm a lab rat.'

'Come right now. I'll get a pot of coffee going. You'll still be drunk, but you'll be more awake. And we'll be able to talk.'

'I just need to grab a shower first. Give me half an hour. Okay?'

'Sure. Listen, please don't drive, Faith. Call a taxi.'

'Don't worry. I would never drive in this condition. I know better than that. I'll be there soon. Thank you, Con. Really. *Thank you.*' She hung up and went to the dressing room to get something to wear. Big choice, she thought grimly, contemplating the primarily black garments hung in a brief, solemn row. 'Gee,' she said aloud, her voice low and brimming with sarcasm. 'Should I wear the black, or the black?' She opened her hand to look at the razor blade, the bloodied edge moist-sticky from the heat of her palm. With a sigh, she dropped the blade into the waste basket, then walked heavily into the bathroom.

In the merciless light, she focused on the mirror to see the same old repellent reflection. '*Look at you,*' she whispered, choked by the sight of herself. '*How did you get to this?*'

One hand braced on the counter, she leaned in close to the glass, scrutinizing her image: the sharp nose, the assertive chin, the high rounded forehead, the misery shining in her eyes like candles in night-time windows. *Jesus! You poor thing. You're a complete disaster.*

Okay, she decided, pushing away from the counter. She'd been given a last-minute reprieve from the governor. *But don't kid yourself,* she told the mirror. *It's just a stay of execution.*

If things didn't change, and soon – maybe tomorrow or a week from tomorrow – she'd climb into the tub and damned well do it. She had ninety-nine more razor blades and plenty of time. After all, according to the birth certificate the Doctors Lazarus had arranged for her all those years ago, she was only a few months away from turning eighteen. Those hundred-odd days felt like forever. But she could keep her razor date with the tub any time at all, so long as the Lazarus clan was out for the evening at one of their 'functions.' And it was a given that the doctors were booked months, years in advance. Their book and the lectures they so liked to give about their adopted victim, *The Stolen Child,* had made them celebrities. So there'd be no shortage of razor blades or of opportunities. All she had to do was check Stefan's diary, decide which evening would work, and then, before getting into the tub, she just had to be sure to take the goddamned phone off the hook.

'This isn't like you at all.'

'Oh, Con' – Faith sighed, too weary and too tipsy to put on the usual happy-go-lucky show – 'it *is*. It's *exactly* like me. I've come to the end . . . of something. Lately, I've been feeling as if it's the end of *me*. I don't know.' She was about halfway back to being sober and she felt terribly tired, too worn down to keep on pretending things were all right.

'Talk to me,' Connie urged, anxious to perpetuate the girl's atypical openness. Only infrequently in recent years was she given to confiding any specifics about her life with the Lazarus family and her feelings about it. 'I can't help you if you don't tell me what's wrong.'

'Everything. *Everything's wrong.*'

'What's "everything?" I thought you were enjoying school.'

'I am. I love school. It's the best part of my life. I mean,' she added quickly, 'I love you and Lucia, her mom and dad. The captain, too. But the Lazarus family. Oh *God*.' She stopped and closed her eyes tightly for a moment, made a face as if she'd tasted something horribly bitter, then opened them again. 'They're making me crazy, Con. I just can't do it anymore.

'It wasn't so bad at the beginning when Monica was around. She was nice, you know? Kind of a lightweight, but sweet. She was good to me, took me places, did things with me. We went shopping and out to lunch; we saw movies. She even took me to the circus, which scared me. She saw that it did and said she was sorry, and we left right away. She had a *heart*, Con. We did coloring books together and she made my school lunches; she came to parents' night at school. But Stefan barely noticed her. He paid more attention to me, not in any kind of parental way, but like I was an endless research project. Asking what I thought of this, how I felt about that. It made me nervous 'cuz I knew it wasn't fair; it wasn't *right*. She was always doing nice things for him and he just didn't get it. He treated her like a potted plant he could never remember to water.'

Connie smiled. 'That's vivid,' she said.

'It's true!' Faith insisted.

'I know it is, sweetie. I was there, remember? I used to come visit you when they were still married. I knew Monica.'

'I was a little kid and it made me feel awful, the way he treated her. Here's this man, this *doctor*, and he's got this lovely wife who cares about him, buys him presents, cooks great meals, does everything she can to make him happy and half the time he forgets to come home or he eats an entire meal without even looking at her, never mind saying this is good or thank you. He was so busy trying to impress his parents. And once he got them involved in the book, that was it. He had no time for Monica. There were endless sessions with his parents, working up each chapter, discussing this and that about me, always about me.

'I watched Monica get sadder and quieter and she just started staying in bed all weekend. I'd go sit beside her on the bed and read my story books to her.' She emitted a damp little laugh. 'I thought it would make her feel better. And sometimes it did. She'd smile all at once and say, "I guess I'd better take you out to buy some more books," or "Let's go get chocolate sundaes," and she'd get dressed and we'd go out. But I could tell she was just doing it for me; she wasn't happy.

'I can't believe she stuck it out for three years.' She opened her bag, saying, 'Con, I really need a cigarette. Do you mind if I smoke?'

'Go ahead.' Connie got up and went to the kitchen, returning with a small crystal ashtray, then curled up again on the sofa beside Faith. 'Tell me all of it, sweetie. Get it out of your system.'

With shaky hands, Faith got a cigarette lit, saying, 'I know these are really disgusting, but they help me feel better . . . because smoking is something that's just mine. You know?'

'I understand.'

'So.' She blew out a plume of smoke, then went on. 'After she left, Monica tried to stay in touch with me. She phoned every week or so and sent little cards – goofy cartoon things, but I loved getting them. Then Stefan got on the downstairs extension one day when I was talking to her, and he told her to stop calling. He said her calls were "counterproductive." As if she was doing something criminal. She went quiet for a few seconds, then said, "She's a *little girl*, Stefan. She needs friends and attention, and people who care about her. DCF should *never* have given her to you. You're not human. You only *look* human. Faith, honey," she said, "just remember that I love you," and then she hung up.

'I never heard from her again . . . She was good to me, Con. The only other person who's paid any real attention to me in all the years since he moved us into his parents' house is Rosa, the housekeeper. If the clan is out for the evening, she'll make her wonderful Mexican food and we'll sit in the kitchen and eat together with good music playing on the radio. I've even been to her house a bunch of times over the years, to hang out with her kids and do dumb stuff like hide-and-seek or play Snakes and Ladders. The rest of the time I'm stuck in the house and the clan studies my every move, my every word – still, *forever* – like a specimen or a TV documentary or something.

'I thought things would change when I started university but it's the same as it ever was. When they got me the car, I thought I'd be free; I'd be able to go places, do things. But no. I drive to Yale every morning, and I'm expected to come back to the house every afternoon. I can't stand it. If I don't get away from them I'm going to lose my mind. I can feel it happening. I can't *eat* in that house; I can barely *sleep* there. The sight of them gives me a stomach ache so I can't eat, and hearing them talking downstairs makes me nervous, so I can't fall asleep. I go to bed at eight o'clock and watch TV with headphones on so I don't have to hear them.

'And weekday mornings, I'm up at five and out by six so I don't have to sit at breakfast with them. I get my class work done at a donut place near the school where nobody bothers me, even if there's a rush on. I have a toasted bagel and coffee while I work and they don't even charge me for refills.'

She took a hard drag on her cigarette, her eyes glossy with unshed tears. 'I feel like I'm dying, Connie,' she said softly. 'I *will* die, if I don't get away from them. What can I do?'

'Getting drunk isn't the answer,' Connie said, remembering

telling Brian Kirlane all those years ago that the last thing the child needed was to be placed under a microscope. There was no satisfaction in knowing she'd been right. But the damage was so much worse than she could have imagined.

'The booze is part of getting the psychopathology just right,' Faith said.

'How?' Connie asked, perennially fascinated by the depth of this girl's intelligence.

'The Doctors Lazarus need empirical evidence to justify every single thing they do or think about me, no matter how insignificant it might seem to anyone else.'

'And?' Connie prompted, brow furrowed, not following.

'If I can convince Stefan he'd be doing the right thing by sending me away, if he thinks he's doing something professionally ennobling, he can be persuaded.'

'What are you *saying*? Please don't make me drag this out of you, sweetie. Just tell me what you have in mind. I will help you in any way I can. You must know that by now.'

'I do. I do. It's just that I have to be very convincing, entirely credible. These people have studied me under their personal microscopes for the last thirteen years. So I can't just pretend . . . it has to seem entirely authentic to them.'

'What does? *What?*' Connie was becoming frustrated.

'This, for one thing.' Faith lifted her skirt up to show the rows of cuts on her thighs.

'My God! What are you doing to yourself?'

'I'm turning myself into a textbook case for them. I've been studying up on the long-term effects of my kind of abuse. The cutting is part of it, so is the drinking. They have to *believe* it, Connie, or they'll never sign off. And I want the guardianship ended. I want their status as executors of my trust fund ended. *I want to live my own life.* If they doubt any part of my behavior for a single moment, they'll keep me tied to them forever. And just the *idea* of that makes me want to slash my wrists.'

'But in a few months you'll be eighteen, legally an adult.'

'I won't make it, Connie.' The tears finally came. 'My being eighteen won't stop him being executor of my trust fund. That goes until I'm twenty-one. And I can't wait that long. I was given that money as a reward for saving the baby.' For just a moment she saw again – as she so often did – a mental image of the baby and was stricken with a yearning to see her that was so intense it was physical. A moment, and then it was gone. She had to take a deep breath to settle herself.

'I want to be able to use the money to have my own place, to pay my school fees if Stefan decides not to keep on covering the tuition.

'I know it's hard to believe, Con, but I felt better about myself when I was living in that van with those two fuckheads. At least I knew what to expect. And they didn't give a shit about what I *thought*. That was my life and it was the only one I knew. Every little kid thinks their life is 'normal.' That was my normal. It was horrible but it was what I knew.'

'I understand,' Connie said in a whisper.

'But when they took the baby . . . when I knew they were going to hurt her . . . that's when I had to try to make it stop.' Wiping her face on her sleeve, struggling to get the words out, she lost the fight to maintain control and cried out, 'And I did it! I made it stop. I didn't let them hurt the baby and they were arrested. I got taken to the hospital where everyone was nice to me. And then that evil bitch from DCF gave me to Stefan. And he and his parents have made me feel so *ashamed*, as if everything that'd happened to me was *my own fault*.

'I was scared a lot of the time with Wolf and Toadman because I never knew what would make them mad so they wouldn't feed me, or where they'd take me next and what would happen to me when they left me alone with some man. But Stefan and his parents *shamed* me, Connie. They turned me into a case study and sold me to the world. I've never had a chance to forget any part of my life with Wolf and Toadman. The Lazarus doctors go on TV and radio, they appear at conferences; they go here, there and everywhere and talk endlessly about what happened to me. They have all the details of everything I was able to tell them all those years ago: they know who did what and as much as I could remember about how I felt. But they don't *know* me. They have *no idea* who I am. They would never, *ever* allow me to forget any of it; they won't allow me to grow beyond the experience. They can't stop probing – as if they're afraid that if it all gets relegated to a part of my history they'll lose their status, their fame. So I'm stuck in the past and it's all fresh in my mind. I might as well still be locked in that van.

'You and Brian and Jan and Lucia, even the captain, you all know me better than the Lazarus family does. Rosa the housekeeper, Monica once upon a time, the people at the donut shop – you all know me better and treat me with respect. But not the Lazarus clan. I'm a convenience to them, like a goddamn public toilet: something to use any time they feel the need.

'If I don't get out and try to live some kind of sane life now, while I can still fight for myself – before they suck my brain out through my ears – it'll never happen. *I have to get away from them.* To do it, to get free, I need to make a deal with the devil I know. I have to hope that somewhere inside of Stefan there's some tiny bit of humanity left that I can reach.' She drew a ragged breath. 'Because if I don't, if I can't get through to him, I'll die! I can't go on this way anymore.'

'Poor you,' Connie crooned. 'Poor old you.' As before, in a hospital room years ago, Connie drew the girl into her arms and silently rocked her until Faith fell asleep, her body shaken by residual sobs. Holding her, feeling the warmth of Faith's slight weight, Connie silently prayed that everything would work out in the girl's favor, because if anyone deserved a happy ending, Faith did.

FOURTEEN

Faith took a swig of Scotch straight from the bottle before going to knock at the door to Stefan's 'library.' So pretentious, she thought, then reminded herself to go in humble or he'd start analyzing her attitude and this chance would be lost – perhaps forever. A notion that made her innards cramp, as if suddenly flushed with ice water.

Without looking up from the papers on the desk he was reading, he said, 'What's up?' No inflection, no interest.

Letting a bit of a slur slide into her enunciation, she said, 'I needa talk to you, Stef'n.'

Now he looked up, a hand immediately moving to stroke his Doctor-Spock's-Evil-Twin goatee. Such an affectation, that goatee. It didn't suit him at all. But no matter. She had his attention. This was the third time in six weeks she'd done this semi-drunken performance for his benefit, each time adding a minor embellishment. Tonight it was the slur. And he was responding as she had hoped he would. The man was a jackal when it came to symptomology – something, she was certain, he'd copied from his parents. Whenever she was in their company she felt as if their mouths were slightly open, waiting to swallow anything of interest she might say or do.

'Sit, talk,' he said.

She allowed herself to lurch very slightly as she sat down in the heavy wooden armchair in front of the desk, her skirt rising, just as she'd practiced, to reveal the razored skin just above her knees.

His eyes absorbed everything, from the lurch to the scabbing-over tail-ends of the cuts.

She hated every aspect of this encounter: the play-acting, the necessary deceit, his calculating aspect, his long-suffering demeanor. *Keep it together*, she told herself. She was fighting for the right to live her life. *Just remember you're doing what needs to be done.*

She could tell that he smelled her alcohol-tainted exhalations, and his eyes kept returning to the cuts. It was all going according to plan. He was taking the bait, just as she'd anticipated he would.

'Are you drunk, Faith?' he asked, showing no anger, only curiosity.

'Oh, no,' she said quickly, then dropped her eyes, adding, 'I just had a small drink for courage.'

'Courage for what?'

'Because I need to talk to you. It isn't easy.' So true. She vowed she would never make anyone feel the way he made her feel; she would never be so oblivious to what was right in front of her.

'Go on,' he said. 'Talk to me.' He sat back in his chair, hooking his thumbs under his red suspenders, a display of expansiveness combined with skeptical interest. 'Tell me what's got you so nervous.' She couldn't help but marvel at the mannerisms he'd acquired over the years, as if he'd seen too many second-rate actors playing doctors in made-for-TV movies. There seemed to be nothing authentic left of him. He was putting on his own performance here. They were two actors without an audience, each trying to upstage the other. She would have to be the more convincing one.

She swallowed, and took a deep, shuddery breath that was genuine. 'I need a place of my own, Stefan. And I need to be closer to school. Commuting every day . . . it's hard.'

'It's a half-hour drive each way. How hard can that be?'

'I-95 is a nightmare. You'd have to experience it to know just how much of a nightmare it is what with the truck traffic and everyone speeding.' He rarely did any highway driving but she could tell he was unimpressed by this argument, so she shifted direction. 'I need a place of my own.' She kept her eyes on his. 'I want a place of my own.' *Don't you cry!* she warned herself. *Don't give him the satisfaction of seeing you crumble.*

'I see. What you're saying is you want to live on your own.'

'Yes, I do.'

'And what's brought this on, all of a sudden?' So patronizing. For a few seconds, she wanted to lean across the desk and smack him, jolt him into reality, into awareness. He was still in there, somewhere. He was; he had to be. If this current persona, this replica of his gelid unyielding mother had subsumed the original Stefan, Faith had no chance of reaching him.

She was experiencing a sudden rise in her body temperature and had to take a few moments to remain calm. 'It's not "all of a sudden,"' she said quietly. 'I've wanted this for a long time.'

'So why haven't you said anything?'

Again, she said, 'Stefan, it's not easy to talk to you.' Her tone was too sharp. She brought it down a notch. 'It's not easy to talk to you, or your parents, but you in particular because my relationship is with you, not with them. The thing is, anything I say in this house could wind up in a book. It's already happened once. Knowing it could happen again makes me self-conscious and nervous.'

'It shouldn't,' he said reasonably.

God! There it was again: the lack of empathy. 'Maybe to your way of thinking it shouldn't, but it does. It was hard enough when I was a little kid living with just one doctor and his wife' – she felt a sudden pang, missing Monica – 'but it's really tough with three doctors. I feel as if I have no privacy.'

'Of course you do,' he argued. 'You have your own suite.'

'I'm not talking about *rooms*, Stefan. I'm talking about my *life*. I need my own place and control of my own money. I don't even get to see the financial statements. I have no idea what I've actually got.'

He leaned forward at this, elbows on the desk, chin resting on his folded hands, eyes narrowing slightly. 'It's substantial. I don't know that you're capable of handling . . .'

Sensing what was coming, needing to derail him from going in that direction, she said, 'Excuse me for a minute,' got up and walked out of the room. She went to the liquor cabinet in the living room and took another swallow of the Scotch, shuddered at the burn of it going down, then returned to the 'library.' Three rows of reference books and a stack of journals, plus the numerous foreign editions of *The Stolen Child* hardly constituted a library. Why couldn't he just call it his office?

'What was that?' he asked, as she slipped back into the chair.

'What was what?'

'What did you just do?'

'I had another drink. I needed it. Talking to you . . .' Abandoning the pretense all at once, needing to know, she asked, 'What *happened* to you, Stefan? I remember the first time we met, when I was at the hospital. You were *nice* to me; you were *sweet* to me. We sat on the floor together and played a game.' Her voice wobbled and tears were dangerously close to the spilling point. 'I know it was part of the analysis but that doesn't matter. You were a thoughtful man, someone kind, someone who listened to me. I really don't know you now.'

Appearing embarrassed, as if being reminded of his younger self was a burdensome bit of his evolutionary history, he gruffly pointed out, 'You were a small child.'

'Yes, I was,' she agreed. 'But I haven't changed – I haven't been allowed to change. I just got older. You've changed, though.'

'What are you suggesting?'

'I'm not *suggesting*. I'm stating a fact. You're not a kind or thoughtful person anymore. You're *Doctor* Lazarus, co-author of a best-selling book about that child – who just happens to be me. But I'm not the resident stolen child anymore. I'm grown up, I'm a *person*!' she cried, her wobbly voice betraying her. 'I want my life! I don't want to be constantly watched, in case I say or do anything of interest, something book-worthy. I just want to be left alone, to let the past be the past.'

'You're drunk,' he said quietly, a measure of sadness entering his tone.

'Maybe,' she allowed. 'Probably. I'm not happy, Stefan. Drinking makes it all more manageable.'

He sat studying her for a time, as she fought to maintain a grip on her emotions. If she lost it and went to pieces, he might never let her go. She couldn't be sure she was getting through to him. It was like psychological surgery.

All at once what had taken place more than a dozen years earlier in the pediatric interview room came back to him in its entirety, every detail crisp, vivid. And he remembered how deeply ashamed he'd been of his arrogant assumptions, and how tender that tiny damaged child had been. She'd comforted him; she'd patted his shoulder and told him it was all right.

And what had he done for her since then? Nothing really, beyond providing the basics: room and board, an education, health and dental benefits – as if she were no more than a live-in employee. But back then he'd helplessly allowed her to minister to him and he'd grieved for the terrible losses she'd suffered. And subsequently, when he'd brought her home after each hospital stay, he was saddened by the physical damage that had necessitated three rounds of surgery and her resulting inability ever to bear children. She'd been stolen and badly harmed. Yet throughout it all she had remained a clever, caring child, eager to learn, able even to laugh.

Gazing at her now, realizing that she had also suffered at his hands and those of his parents, he wondered how he could have forgotten that initial meeting. How had he managed to misplace his recall of the tidal emotion she'd aroused in him, and the sudden knowledge that he had very little to bring to the table? The child had more life experience than he did; she had more understanding of pain, of betrayal, of the often casual cruelty of people, than he did. She was fearful yet remarkably brave and truthful. He'd known at their first meeting that he was not up to the job of dealing competently with her. Yet he'd gone forward regardless, sensing that he could profit from his involvement with her. And he had profited. In truth, he had made much use of her, just as her kidnappers had. Only the manner of use was different. But, use was use. Indisputable. And he'd been rewarded with international recognition and a third of the substantial income derived from the perennial bestseller he'd penned with his parents. The only honorable thing he'd done was to put half his share of the income from the book into her trust fund.

But early on self-interest had blinded him. And his parents had always been blind, even to each other. They co-existed under forbearance, probably because few other people would have tolerated either one of them. They were cold, clinically detached people who claimed to live lives of the mind. They were disdainful of those who lived emotional lives, which was why they were teachers and not practicing psychiatrists. The cool intellect was God. And that belief rendered them incapable of being of therapeutic value to others.

They should never have become parents, he realized now. They had no patience – not with each other, with their students, or with him. As a youngster he'd learned not to seek them out with his hurts or problems. Until she died when he was eleven, he went upstairs to his grandmother, his father's mother, for soft Russian-accented words of consolation and understanding, for gentle hands, warm embraces, the scent of Chanel No. 5, and a welcoming lap and illicit sweets. He never fully recovered from the loss of her and even now she sometimes came to him in dreams from which he awakened quietly bereft, with a deep ache of longing in his chest.

He'd never loved his parents the way his few friends loved theirs. He respected and feared their authority, admired their austere but handsome features, and their academic accomplishments. So he'd worked hard to win the approval of his ever-elegant, stately mother (hair in a careful knot, cashmere sweaters, pearl necklaces, dark suits with slim skirts, low-heeled pumps on long, narrow feet) and his perpetually frowning father (short-back-and-sides with a touch of brilliantine, Brooks Brothers button-down shirts under Shetland pullovers, gray flannel slacks and navy blazer, Bass loafers) and ultimately he'd succeeded – to a degree – by sacrificing this girl to their inspection. And they went avidly at his offering, almost drooling at the tasty morsel he'd brought into their lives.

She had become a permanent reference source in the house. Not a person. She had taken over his position as the observable resident specimen. But to her credit she had never capitulated to his parents the way he had. Always polite, always accommodating but always keeping a little distance, she had never shared her innermost thoughts with them. She had learned at a very early age to conceal herself in plain view. She had gone to Connie in much the same way he had gone to his *bubbe*.

And now he also realized with a jolt of understanding that Faith was the only person in the household who did genuinely live a life of the mind. His parents were poseurs, generally

respected but almost universally disliked by their peers. And
he'd abandoned his practice to join up with them, acquiring
props and mannerisms en route: the beard, the suspenders, the
abrupt and dismissive manner of dealing with people. No
wonder Faith found it hard to talk to him. He'd been so busy
attempting to emulate his parents that he'd lost most of his
best qualities. He had become the polar opposite of his grandmother's beloved and lovable *boychik*.

He looked at Faith now and experienced again a strong
degree of the heartbreak that had overwhelmed him years ago
in that interview room. He was indebted to this girl and felt
now a sudden, powerful sense of obligation to her.

'Faith,' he said softly, 'I think you're right. I think you do
need to have a place of your own. And I'll agree to give you
what you want if you'll do something for me.'

Instantly hope-filled, aware that he'd undergone some sort
of transformation, she said, 'What?'

'I'd like you to go for residential treatment.'

She blinked slowly. This was not unexpected and very
reasonable, given the extent of her performance. She had
convinced him. But more than that she'd managed to call him
back – perhaps only temporarily – from that place he'd gone
to soon after he'd brought her home to the cozy little house
he'd shared with Monica. 'Where?' she asked.

'I know of a good place upstate, near Kent. I'm confident
I can make a phone call and get you in. If you'll do the program
and get yourself sober, I'll arrange to sign off on the guardianship and as executor of your trust fund.'

'How long would I have to stay there?' she asked, hoping
not to miss any school. She was trying to do her BA in two
and a half years. She couldn't afford to lose any credits.

'I think it's two weeks, maybe three. I believe you need
twenty-four hours without drinking before they'll accept you.
That would mean the day after tomorrow. But I'll know more
after I phone up there and speak to someone in admissions.
Will you do it?'

'What about your parents?' she asked. 'Won't they have
something to say about it?'

'Actually, no,' he answered. 'I'm your legal guardian for

another few months, but that's merely a technicality. My parents have no legal standing where you're concerned. I am responsible for your well-being and, frankly, I don't think I've done too great a job of it. I'd like to try to make it up to you and this would be the first step. Will you go?'

It was an apology. She could scarcely believe it, but she certainly wasn't going to reject it. All at once he resembled the man who'd broken into tears in that room with all the mirrors; she remembered how surprised she'd been, only in the past day or two having ever seen grown-ups cry. 'What kind of place is it?'

'It's upstate in the mountains. They have an excellent track record. And if we can get you in right away, because it's coming up to the Christmas break, you won't miss more than a few days of classes, if any. If you'll let me, I'd like to drive you up there, get you settled.'

'Okay,' she agreed, reasoning that it couldn't possibly hurt her. As long as she was out of this house, away from his parents, it was a major step in the right direction. 'I'll do it. But will you promise me that if I go there and complete the program you'll let me take charge of myself when I'm finished?'

For the first time in years, he smiled at her. He was suddenly present, no longer posturing or performing. 'I will put it in writing and have it notarized,' he promised. Then, the smile dimming away, he said, 'It's the least I can do. I think I've done you more harm than good. It's . . .' He shook his head sadly.

'I think you meant to do good.'

For the second time in his experience with her, he was choked with sorrow for the losses suffered by this misleadingly frail young woman. 'I'm sorry, Faith,' he said. 'I never intended to make you so unhappy. Somewhere along the way everything got very mixed up.'

'You should get your own place, too, Stefan,' she said sagely. 'Maybe you'd be happier.'

He could only stare at her, once again able to see the old, sympathetic soul gazing out at him through the dark windows of her eyes. 'I'd forgotten what a sympathetic and generous person you are,' he admitted. 'I won't ever make that mistake again. I hope you'll allow me to go on being a part of your life.'

'Of course I will. You're the only parent I've ever known.'

He couldn't respond to that or he risked breaking down, so he addressed the practicalities. 'I'll continue to pay your school fees, the cost of your stay for treatment, and all your expenses,' he added. 'So don't worry about any of that.'

'Thank you, Stefan. I appreciate it.' Everything inside her had lifted, was rising buoyantly. She was going to be free. More than that, the man she'd first known had reappeared and was looking at his surroundings with visible dismay. And she knew with certainty that he was going to move out, too. She and Stefan were going to leave his parents on their own to figure out how to live alone again.

FIFTEEN

Hay's eyes were caught and then helplessly kept returning to the young girl alone at a table at the far end of the barn. She didn't look old enough to be there, but of course she had to be. The age limit was eighteen. Long brown hair and shapeless black clothes gave her a frail, waif-like appearance and she had a sorrowing aura that relentlessly drew his attention.

He couldn't help noting that she waited until almost everyone had been through the food line before she came down the length of the room to the serving window. Up close he studied her pale, delicate features and deep brown eyes, the glossy dark hair that fell forward from a center parting and partially concealed her face. This, he thought, was a child in hiding. He felt immediately protective of her, touched by her state of distraction.

'How about some of this perfectly roasted chicken?' he asked, drawing her attention.

Faith tuned in to see a big, bearded fellow smiling at her. In a food-splattered apron, with a blue-printed kerchief tied over a red-brown ponytail, he looked like a cheerful lumberjack. He had clear grey-green eyes, warm with kindness.

She looked down at the aromatic array of food and said, 'Yes, please.'

'White or dark?'

'Either is fine, thank you,' she answered.

'Excellent. And some nice buttery mashed potatoes with a hint of dill?'

She couldn't help returning his smile. 'Yes, please.'

Encouraged, he asked, 'Perhaps a *soupçon* of green beans?'

Still smiling, she said, '*Oui, merci, monsieur.*'

'*Il me fait plaisir, mademoiselle.*' He made a demi-bow, saying, 'Hayward, *à votre service.*'

'I'm Faith.'

'*Bon appétit,* Faith.'

'Thank you, Mister Hayward.'

She carried her tray off toward the distant unoccupied table and Hayward watched for a moment, then returned his attention to dishing up food to the last of the latecomers. He was intrigued. Despite her very youthful appearance, there was nothing particularly young about her. She seemed careworn and weary, and alarmingly thin. Little Faith was well-mannered, smart as a whip, and very alone – plainly anxious to keep to herself. A troubled soul, yet possessed of a lovely sense of fun. There was definitely whimsy in those vivid red-painted fingernails.

By the time everyone had been served, he spotted the girl heading out of the barn, head bent in the act of lighting a cigarette as the door swung closed behind her.

The Farm was not the institutional structure Faith had imagined it would be. There was a cluster of well-kept houses – some considerably older than others – situated around what had once been a working farm. Grassy areas spread off to either side under patches of snow, with benches invitingly positioned here and there. Trees and bushes everywhere, and naked flower beds demarcated by whitewashed rocks. The entire place sat in the broad cupped palms of surrounding hills.

With her free hand she pushed the snow off one of the benches that overlooked the valley below and sat down, smoking her cigarette and savoring her first taste of brand-new freedom. People here seemed to leave each other alone; they understood the need for privacy but were available if someone needed to talk.

For the first time in too long, she'd actually been hungry and the food had been delicious. And best of all, no one seemed to care if she ate, or how much, which made it possible for her to eat in peace for the first time in more than a decade. She sat very still now, enjoying the fullness that pushed out her belly, and she imagined her organs hard at work dealing with what she'd consumed. Protein was being sent here, carbs went over there. Her internal machinery was humming away, happy to be back at work tending to her neglected body.

She had expected the people here to be deeply serious and so had been taken off guard by the amusing little exchange with . . . What was his name? Hayward . . . A nice man, with gentle eyes. Educated. Someone who looked like a lumberjack but spoke effortless French.

Gazing up at the very clear, very blue sky, the frigid air biting at her ears, she fretted about her dishonest replies to the sheet of twenty questions she'd been given to complete shortly after arriving early that morning. Some of her answers had been essentially truthful: yes, she felt remorse after drinking. Yes, she drank alone. Yes, she drank to escape from worries or troubles. Thinking of those questions and her replies, she felt a sudden spasm of anxiety. She was here under false pretenses. Maybe they'd recognize that and kick her out, send her back to the Lazarus clan. She couldn't let that happen. No matter what, she was never going back to that house.

Smoking her cigarette as she gazed out over the snow-covered land spreading off into the distance, she felt she was in a safe place. She wanted to stay. She needed this time to get healthy, to build up her mental as well as physical strength. She had to stay.

'Would you mind if I sit with you?'

She looked up. The kerchief was gone and he was wearing a bulky down jacket. 'No, that's fine.' Her gaze returned for a moment to the view, then she watched as he pulled the makings from his jacket pocket, quickly rolled a cigarette on his knee, returned the tobacco and papers to his pocket and got his roll-your-own lit. Then exhaling a plume of smoke, he said, 'So, I assume you just got here this morning.'

'You assume correctly.'

'Beautiful, isn't it?'

'It's not what I was expecting,' she admitted.

'Hardly anyone ever expects this.' With a sweeping gesture he indicated their surroundings. 'I think it's a big part of the magic. It certainly was for me.'

'Magic?' she glanced at him for a moment, then bent forward to extinguish her cigarette in the snow. She fished a tissue out of her pocket and wrapped the butt in it, to throw away later.

He gave her points for being respectful of her surroundings.

'Most of us are pretty wrought-up when we get here. The atmosphere, the beauty, they have a calming effect.'

She nodded, eyes back on the valley below. 'I can see how that would be. Have you been here a while?'

'Nine years. I came as a guest back in the summer of 'seventy-four and never left. I've been on staff for all but six weeks of that time.'

'How does it work?' she asked.

'You mean what should you expect here?' She nodded again and he said, 'What do you hope for, Faith?'

'In general or from this place?'

'Either, both. You're very young. Everything's in front of you.'

She wasn't sure what to say. 'I'm only young in years. Is it safe to talk to you?'

He smiled, then took another drag on his cigarette. 'I'm not going to repeat anything you tell me. Everything that's said here is treated as confidential.'

'Really? For everyone?'

'If you want to share information, it's entirely up to you. The Farm follows AA guidelines. And AA is an anonymous program. You don't have to attend the three meetings a day but you'd be missing out in a big way if you didn't.'

'Missing out on what?'

'On some sensible steps and a way of thinking that will make life easier in a lot of ways.'

'So no one's going to be monitoring what I do?'

'There's a little bit of that,' he explained. 'We all keep an eye out for problem situations, like two guests getting romantically involved. Or someone smuggling in substances. But basically, this is a retreat, a place where people can get away from the craziness of their lives for a time, where they can calm down and start coming to terms with their problems.'

'I see.' She wondered if Stefan had realized that when he'd chosen to send her here. 'It does feel very calm here.' She paused for a few seconds, then said softly, 'What I want is to be left alone.' Quickly, she added, 'I don't mean you.' Looking away, she said, 'I don't ever want to be watched and studied again, treated like a collection of symptoms, not like a person.

I had to do some fancy dancing to get here and it's going to take time for me to get used to being free.' She couldn't bring herself to express her fear that she'd be discovered a fraud and sent away. It was a discussion for another time.

He busied himself snuffing out his cigarette, taking advantage of that brief time to consider the possible implications of her words, before saying, 'Freedom is most often a state of mind.'

She regarded him sadly as she said, 'For me, it's been a state of being, Mister Hayward, a kind of domestic prison. I've never been a free person.'

'I'm sorry to hear that, Faith. I know a bit about different types of prisons. And, please, it's not Mister. It's just Hay.'

'I'm sorry, too,' she said, understanding intuitively that he wasn't referring to any kind of penal institution. 'Everything I've said and done for the last thirteen years has been watched, judged, and written down for publication. Aside from a few people I've been truly close to but don't get to see very often and the staff at the coffee shop where I have breakfast and study before class every weekday morning, you're the only other person I've had a viable conversation with since I was five years old. It's a long story, and the perfectly roasted chicken and buttery mashed potatoes with dill have made me sleepy.' She offered him an apologetic smile. 'I hope you won't think I'm rude but I'm going to go to my room and have a nap.' She got to her feet. He followed suit and she looked up at him. 'I've enjoyed talking to you, Hay. You listen but you don't push.'

'It's mutual,' he said, with the strongest feeling that this girl and Tally had a lot in common. It had to do with their withdrawn aspects and their clearly superior levels of intelligence. They were two women who appeared to be looking outward from invisibly enclosing areas of isolation. Yet, most rewardingly, they both had unexpectedly well-honed senses of humor. 'I don't have too many viable conversations either,' he went on. 'Just one quick thing before you go. On Saturdays friends and families come to visit the guests. In the evening, there's a roast beef dinner followed by an open meeting. Will your family be coming to see you?'

'I have a guardian, not a family. And no, he won't be coming. I asked him not to.'

'Then if I may I'd like to talk to a friend of mine, see if she'd care to come. I can't help thinking the two of you would hit it off. She's a lovely woman.'

'Okay. That'd be fine. If she's your friend, I'm sure she's someone I'd like to meet.'

'Wonderful! Have a good nap, Faith. I'll see you later.'

'Thank you, Hay.' She looked around, getting her bearings, then started off toward the house where the women guests stayed.

He watched her go, head down, hands jammed into her coat pockets. Her words were echoing inside his head. That tiny girl was the repository of some terrible tragedy. And he felt an immediate kinship with her, intimately acquainted as he was with the elements of tragedy. Its dimensions were acid-etched on his brain, permanent and only intermittently escapable.

He telephoned Tally the next morning after the breakfast clean-up was completed and asked if she'd like to come to the Saturday night dinner.

'I thought I might persuade you to take some time off from stripping the wainscoting,' he said, which got the laugh he'd hoped for. 'The food's very good and there's an open speaker meeting after. I think you'd enjoy it.'

'I'm not a terribly social person, Hay,' she said carefully.

'You don't have to be. It's just about eating and listening. You don't need to talk to anyone beyond saying hello. Not even that, if you're not up for it. The atmosphere is always pretty festive, a whole bunch of folks feeling optimistic for the first time in a while because people they care about are getting well again, finding themselves. They're starting to resemble the people they used to be and that's a special thing; it seeps into the air.'

'You make it sound like a party.'

'Well, not a party per se, but a celebration of sorts. I'll be more than happy to pick you up and bring you home again, so you don't have to worry about finding a new place in the dark.'

'Good food and a good speaker, a festive mood, plus complimentary pick-up and delivery. How could I resist such an invitation? I will accept. Thank you for thinking of me.'

'The downside of the invitation is that you'll be on your own for about forty minutes while I do the dinner service. I'm covered for the clean-up afterward, but I'm needed at the serving window for the main event. You could bring a book and read, if you like. Or you could just relax and people-watch. I'll be happy to swing by and pick you up around five thirty. Will that be okay?'

'Okay,' she agreed. 'I'll see you on Saturday. Just please don't expect me to be the life of the party.'

'I have no expectations, Tally. I'm happy you're willing to come. I really do think you'll enjoy it.'

'If I don't,' she said with a laugh, 'I foresee some paint stripping in your future.'

'Fair enough,' he said, then hung up the office phone and headed out to the truck. He was going to drive over to the Westfalls Mall in Farmington to buy a new shirt or two, maybe some slacks. Then he'd get a haircut, have the beard trimmed. It'd been too long since he'd paid any real attention to his appearance and all at once how he looked mattered again. He wasn't going to revert to the fellow who'd bought his clothes at Brooks Brothers and fit right in with his classmates at Princeton. That poor bastard was long gone. Sometimes that guy felt to him like a close friend who'd died. He was never coming back. And that was sad.

As he drove down the long driveway toward Route 7, he had a powerful sense of occasion. Nothing specific, but it was very real. Things were about to change.

SIXTEEN

Three days into her stay at The Farm, Faith was no longer worried about being sent away as an interloper but she remained self-conscious, uneasy. After all her years with the Lazarus clan she knew her anxiety level wasn't going to start diminishing in a mere matter of days . . . if ever. She accepted that reality and sat alone for meals, bringing along her copy of *Alcoholics Anonymous*, which everyone referred to as The Big Book to read while she ate – a successful ploy to discourage people from trying to engage her in conversation. Beyond an exchange of greetings with other guests in passing and attending the three daily meetings, she kept to herself. Having learned that she wasn't obligated to speak at all during the meetings she was able to listen – and to read – with genuine interest, absorbing the basics of the program and finding it all very sensible, very well-conceived.

She was nervous about the Saturday night dinner and meeting Hay's friend. Her instinct was to stay away. There'd been a couple of occasions at school when classmates with whom she was on speaking terms suggested she might like to read this hilarious book they'd just loved. Each time, without fail, Faith had found the book in question not only not funny but unreadable. She suspected that being introduced to someone with whom she'd 'hit it off' was going to be the human equivalent of the highly recommended unfunny books.

But she liked and trusted Hay. It was instinctive. In the same way she'd entrusted herself all those years ago to Brian, letting him wrap her in a towel and carry her through the store, looking for Wolf and Toadman, she was truthful with Hay, letting his kindness serve as a kind of protective blanket. It was safe to talk to him and she had the feeling that, as with Brian, this man could become an ongoing presence in her life.

They'd had two more conversations since that first afternoon outside on the bench – once after the evening meeting that same day, and once the previous afternoon. He was consistently soft-spoken, thoughtful and good-humored. He took her seriously, gave weight to what she had to say, and laughed with her over things she found amusing. He was fatherly, protective without being overbearing. And given that some part of her was always in search of her parents, he qualified as someone worthy of considering in parental terms.

The dinner was obviously so important to him that he'd visited a barber and as a result looked much younger and no longer like a lumberjack, more like a gentleman farmer. She hadn't had the heart to refuse him.

She was standing just inside the door to the barn when he asked, and she agreed to come a bit early that evening, even though the thought of it made her stomach muscles clench.

'Just so you know,' he warned, 'every table will probably be occupied. It's a big night and there's usually a full house.'

'Okay, I've been warned,' she said seriously. 'Do people get all dressed up?'

'Not at all. Wear whatever you want. It's not formal.'

'That's a relief. I don't do formal.'

She sounded like Tally, and he was more and more convinced that introducing the two of them would be a good thing – for both of them.

'Thank you, Faith. I appreciate it.'

'You're welcome. I'll see you and your friend later,' she said, pulling her pack of cigarettes from her pocket and heading for the door.

He returned to the kitchen to help with the clean-up, praying he hadn't misread these women. He'd never done anything like this and there was always the possibility – however remote – that they would take an instant dislike to each other and the evening would be an utter failure.

'You got your hair cut,' Tally observed when she opened the door to him that evening. 'And trimmed the beard, too.'

Touching a hand to his goateed chin, he said, 'My first visit to a barber in years. I'm still not used to it.'

'It's most becoming. You look very civilized.' She smiled and stepped outside, pulling the door closed.

'Less of a wild mountain man,' he offered.

'Exactly. I don't think you'll be frightening any little old ladies.'

'Well, I'm glad to hear that,' he said wryly, as they descended the porch steps and headed to his truck. 'It's good to see you, Tally.'

'And you,' she said, as he held the passenger door open and she climbed into the warm cab. Typically considerate, he'd left the car running. It was their third meeting since the night of the snowstorm and she'd come to recognize that his civility was ingrained. He was a well-bred, considerate man; gentle and thoughtful. Good company.

Faith sat alone at her usual table turning a glass of water on the tabletop, something to do with her hands while she waited for Hay and his friend. She was grateful for the echoey emptiness of the barn that allowed her to gather her thoughts, seeking to remain calm. The only sounds came from the kitchen where the dinner preparations were well underway. The smell of roasting meat was so heady she wanted to close her eyes, put her head down on the table and go to sleep.

She'd eaten more in the past three days than she had in years. She could feel the weight-gain. It was as if a hidden switch inside her had been turned on and she couldn't wait for mealtimes, no longer staying back to be the last in the food line but moving forward, often to be the first. Which prompted Hay to offer a big smile before he recited the offerings to her, usually with French descriptions.

Now, dreamy in the rich aroma drifting through the huge space, she thought about the place of her own she planned to get once she had access to her money. She wanted to learn how to cook. She'd take classes somewhere or buy videos that would lead her step by step through food preparation. She didn't care if she got to be the size of a Sumo wrestler. So her first thought about a home of her own was of a kitchen with well-stocked cupboards and a crowded refrigerator; a brightly lit room with every conceivable appliance where she'd produce headily aromatic meals to eat at a leisurely pace; meals to share with Connie, or Brian and his family, possibly even Stefan, once he'd settled into his new place. Maybe a party with all of them. She could envisage that. She wanted to eat with friends. One of the new rules for her life would be her refusal to eat with people who made her uncomfortable.

She didn't want a house. That would entail too much maintenance. But a condominium would be good. A place where outdoor chores would be taken care of automatically, but indoors would be entirely her own, just as she wanted it. A wonderful kitchen, a big living room with a fireplace . . .

Hay's voice saying, 'Faith, I'd like you to meet Tally,' startled her. Heart thumping, she jumped to her feet, not knowing what she was doing, unfocused, dragging her thoughts into the moment as her eyes slid off Hay and landed on a face that belonged to a movie star. Beautiful yet with melancholy eyes Faith recognized from her own miserable encounters with mirrors. The woman offered a smile and an out-held hand.

'I'm sorry,' Faith got out. 'I was . . . daydreaming . . . Hi!' She took hold of the woman's slim hand, looked into her eyes, and felt a seismic jolt. The woman felt it, too: recognition and an instant understanding of each other. It was as if they'd once spent time together – intense, concentrated time so that they knew one another intimately. Tally's expression turned quizzical and she searched Faith's eyes, keeping hold of her hand. What was happening here? When had they known each other?

Tally saw a little girl with an old woman's eyes, delicate features half-hidden behind an abundance of long gold-brown hair; a child in appearance, with painfully undernourished limbs. Her hand was small and warm and firm, and Tally had the arbitrary notion that this ethereal child would simply drift away if Tally relinquished her grip. Improbably, she felt somehow responsible for keeping the girl tethered to herself. She'd met someone important here, and Tally didn't want to lose her. She had to know what this meeting signified. For the first time in many years, her heart was stirred fully alive. It was beating importantly, alerting her to a revival of all her senses.

Hay broke into the moment. 'I've got to get into the kitchen. Take care of each other, you two,' he said, and hurried off, satisfied by what he'd witnessed. He'd known in his bones that these two women needed to meet. There'd visibly been an instant connectedness he'd anticipated, as if a lengthy separation had been brought to an end. A reunion of people who'd never met but who were deeply familiar to each other – and to him. He'd felt it the moment he'd seen Faith, had sensed the restorative effect she'd have on Tally and, in turn, the maternal consolation Tally could bring to Faith's plainly orphaned spirit.

Unsettled, Faith said, 'We should probably sit down,' then waited for the woman's hand to leave hers, feeling briefly chilled when it did.

'You seem so – *familiar*,' Tally said. Then she smiled again and said, 'But that's impossible.'

'You do, too,' Faith said. 'And it *is* impossible. I'd definitely remember if we'd met before.'

Tally shrugged off her jacket, draped it over the back of her chair and sat down.

Faith resumed her seat, unable to take her eyes from the woman. 'I'm probably being rude. I lack social skills,' she said.

'That's not so.' Tally disagreed with a shake of her head. The girl was a small island, she thought, alone in a vast sea of uncertainty. 'You're probably just not used to being away from home.'

'I don't *have* a home,' Faith said quietly, 'only a place where I've had to be until now.'

With a slight frown, Tally asked, 'How can that be?'

'Nobody knows who I am.' Faith couldn't believe she'd said that aloud, but she wasn't sorry. It seemed as if she'd been waiting her entire life to talk to this woman. For the briefest fragment of time, she wondered if she was meeting her mother. She wished it were so, but she knew it wasn't. Tally wasn't old enough; they bore no resemblance whatsoever to each other. What Tally did offer, though, was a rare acknowledgment, an acceptance that no one else had ever provided. It felt as if a long-sealed door had silently opened and Faith was able to enter a place where she could finally know how it felt to belong – as a child to a parent. That knowledge was here; it resided in Tally and the transfusion of feeling had already begun. Inexplicable but undeniable.

Tally leaned on her elbows, closing the distance between them. 'Why not?'

'I *never* talk this way,' Faith told her. 'I don't tell people about myself. I have no idea why I'm saying these things to you.'

With the sense that time had ballooned around them, enclosing them in an elastic moment, Tally knew that this was a meeting that could never be duplicated, no matter how many times they might meet again. Like a chapter from a science fiction novel, they were meeting in a space out of time where who they were could be safely revealed – but only to each other. A cosmic gift? Karma? It was impossible to know, but it was ordained somehow. And they both felt it.

'Should I tell you something that *I* never tell anyone?' Tally asked, swimming in the warmth of the girl's deep eyes.

'Yes. Please.'

'I've spent the last fifteen years in prison. I was released just a few months ago.'

'*God!* Why?' Rather than alarming her, Faith felt utterly sympathetic. She knew that whatever the reason for Tally's being in prison, it was wrong.

'It's too long a story, but I'll tell you about it later, if you like.'

'Yes. I'd like that.'

Tally reached out and took hold again of Faith's hand. 'I know it's not possible, but it feels as if I know you.'

'I feel the same way. It's so strange. But good . . . as if I've been waiting all this time to meet you.'

'Exactly,' Tally agreed.

'I've spent the past thirteen years with the Lazarus family,' Faith said softly, in the throes of a confessional need she'd never before experienced. Her voice diminishing to a husky whisper, she confided, 'I'm a famous stolen child.'

A gloss of tears suddenly appeared in Tally's eyes. '*The Stolen Child*? That book? It's about you?' Tally remembered sharing the book with her cell mate Bertie. It was the only time they'd ever discussed one of the books they'd shared. Tally had been overwhelmed with dislike of the doctors who'd written it, feeling that they'd capitalized on the child's misfortune. And Bertie had agreed quite volubly. 'Poor little tyke. They oughta be *ashamed*!' she'd said with disgust.

Faith said now, 'It's about who they *thought* I was. But I've *never* been that person. All I ever wanted was to find my family – to go home. I could never stop thinking that somewhere out there' – a sweep of her hand indicated the world beyond the barn – 'I had a mother and father who didn't know where I was. I wanted to find them. I've always wanted to find them; I probably always will.'

'How is it possible we're telling each other our secrets?' Tally wondered aloud. 'We met two minutes ago but I feel as if I've always known you. Do you think it's because I read the book?'

'Maybe. But I've never read about *you*.'

They stared at each other for a long moment, then spontaneously began to laugh.

'Hay was right,' Tally said, glancing over to see that people were filing into the barn.

Following her eyes, Faith said, 'We'll talk later, after dinner, won't we?'

'Absolutely,' Tally promised.

'I feel as if you came tonight just to visit me . . . as if you're family. For a minute, I wanted you to be my mother, to have found me finally.'

'I had a daughter who died,' Tally said softly. 'She was five months old. Her name was Anna.'

'Oh, no!' Faith felt the loss like a blow to the midriff that curled her forward over the sudden pain. 'I'm so sorry.'

They sat silent for a time, their hands still joined. Then: 'The food smells wonderful,' Tally said, letting go – a signal. 'All of a sudden I'm very hungry.'

'Me, too,' Faith said, understanding. She looked over to see people settling at the nearby tables; the room all at once abustle, voices falling over each other, rising in volume. 'How did Hay know we had to meet?' she had to ask.

Folding her arms on the table in front her, Tally thought about that, realizing something she'd known about Hay from the outset without actually considering it. 'I think perhaps we've all been prisoners in one way or another. And he

recognized that. Maybe not consciously. Sometimes we follow
our intuition without knowing why. He's told me very little
about his life; it's not anything he's said. But it's something
about him that I've felt. And now I think he recognized that
same thing about you and me . . . I think he intuitively felt it
was important for the two of us to meet.'

Faith thought that made sense, and automatically she looked
over at the serving window where Hay was setting a huge tray
down on the steam table. The usual blue kerchief was tied
over his hair, a clean white apron wrapped around his middle.
His eyes lifted as if he felt the weight of her gaze and she
waggled her fingers at him. He smiled at her then stepped out
of view, back into the kitchen.

Faith ate quickly, savoring the end-cut piece of roast beef Hay
had kept aside for her. Everything was delicious: the moist beef
subtly seasoned, the carrots sweet, the potatoes buttery, the
gravy smooth and rich. Her appetite was enormous, and she
was relieved to see that Tally, too, was eating quickly, hungrily.

Their eyes met, and again, they grinned at each other.

They'd dived instantly into intimacy as if leaping from the
top of a tall waterfall, dropping into a plunging torrent that
had deposited them upright in a soothing, frothy pool at its
base. They had, in meeting, been magically freed of all prior
constraints. Even in silence, they were communicating. Both
of them felt happier than they had in a long, long time with
the sense that long-missing parts of themselves had been magically restored.

Now and then finding his sight-line clear, Hay glanced over
to the table, elated to see Tally and Faith, both of them easy
in their demeanor, interacting like long-time, close friends,
their conversation intercut with sudden laughter.

With the food service complete, when he brought his plate
of food to the table and sat down with them to eat, all three
of them laughed spontaneously. It was exactly as he'd hoped
it would be – ordained, somehow. Something damaged on
Asian soil, something more lost on familiar ground, was being
returned to him in a way he could never have imagined.
Mentally he thanked his higher power for this unexpected but

hugely welcome gift. Once again he was part of something that had all the constituents of a family and he felt a rush of love for these women. His gratitude was beyond measure. They each no longer had to feel alone. The little girl pretending to be an alcoholic could stop pretending. The woman pretending not to care about her life could end the pretense. And the man pretending to relish his isolation could dine at a table with people for whom he was amassing a wealth of feeling.

SEVENTEEN

F aith could barely concentrate on the evening's speaker. Her thoughts tumbled distractingly. She wanted to talk more with Tally and Hay. She wanted to know about the roads they'd traveled to arrive at this point in time as the people they were now. She herself had been profoundly affected by Margery Briggs's decision to put her in the care of the Lazarus family. Had the woman been better equipped for her job, had she been less of an elitist and more sensitive to the children who came under her jurisdiction, she'd have chosen to place Faith with Brian and his family, or with Captain Garvey and his. Connie would have been ideal but her lack of a husband eliminated her from consideration, which was a rule so stupid that Faith couldn't think about it without becoming infuriated.

Margery Briggs had made a decision that could never have been construed as being in the best interest of the child. But she'd had the authority to make that decision, and her choice had shaped Faith into the person who'd used a risky and devious ploy in order to save herself. Twice in her life she'd relied on her native ingenuity to escape from dangerous situations: once to save the baby and now to save herself. Literally. The Lazarus clan had brought her to the brink of suicide, so contaminated was she with self-loathing by the images they had kept forcing her to revisit, never allowing her to clear her mind. But she'd escaped and life all at once felt livable again. She could continue on toward a future of helping children, caring for them, saving them, if possible. She would use her experience to intervene when needed, to effect change, to offer sanctuary, however briefly. Somebody had to speak up for the babies, and she could do that.

She couldn't help sensing there was truth to Tally's suggestion that all three of them had been imprisoned in some fashion. Although she hadn't previously thought of it in those terms, she could see now that her years in the Lazarus home had been an esoteric form of imprisonment. The only possible reward to be garnered from the experience would be financial, once Stefan made good on his promised settlement. And she didn't doubt he'd keep his word. He was many things, but not a liar. In only a couple of days he'd become once more recognizable as the young man who'd sat on the floor and played games with her at their first meeting, the young man who'd been sitting at her bedside each time she'd awakened from another surgery. That young man had had great empathy, and it seemed to have restarted again, as if he'd lived in some arcane cryogenic state during the intervening years.

All she wanted now was to get to know Tally and Hay and learn how their experiences had shaped them. To her mind, it was like random child's play. The transient placement here and there of dolls in the control of heedless children had defined three people's lives: their memories, their behavior, their very existence. And tonight she was relieved to learn that hers wasn't an isolated case; that other people had done whatever needed to be done in order to survive. Intellectually of course she'd always known that, but she'd still felt alone, locked inside herself – trapped in that fancy spider's web of a house.

At last the meeting came to an end and people were either streaming over to talk to the speaker or putting the tables and chairs back in place, carrying full ashtrays to a table near the kitchen before filing out of the barn. Hay got up, saying, 'Why don't the two of you grab seats and I'll get us some coffee.'

Faith sat quietly for a moment, then told Tally she was going to get an ashtray. 'I really need a cigarette,' she said apologetically. 'I'll be right back.'

After making her way through the slow-moving crowd and emptying one of the ashtrays, she got back to the table as Hay returned carrying a tray with mugs of coffee and a plate of cookies. Taking note of Faith's cigarette, he put the tray on the table, saying, 'I've been wanting a cigarette, too. Will you be all right with both of us smoking?' he asked Tally as he sat down, prepared to pull his tobacco and papers from his pocket.

'Smoke, you two,' she told them. 'I really don't mind.'

'Tell me,' Tally asked Faith, surrendering to her curiosity. 'What will you do when you leave here?'

'I'll be going back to school and looking for a place of my own in my free time.'

'Aren't you a bit young for your own place?' Tally asked.

'As far as anyone knows, I'm almost eighteen. That makes me "legal." I'd like to be closer to school. Right now I'm spending a lot of time driving back and forth every day. I'm a sophomore at Yale, in pre-med,' she elaborated.

Hay was impressed. 'I thought you were maybe a junior in high school.'

'Everybody thinks that.' Faith shrugged, giving him a smile. 'I'm used to it. But I've always wanted to be a doctor, a pediatrician specifically.' Turning to Tally, she asked, 'I know it's kind of pushy of me, but will you tell me about prison, about what happened?'

Bemused, Hay took a drag on his cigarette, waiting to hear what Tally would say. Obviously, the two of them had engaged in some intense conversation before he'd been free to join them earlier with his dinner plate.

'I was young and impatient once, too,' Tally said generously, offering Faith a smile, then including Hay. 'Here's the abridged version,' she began.

'In the spring of 'sixty-five I was working on my BA thesis at the San Francisco Art Institute, and trying to decide if I really wanted to start graduate school in the fall. I was pre-enrolled but very uncertain. My immediate plan was to head home to Nevada and take the summer at the ranch to decide on a direction because nothing appealed to me. I considered myself an emancipated woman, modern and forward-thinking. I wanted to *do* something, have some kind of career, but I didn't want to throw away the tuition money if my interest turned out to be in some area that wasn't covered at the Institute.' She took a slow breath, and said, 'And then I met Clayton and everything changed.'

Just as he had all those years ago in reality, he stepped now into her recall: clear-eyed and smiling, with a country boy's sturdy build and unaffected manner; a perfectly beautiful young man with direct blue eyes and a well-shaped mouth, asking to borrow the salt from her table in the cafe.

She was alone. He was alone. He asked if he could share

her table. She said yes. Lunch evolved into a lengthy laugh-punctuated conversation that continued on to become a rambling walk through the city with a pause for a takeout dinner of hamburgers and fries eaten on a park bench, and ended just before midnight when he escorted her back to her apartment and kissed her cheek before heading off to his boarding-house.

He was an orphan who'd been raised by his only relative, his mother's laconic unmarried Uncle Bradford who'd owned a dude ranch in central Wyoming. Deeply sensitive, aware of nuance, immensely talented and kind-hearted, Clayton was – with the inheritance from Bradford's estate – completing his degree in the photography program at the Institute that had been started by Ansel Adams.

Despite the rural upbringing that had begun for him at the age of six following his parents' death in an automobile accident, Clayton preferred shooting urban scenes, often subtly hand-tinting black-and-white images with faint colors to lend them surprising softness and warmth.

Tally loved his work; she loved him. Their feelings for each other were immediate and absolute. When he revealed that he was on a student deferment and would be inducted into the military following his graduation in June, she said, 'We'd better get the license right away then.'

Purely as a formality, because she so rarely saw them, she'd phoned to invite her parents to the ceremony. As Tally had anticipated, her father initially sounded pleased for her and said he was willing but, his tone changing and voice dropping to a near-whisper, admitted that he had to turn the matter over to her mother, who immediately came on the line, angry. 'We have an *important* luncheon booked that day! You can't seriously expect us to change our plans on such short notice! This is *so* typical of you, Natalie. You never think of *anyone* but *yourself*!'

When she called him, Warren exclaimed, 'What wonderful news! I'll call Alexis right now. We will be there, Tally!'

In keeping with her status as an emancipated woman, she chose to keep her own name. Clayton didn't mind. She was nineteen. He was twenty-one. Eighteen days after they met, they went downtown to City Hall and got married. Warren and Alexis happily witnessed the ceremony, then insisted on taking the newlyweds to lunch at The Top of The Mark.

The next day a courier delivered an envelope that contained a check for ten thousand dollars along with a note that said, 'I am sorry we couldn't be there. I wish you both every happiness. Love, Dad.'

Surprised and touched, she wrote a thank-you note and sent it to his office where she knew he'd actually receive it. Anything sent to the house would be intercepted by Ivory who was likely, first, to raise hell with her husband for daring to send any sort of gift to their daughter without consulting her and, second, she would destroy the note. In doing all this, it would never have occurred to her that she'd confirmed Tally's receipt of her father's gift. It was safer to circumvent her mother altogether and deal directly with her father who, every now and then, revealed a functioning heart – something her mother did not possess.

Their honeymoon was a long weekend at the ranch. Clayton fell in love with the place. 'It feels familiar, like home,' he declared, quickly deciding that next to the porch with its panoramic view, his favorite spot was a wide tree trunk by the river where he was content to sit with a book, looking up every now and then to watch the river water rushing past.

Alba and Joe Seven Moons took to Clayton on sight and, at Tally's insistence, sat down with them to the standing rib roast celebration dinner that Alba prepared.

When they returned to the city, Clayton moved into her quaint apartment on Potrero Hill. They worked slavishly to complete their theses, his on the effects of sunlight on the urban landscape in photography, and hers on the issue of what forms might legitimately be considered contemporary art.

After defending their papers, they returned to the ranch to spend their final week together before he was to report for duty. He didn't want to go but believed it was the honorable thing to do. One defended one's country, his great-uncle had told him. During the war, Clayton's dad had been a private in the army, based in Italy, and Uncle Bradford had been a captain in the navy, seeing action in the Pacific.

'It's only a year-long deployment,' Clayton assured her. 'Then it'll be behind us.'

That one year lasted forever, her longing for him initially relieved by his frequent letters. But they came less and less often until his last one arrived three months before he was discharged. The long silence worried her.

A year later, a haggard stranger came back. Thin to the point of emaciation, his pants were held up by a length of rope. His fair glossy curls had given way to a buzz cut so short that in sunlight he looked bald. His complexion was ashen, dry; his cheeks and somehow faded eyes were sunken. His nails were bitten to the quick, blood-rimmed, and he chewed on his fingers constantly, unable to hold a conversation of any length. He clung to her as if she was all that stood between him and a terrifying descent into frigid darkness.

A month after he returned, he gathered all his prints and negatives and built a bonfire in back of the house. He couldn't be persuaded to save any of his work. Jaw clenched, eyes narrowed, he stood chewing on a forefinger, watching until the fire burned to ash. Tally stayed to one side, trying to understand what was happening, able only to believe that what he'd experienced in Viet Nam had been too dreadful to tolerate. His very being had been altered by the experience.

She thought he might rally when her pregnancy was confirmed. But he shook his head. 'It's a mistake,' he told her, anxious and fearful. 'This isn't a world fit for children. You should get rid of it while you can,' he said with frightful solemnity.

'I *want* this baby,' she said quietly, wounded. 'And once you meet him or her, you'll want the baby, too.'

'No! It's a mistake,' he said again.

She tried to get help for him, arranging appointments Clayton refused to keep. 'Please let me help you,' she asked repeatedly.

He just shook his head and walked off to the river's edge where he'd sit unmoving for hours simply staring at the water. He no longer read or listened to music. He just sat, looking out but, in reality, gazing inward.

She tried to comfort him, tried to get him to talk. Nothing

worked. The gifted, sensitive man she'd known was in hiding or perhaps gone forever. Nothing she said or did had any effect. He was fretful, jittery. He'd lost the ability to smile. He couldn't eat more than a bite or two of anything. He had nightmares that caused him to cry out, startling both of them into wakefulness. He wept without warning, inconsolable. She'd gaze into his eyes, searching, but unable to find him. She had no idea who this person was but she couldn't give up trying to retrieve the man she loved who had to be still somewhere inside him.

When she returned late one afternoon from her regular monthly trip to Carson City for a check-up with her obstetrician, she found the driveway crowded with emergency and police vehicles. Her heartbeat turned chaotic, her mouth went dry. Alba had been keeping a watch out for her and came running to steer her away from the house. 'Don't go in,' Alba warned her. 'Come with me, Tally, please come with me.'

But of course she went in, entering in time to see the paramedics cutting Clay down from the center beam in the living room. The coroner, the sheriff and several deputies stood by, watching. They were terribly gentle with him, lowering his weight into the body bag on the waiting stretcher, zipping closed the lurid black container before bearing him away. The coroner was holding Tally's hand but she didn't notice until she turned to watch the paramedics directing the stretcher out to the ambulance, when the warmth of the hand enclosing hers penetrated the chill that gripped her. She couldn't speak, couldn't think.

She was twenty-one years old, six months pregnant, a widow.

Ten weeks later, Anna was born. And for the first time since Clayton died, Tally felt warm. Alba and Joe fussed, insisting on babysitting Anna the first night home so Tally could get some rest. Seeing the baby in Joe's strong brown arms was comforting. As she lay down to nap, Tally couldn't help thinking things were beginning to look a bit brighter.

Anna was easy, a jolly baby who loved to eat, loved to sleep, loved being cuddled and sung to. She had thick dark curls and chubby limbs and her eyes quickly turned the familiar crystal blue of her father's eyes; she splashed happily with excited energy while being bathed in the kitchen sink. She made giddy noises as her hands smacked at the water. Alba stood by with a towel, ready to receive the baby for the nightly ritual of cooing and cuddling and then a feeding with her mother before bed.

Then one morning five months into her motherhood, Tally got up and went to get Anna for her morning feed. She looked into the crib to see that the baby lay motionless. Her skin was cool. Tally couldn't breathe, and held the baby, trying to think what to do. She felt her mind starting to melt.

The same paramedics came again and so did one of the deputies. Anna couldn't be revived. The assistant district attorney arrived, as did the coroner, and they talked quietly with the paramedics while Tally clutched the baby, trying to will her awake, trying to infuse her body with vital warmth.

'I'm so sorry,' the young lawyer said consolingly, a hand touching lightly to her shoulder.

'So very, very sorry,' the coroner said.

Then they went on their way.

Joe and Alba gazed on in shock as Tally begged the paramedics to explain what had happened to Anna, to explain how she could just go to sleep and not wake up again. The older of the two EMTs, Paiute-Shoshone like Alba and Joe, with a much lived-in face, said softly, 'It happens sometimes. It just happens, and there's no explanation.'

Tally couldn't absorb that and continued rocking the baby in her arms until, finally, Alba convinced her to let the paramedics take Anna. 'You'll see her later,' Alba said.

'She'll still be dead,' Tally replied, noticing the depth of the wrinkles surrounding Alba's eyes. She realized she had no idea how old the woman was. In her late sixties, maybe her late seventies? She looked ancient. Why had Tally never really looked at her before?

Alba eased the baby out of Tally's arms and surrendered her to the older paramedic, then held Tally gently, securely, while Joe went with the men out to the ambulance.

It was over. Dead husband. Dead baby.

But no. It was an election year and the district attorney wanted to make a case out of Anna's death. So despite the assistant district attorney's angry argument that there *was* no case, that according to the paramedics and the coroner, there was no evidence of any physical harm to the baby, the DA charged Tally with second-degree murder. A murder trial would make the district attorney the center of attention, especially if she tried the case herself. It would ensure her re-election.

Tally found an old Chanel suit of her mother's that seemed perfect for the occasion and wore it when she surrendered herself to the surprised sheriff, who said in an undertone, 'Go home, girl, and talk to your lawyer.'

'Just lock me up and be done with it,' Tally said tonelessly.

'Natalie Paxton, I've known you your whole life. You're no murderer. You've had lousy luck and that's the God's honest truth. It's a goddamned shame. But you're young; you still have a future. Don't go along with this bullshit! There's no case!'

She was deaf to his words.

When she learned what Tally had done, Alba immediately phoned Warren and he got on the next flight, arriving at the jail in a rental car that afternoon.

'We'll fight this,' he told Tally, having made some calls from the airport before he'd boarded his flight. 'They have no grounds. This DA is blowing smoke, making noise to get attention so she can win re-election.'

'I don't care, Warren,' she said, defeated. 'I just don't care.'

'Tally, the penalty for second-degree murder is fifteen years in prison!'

'I don't *care*, Warren.'

'If you plead guilty, Tally, if you allocute, it can't be undone. Let me get a Nevada criminal lawyer in to defend you. Any halfway decent attorney will get the case thrown out. For chrissake, a first-year law student could get this thrown out!'

'Thank you for caring, Warren. Would you please draw up papers to transfer ownership of the ranch to Alba and Joe? Annalise would have wanted them to have it. And will you take care of everything for me while I'm away? Whatever needs doing.'

'You know I will,' he told her with unshed tears in the rims of his eyes.

'Good. I'm very tired now. I'd like to lie down.'

Seeing she would not be swayed, he kissed her forehead and left her there.

In a special session the next day, with only Warren, Alba and Joe in the courtroom, Tally waived her right to counsel and confessed. 'I must have done it,' she told the judge. 'No one else was there.'

Even the judge asked her to reconsider, but Tally said, 'Let's finish this,' and sentence was passed. Fifteen years, as Warren had warned. She didn't care; she was beyond caring. Her life had started to unravel with Clayton's death and had ended with Anna's. She was as dead as they were.

'And that's the story,' Tally said, taking a swallow of her now-cold coffee. 'The district attorney did not win re-election, by the way.' She looked down to see that Faith's hand was wrapped around her own, as if tethering her to the present. She looked into the girl's eyes and for a moment she knew how it might have been to be mother to an eighteen-year-old Anna. It was possible, she thought, that surrogates appeared through some cosmic mutual need. Whatever it was, Faith felt to Tally like an unexpected and very valuable gift: a daughter to stand in for the one she'd lost.

You can be my mother, Faith thought, sensing Tally's thoughts. *I want to be a daughter. I need so badly to be someone's child.*

Hay's thoughts were on the dead soldier and he recalled Tally's comment that day they'd spent together in the snow-storm. He remembered saying to her, *Those of us who did come home . . . we weren't the same.*

And she'd replied, *No. Not the same at all.*

'Maybe,' he said quietly now, 'it had something to do with Clayton's philosophy on sunshine. To me, it didn't feel as if the sun ever shone benevolently in 'Nam.' He shook his head. 'Things happened over there . . . beyond belief. It was hard to wrap your mind around the stuff that went on. And most of the guys were still teenagers. So young, too young really . . . It was like some novel of insane horror fiction, a book that just would *not* end.'

Gazing intently at Hay, Tally said, 'Clayton talked all the

time about how the sun didn't shine anymore. I couldn't make sense of what he was trying to tell me, no matter how hard I tried.'

'No one who wasn't there could *ever* make sense of the things that went on, Tally. There was no rhyme nor reason to any of it.' He took a deep breath and shook his head again. 'We ended up with thousands of dead kids and five or ten times as many wounded or eternally damaged ones. And for no real reason.'

His eyes on his hands as he rolled a fresh cigarette, he said, 'I signed up as a translator. Completely clueless.' He shook his head, a mix of disgust and bewilderment in his expression. 'My mother was French. We lived in Paris the first five years of my life,' he explained, glancing up briefly. 'My dad was head of the European arm of an American corporation. Anyway' – another shake of his head – 'I was just graduating from Princeton with a major in French and a minor in communications. I was fluent, thanks to my mother, and the military needed French-speakers in Viet Nam. The recruiters offered most of the guys in my graduating class commissions. Second lieutenant. I didn't think of it as going to war. It just seemed as if it'd be an interesting job with an impressive-sounding title.' He rolled his eyes at his youthful naivety. 'There was no limit to my ignorance.' He paused to light his cigarette, then said, 'The short version is I was captured just walking along the street in Hanoi one afternoon. They thought I was someone important because of the uniform and the insignia. Two men grabbed me, threw a burlap bag that smelled of chickens over my head and shoved me into the back of a car. I couldn't believe what was happening. And they refused to believe I had nothing of any value to tell them. So after their efforts with small hand tools failed to get them any useful information, despite my willingness to spout their propaganda or say any damn thing they wanted me to say, I got put into a "black box" for seven months.'

His eyes filled and he had to pause to pull himself together. Even all these years later, the mere thought of that box made him feel he was on the verge of death, unable to breathe or see properly. Terrifying shapes in the narrow darkness, eerie sounds in the near distance, the sense that insects were crawling over him so that he couldn't stop clawing at his skin.

He took a hard drag on his cigarette, then continued.

'After the first couple of weeks I couldn't think my way past it. I just cried all the time. Couldn't stop. Could *not* stop. Pitch black, no room to stand up. Everything got utterly distorted. Even when they let me out for an hour now and then I couldn't function. I remembered how to do things, simple things like washing myself, but it took me some time to actually do them. I could feel myself slipping away, letting go. And all the time I kept crying, on and on.

'I probably would've been in the box a lot longer, until I lost my mind altogether or until I died, but a group of relatively new POWs staged a breakout. And suddenly I was outside, able to move, and there was a bit of light again in the world. By the second day out, the tears stopped.

'The newer guys brought along the older ones who were still mobile, and we all helped carry the ones who couldn't walk; everybody helping everyone else. Somehow, amazingly, the whole group was able to cover the miles to Hanoi.

'About half of us were given honorable discharges and after getting checked out by the medical staff, we were to be shipped home. The rest of the guys were given a few weeks' R & R and then put back on active duty. I was one of the group that got discharged – for which I was then and still am now grateful to the bottom of my soul. I'd been terrified that they'd make me stay in country.

'While I was awaiting transport, all I could think about was getting home to my parents, especially my father. We were very close . . .

'Then the mail caught up to me – a big envelope stuffed with almost a year's worth. I learned in a letter from my father's lawyer that there was nothing left of home. A dryer fire set the house ablaze one winter night five months earlier, and my parents were asphyxiated in their sleep.' He gazed off into space for a long moment, then shook his head yet again and took another drag on his cigarette.

'I took a couple of downers one of the other guys en route home offered me. And for the first time in a year I slept through an entire night. It felt like a gift, beneficence. I woke up feeling physically a little stronger and mentally shredded. I started shopping among the men and by the time I was on-board the transport home, I'd amassed enough pills to help me sleep for a thousand nights.

'I went through them in less than three months,' he confessed. 'I started taking speed to stay awake and Benzos to go to sleep. Day and night got turned around. I moved out of the motel room I'd been renting and put a tent up in what used to be the back yard of our house in New Jersey, behind the ruins, amid the debris. I lived in the tent until the neighbors complained and the police started coming around to warn me. I was making a lot of noise day and night and didn't even know it. The neighbors wanted me gone but I didn't know where to go. So I stayed in the tent and tried to keep quiet – I actually put tape over my mouth. Picture it: this not very clean, grisly guy, sweating and shaking, popping pills and living in a tent. No wonder they wanted me gone. I was scaring people but nobody would come near me.

'The only one who cared was my high school friend Katie Henshaw's mother. She would check on me every few days, bring me a plate of food now and then. And one afternoon she walked down the road and sat with me on what used to be the back steps of my house. She held my hand and told me how Katie had OD'd while I was in 'Nam. Mrs Henshaw said she felt she hadn't intervened in time with Katie but she was damned if she'd stand by and watch me die in front of her. "I did all the homework and begged Katie to let me send her to The Farm up in Connecticut," she told me. "But Katie wouldn't listen. She insisted she was just *dabbling*, didn't have a real problem, she was in control of it. A couple of months later she wound up dead at a room-by-the-hour motel on Route 22 with a needle still in her arm. It's a cliché, until it's your kid," she said. "Hayward, your parents would be devastated to know you were doing this to yourself," she said. "I loved your mom and dad; they were good friends and helped me tremendously when Katie died. If you'll agree to go to The Farm, I'll drive you there myself. Please let me do this for you."

'So I agreed and she brought me here, told me to phone any time if I needed anything or just to talk. It's almost ten years later and Mrs Henshaw died of a stroke three years ago. I still miss her. Her kindness saved me and I'll never forget that.' He took a last hard drag on his cigarette and stubbed it out. 'Anyway, the thing of it is, most of the time these days, when the sun is shining, I can see it, I can feel it. I was lucky.'

'Hay,' Tally said softly, 'that black box experience. Is that why you're living in a thrown-together shack in the middle of nowhere at the top of a hill?'

'Basically, unh-hunh. If I need to be outside, I'm there instantly.'

'I'm so sorry,' she said.

'Don't be, please,' he told her. 'Things are fine. It's a working situation.'

'You know something?' Faith interjected, getting the attention of the other two. 'We are three seriously messed-up people!' she declared. 'I am *so* glad I've found you two. I thought it was always going to be just me.'

Tally and Hay just stared at her.

'Well, it's a lot easier being with you guys than being messed-up all by myself.' Faith defended her assertion, unable to stop the smile that was overtaking her face.

Hay let out a yelp of laughter. Tally put her head down on her crossed arms and laughed helplessly.

'Really!' Faith insisted. 'Why are we *laughing*? It's the truth. We've had such fucked-up experiences. Are we crazy to be sitting here, laughing?'

Lifting her head to look at this girl she'd taken instantly to her heart, Tally said, 'It *is* the truth. And we probably are crazy. I think we're laughing because the three of us are all cried out. It's time for some lightness. It doesn't mean any one of us is over the proverbial hump. But we've actually got each other to talk to. And, dear one,' she addressed Faith, 'it was the way you said it. Misery truly does love company.'

'I have to tell you,' Faith whispered. 'I'm not really an alcoholic.' She looked around furtively, as if there might be someone present she'd overlooked who would hear and report her as the imposter she was.

'Never thought you were,' Hay said. 'But I knew you had a really good reason for being here, and that's all that matters.'

Before leaving her outside her room, Tally and then Hay hugged her. Faith could still feel their arms for quite some time after she'd gone inside. As if her parents – or two people who felt parental – had at last found her.

When Hay pulled into her driveway a short time later, Tally turned to him. Her hand on his arm, she said, 'Would you like to spend the night?'

In answer, he put the truck into Park and pulled the key from the ignition.

INTERLUDE
1987

EIGHTEEN

When the telephone rang early one morning in October, Tally assumed it was either Faith or Hay. Thrown, she heard, 'Hello, Tally, it's Dad.'

'Dad! How *are* you?' Tally exclaimed. 'It's so nice to hear your voice. But how did you get my number?'

'I called Warren,' he explained. 'I've been wanting to talk to you for a very long time . . . but, well, you know.'

'I know.' She did. Her mother famously controlled the things her husband did. Tally had known since early childhood that her father had the idea – not altogether arbitrary – that Ivory would know of any unapproved actions he might take and would punish him accordingly. So he tried not to do anything to upset her. Ivory tried to control Tally too, but couldn't. Tally was defiant because she knew her mother had no feelings for her. Childhood mishaps were seen to by the housekeeper or by her father. Ivory had no interest in dealing with the messy realities of childhood. Until her grandmother explained matters, Tally couldn't make sense of her father's consistent capitulation to his demanding wife. Tally knew that her father loved her, but it was a secret between the two of them that they tacitly kept from Ivory.

'I am the bearer of news which I don't think will be particularly sad from your viewpoint,' he told her now.

'It's about Ivory, right?'

'It is. She died the day before last. I'd have called you sooner but there was a lot that needed my immediate attention, including her cremation yesterday. There was no service, no ceremony of any sort. No one would've come. She'd alienated everyone she'd ever known.'

'What happened?'

'Heart failure. Just dropped down dead in the kitchen, right at the peak of one of her typical rants while I was having a piece of toast and some coffee and reading the morning paper.

She liked to spend the night-time hours planning what she'd say. I'd become so good at blocking her out that it took me a moment or two to realize what'd happened.'

Tally's immediate thought was that one had to possess a heart in order to have it fail. But she kept that notion to herself, and said, 'I'm sorry, Dad.'

'To tell the truth, Tally, I'm not.'

'Really?'

'Really. My feelings for your mother began to change when she refused to attend your wedding. From that point on, I couldn't keep ignoring her self-centeredness and her terrible treatment of you. Our relationship was never the same from that point on. You were always a good girl, Tally. I was wrong to allow her to behave as she did, wrong not to take a stand.'

Very touched, Tally said, 'I appreciate your saying that.'

'It's the truth. I closed my eyes to her behavior out of habit. I should've been there in Nevada when you needed your family, regardless of your mother's horror at being the parent of a quote unquote murderer. I am deeply ashamed of my failings as a parent. To lose your husband and then . . . I knew you hadn't harmed your child . . . I should've ignored your mother's idiocy and your insistence that everyone stay away. You're my only child and I didn't take the initiative to support you when you were most in need. I never called your mother to task, ever, about anything. There were an awful lot of things I allowed to just slide by, unchallenged. I grant you I was weak but I was never heartless. I loved you; I was proud of you. I should've got on that plane with Warren, and been there for you.'

'Thank you, Dad. That means a lot to me.' It meant so much that she felt suddenly shaky. 'How are you managing now?' she asked tactfully, reeling from this remarkable blanket apology.

'I'm relieved,' he declared. 'I have a lot to do here but I was hoping you might be persuaded to come for a visit.'

'I don't need persuading. I would love to see you, Dad.'

'And I you. I'll be happy to put you up here at the Fairmont.'

'You're not at the house?'

'I can't *stand* that house. It was always horrible and it hasn't improved with time. I've stayed here two or three nights a week for years but I moved in bag and baggage the day your mother died. Of course she was convinced it was a "love nest." That's what she was carrying on about when she died. Anyway, I plan to sell that atrocity of a house, flocked wall-paper and all.'

She laughed softly, thinking he sounded like Annalise. 'You're full of surprises.'

'I suppose I am,' he agreed. 'I definitely feel liberated. So, will you come see me, Tally?'

'Of course I will. I'll see about flights and let you know when to expect me.'

'I hoped you'd agree,' he said, audibly pleased. 'So I made a reservation for you on a flight out of Bradley this evening. Is that too much pressure?' he asked anxiously.

'Not at all. I have a close friend who'll be happy to drive me to the airport. What time is the flight?'

He gave her the details; she made notes, then said, 'I'll see you soon, Dad.'

'Thank you, Tally. I'm so looking forward to seeing you.'

'Me, too, very much.'

As expected, Hay offered at once to drive her to the airport. 'Are you excited?' he asked.

'Actually, I am. My father sounds like a changed man. Perhaps he'll come visit sometime soon and you'll get to meet him.'

'I'd like that. I'm happy for you, Tally. I can tell this is a big moment for you.'

'It really is. It feels like a gift – for both of us. To have lived for more than forty years with my mother, he deserves a special award. To have survived with his brains not scrambled deserves an even more special award.' She laughed. 'Someday I'll tell you about my mother and how she ruled my father's life. But he sounded very chipper. I've never known him to sound that way. My grandmother said once that my mother held the keys to his psychosexual well-being.'

Hay now laughed. 'Your *grandmother* said that?'

'She did. She also said my dad was as set in his ways as a concrete patio.'

Hay chuckled appreciatively.

'She was fabulous, Hay. My grandmother was beautiful and

clever, and funny, incredibly intelligent. I still wish I could phone her up or visit her. So often she's in my dreams and I wake up feeling the loss all over again. I miss her deeply – always. She was my true family and she died too soon.'

Hay nodded. He knew how that could be.

At the gate, he put his hands on her shoulders and said, 'Call me, okay? Let me know how things are going.'

'I will,' she promised.

'And let me know when you're coming back. I'll pick you up.'

'I will,' she said again. 'Use the house if you need a shower or just want to watch TV or sleep indoors. Feel free, Hay. Oh, and please give Faith a call, fill her in. She's welcome to use the house, too, if she wants to come up.'

'Consider it done.'

Hay got to the airport early and spent forty-five minutes drinking coffee and reading a paperback novel one of the guests at The Farm had left behind. The coffee was terrible and so was the book. He kept checking the time, anxious to see Tally. It had been a long week, with a couple of brief calls from her. Without ever having discussed it, she knew how he felt, and the calls were for reassurance. She would come back; they would see each other again. He was not locked in a mental form of black box but was merely in a temporary holding pattern, entrapped only by dark imaginings that didn't want to quit.

Being separated from Tally for the first time had brought him a new, unexpected set of fears that also included Faith. After almost four years of knowing each other, all their prior constraints had been unlocked and they'd become comfortable sharing their thoughts. Together, they were safe.

They'd evolved into a family and then, suddenly, a week without both women nearby had shaken him. During the time Tally was away in San Francisco and Faith was putting in ever-increasing hours at school in New Haven, the fear of losing these women grew to unbearable proportions. He couldn't stop worrying. He kept telling himself to get a grip;

reminding himself that no amount of fretting would alter the destined course of events. But he was suddenly incapable of riding along contentedly, confident Tally and Faith would return.

For years he'd been working diligently to repair the cracks and crevices in his psyche. He knew he was unlikely ever to complete the task but during the past few years he'd given less thought to life's darker possibilities. Only occasionally had he considered how he might feel if the components of this replacement family were to be lost to him. But just a week's separation had revealed him to be vulnerable in an entirely unexpected fashion. He had temporarily lost his hard-won ability to live in the moment. During the week-long separation he found himself silently pleading with fate to be kind to him because he didn't think he could make it without the women he loved. One week on his own and he was a mess.

He positioned himself at the gate twenty minutes before the plane was due to land, taking deep breaths to stay calm while snapshots of disasters clicked on and off in his head. *Stopstopstop!* He kept closing his eyes, trying to refresh the interior landscape, trying to smooth the surfaces. Then Tally appeared at the head of the gangway and his heart surged, while a helpless smile took hold of his face. Disaster averted; life would go on. She had come back.

With a big smile, she hurried toward him, a dapper older man following in her wake. Instantly, Hay realized it was her father and his smile dimmed slightly. But no matter. His fear dissolved as she opened her arms and hugged him close. He rested his cheek against the top of her head, inhaling her subtle fragrance as his heart racketed, a frantic tattoo. Then, keeping an arm around her, he extended a hand, saying, 'Hello, sir. If you're not Tally's dad, I'm going to be very embarrassed.'

'No need. You are not wrong. Tyler Paxton,' her father introduced himself, taking hold of Hay's hand. 'I've been hearing a lot of good things about you, Hayward.'

The man had a direct clear-blue gaze, an affable manner, and a firm grip. Hay's frayed nerves began to settle. He'd worked himself into a state for no reason at all.

* * *

Tally thought her father looked remarkably youthful for a man of sixty-four. He seemed to have shed years daily since Ivory's death so that he looked like the younger brother of the man who'd met Tally at the airport in San Francisco. She couldn't help thinking how pleased Annalise would have been to know that her son hadn't been entirely taken over by his wife. In the aftermath of her death he was coming to life, displaying a sensitivity whose concealment during the years of his marriage had to have cost him dearly.

Annalise had believed her son was in sexual thrall to Ivory and at the outset – the younger man meeting the sexually sophisticated woman – that was undoubtedly true. But based on remarks her father had made in the course of the past week, it was evident that lust had long-since been supplanted by sufferance. It was Ivory's periodic but powerfully convincing threats to do away with herself should she ever lose him that had kept him tethered to her. 'It was like belonging to a cult,' he said. 'There's always the possibility that what the leaders threaten might happen actually will. The idea that I would be responsible for her death . . .' He shuddered. 'I didn't have the guts to say, 'Go ahead and do it.' Because I believed she would. I *knew* she would. She was that determined to have her way.

'So I stayed with her but was no longer available to attend her "important" dinners. Lunches were out of the question due to business commitments. It drove her wild, but I found other things to do in the evenings – primarily grabbing a bite to eat somewhere, then taking in a movie, or dining with old friends. And then she started having all sorts of plastic surgery to keep herself young-looking, but she just managed to become grotesque, her face tight and flat like a trampoline, little scars tucked under her ears, in her hairline. She was seventy-three and dressing as if she were still in her twenties.'

Tally was surprised. She'd had no idea her mother was so much older than her father.

'Now I've been freed,' he told Tally over dinner that first evening. 'I feel as if I've had some kind of oxygen infusion and can take deep breaths.' He gazed at her for several seconds, then said, 'I'm so very happy to see you. You're a gracious soul, to fly here at the drop of a hat and listen to my rantings when I've been so remiss as a parent.'

'You're my father. There's nothing gracious about wanting to see you.'

'Forgiving then,' he amended.

'I never blamed you – for anything. I always believed Ivory wasn't quite right in the head, and I wondered why you put up with her.'

'Exotic blackmail,' he said flatly. 'But it's not too late for us to have a relationship, is it?'

'I would like that very much.'

'I will try to make up for lost time,' he promised, 'and be a good father.'

The house was even more crowded than Tally remembered. She and her father went room by room, appending red stickers to the relatively few items he wished to keep. A removal company came the next day, collected the pieces and moved them into a storage facility. The house sold in three days, the new owners happily paying the full asking price (which was low by current market standards) and taking it as-is, all the furnishings included.

Tyler asked all about her new home and about Connecticut, and mentioned in passing that he'd always wanted to see the east. Tally at once invited him to travel back with her and stay for as long as he liked in one of the guest rooms.

During the flight home, she told him about her surrogate family: her replacement daughter Faith, the brilliant medical student, and about Hay, not quite sure how to define her relationship with him. 'He's gentle and generous and damaged – all three of us are. When I don't see or speak to either or both of them for a few days, I feel the loss. We three grew very close, very quickly.' Her father nodded soberly. He understood.

'I wonder often if it's the losses, the damage, that actually makes us human,' he said. 'Forgive me for paraphrasing Tolstoy,' he elaborated, 'but happy families are on the boring side. Unhappy families are difficult but with some sympathetic glue can be very –' he searched for a word, then said – 'worthwhile.'

She could only gaze at him in wonderment for a long moment. She never would have imagined he was of such a reflective bent. They were going to have to start from scratch and really get to know each other – a very gratifying idea.

Faith got on the road early on the Sunday morning after Tally's return, excited by the prospect of meeting her father. To be reunited with a parent had always been Faith's fondest wish, and if it couldn't happen for her, she was happy that it happened for Tally. Throughout the drive upstate, she tried to imagine the man. She had a well-formed mental image of Ivory based on throwaway comments Tally had made about her, and Faith had tried but failed to form any image of the sort of man who would tolerate a woman who could be so cruel to her own child.

She knew Tally wouldn't have brought him back with her unless he was unlike the heartless woman he'd married. Faith had known early on how men could be driven by their sexual needs . . . many of them reliant on children for fulfillment . . .

She punched in the rock station she'd programmed for moments when her thoughts turned in that direction, and hiked up the volume. Someday, perhaps, when she thought of her childhood experiences her stomach wouldn't go tight, with panic overtaking her brain, as she went tumbling down a black tunnel in instant turmoil.

She was a good deal calmer now than she'd been when living in the Lazarus house. And she'd be better still when her condo consisted of more than a well-outfitted kitchen and an otherwise barely furnished place with a bed for sleeping, a dining table where she ate and studied when she wasn't putting in ungodly hours at school, doubling up on courses, writing papers and reading, reading, reading. Her only concession to pleasure during the school week was a Bang & Olufsen shelf stereo system with a growing collection of classical CDs. Furniture was in the future, after she completed two more years of med school, followed by a residency, then licensure and certification. After all that, she'd be a pediatrician, finally able to hold and marvel daily over babies, satisfying a permanent-feeling, admittedly irrational desire to see baby Gracie one more time.

Her routine was interrupted about once a month when Brian insisted she take a break and come to the house for supper with the family, or when Connie phoned to say she was on her way over with food. And every few weeks, Stefan took her out to a meal or invited her to his ultra-modern condo in North Haven for a simple dinner he cooked himself. Now that he had distanced himself in every way from his parents, he'd become much more relaxed and easy-going, and he and Faith had grown close. He now played a recognizably parental role in her life, for which she was grateful. He oversaw her finances and was always available to talk – about anything, especially about the rigors of completing a BA and medical school in less than the mandated four years each. He'd done it in seven years. She was going to finish in six and a half. The residency requirements were fixed at three years. She had a lot of time still to put in and Stefan had become a welcome source of comfort and encouragement.

Tally appeared at the door incandescent, as if lit from within. And her embrace was warmer, more intense than usual. 'Leave your bag in the hall and come meet my father,' she said, towing Faith by the hand to the living room. There, her arm secure around Faith's shoulders, Tally said, 'Here she is, Dad. Here's Faith!'

Her father had the effortless good grooming of a man of taste, someone socially at ease. He came beaming across the room, and Faith stepped forward, automatically offering her hand. She felt suspended in time and space, absorbed by his eyes, actually *seen*. He said, 'How wonderful to meet you!' and bypassed her hand to embrace her. The softness of cashmere and the clean scent of citrus, the warmth of his smooth-shaven cheek against hers: a stunningly intense moment. She burst into tears. Shocked and chagrined, she wanted to apologize but couldn't speak for several seconds while Tally's father gently kept hold of her. It was an unparalleled experience, one she knew she would always remember.

At last, she stepped back from him, wiping her eyes with the back of her hand. 'I didn't know I was going to do that,' she blurted, then found herself laughing foolishly. 'It's so good to meet you,' she told the man, wanting impossibly to stay right there with him and Tally forever. He was altogether lovely, and for the briefest moment she was deeply jealous of Tally. Then, ashamed, she pushed the feeling away.

'It's good to meet *you*, little Faith,' he replied with a smile, giving her his handkerchief. 'You're even dearer than Tally said.'

'*Qu'est-ce qui se passe?*' Hay asked, wiping his hands on a dish towel as he came hurrying in from the kitchen to Faith's side.

'*Ce n'est rien,*' Faith assured him with a hug. '*Je me suis émotive pour aucune raison.*' It was true: she was emotional for some reason.

'*Es-tu sûr?*'

'*Je suis sûr.*'

'Okay. Food's almost ready, everyone. Three minutes,' he announced, and hurried back to the kitchen.

'Where did you learn your French?' Tyler asked.

'The Country Day School,' Faith answered. 'And Hay's mother was French,' she added. 'For some reason, he spoke to me in French the first time we met, without even knowing whether or not I understood. It made me like him at once.'

'I can see how that would be,' Tyler said. 'My mother, Tally's grandmother, was born in Sweden. Sadly, the only word I know, courtesy of the exquisite Annalise, is *skål*. Quite rightly she considered me something of a dunce.'

Faith laughed. 'What do you think of Connecticut so far?'

'It's splendid. The autumn colors are magnificent. I think I'd like to stay in this part of the world.'

Surprised, Tally said, 'Really?'

'If you have no objection, I'd like to find a place nearby, settle in and try to make up for lost time with you.'

'That would be wonderful,' Tally said softly. 'I would love that.'

Faith could feel herself getting choked up again and excused herself to go help Hay in the kitchen. He looked over at her and smiled. 'We're set to go,' he told her, 'if you want to grab the salad.'

'Okay, Chief.'

The family had expanded and she was rooted in its midst, taken to its heart, no longer the stolen child. Straightening her shoulders, she reached for the bowl and, smiling helplessly, carried it in to the dining room. Home.

PART THREE
MAY 2003

NINETEEN

During the years of her medical practice, Faith had heard many babies crying. But this was different. Intuitively, she knew this wasn't about hunger, or colic, or the need for a clean diaper. This was something else completely. The moment she heard the sound from the reception area an awful sense of recognition attached itself to her like the needle-toothed jaws of some savage creature.

When she finally got to the examining room, the baby was in the father's arms, struggling, red-faced and shrieking, refusing the bottle he was directing at her mouth. At once, the father struck Faith as all wrong. Plainly frustrated by his inability to deal with the baby, he was fighting for control, trying again, then again, to get the baby to take the bottle. Sweating and angry, he struggled to conceal his anger, trying to appear like a concerned parent. It was a battle and he was losing. Clearly, he had no love for this child, no essential connection to her. Even an inept but caring parent would have had more of an idea what to do for the baby. This man was not a parent.

Faith took a quick look at the chart. Having listened closely to what was going on outside during each visit to the small patients in the other examining rooms, she was aware that this baby had quieted while Fran had measured and weighed her, done her vital signs. But the moment Fran had left the room, baby Jill had resumed her screaming.

'What seems to be the problem, Mr Brown?' she asked, lifting the five-month-old out of the man's arms. Silently Faith said, *Don't be afraid, baby girl. I'll take care of you.* As if she understood the silent message, the baby clutched at her, winding one hand into Faith's hair, the other gathering a fistful of Faith's sleeve. She pushed herself tight to Faith's chest – a fear-induced prehensile response: latching on to someone who instinctively felt safe to her. Her wide blue eyes searched Faith's expression, chest heaving with sob-echoes.

Mr Brown looked irate and embarrassed, as if he wished he'd never encountered this child and was trying hard not to let it show. 'She's got a bad diaper rash,' he said, dropping exhaustedly into one of the two chairs in the room. Faith felt the heat of the baby's face as she dried her tears, and breathed in her smell of formula and stale urine, aware of Jill's sturdy heart thudding – a rhythmic signal against her breast. Messages in arterial code.

Automatically she smoothed the damp wheat-colored curls at the back of the baby's head and stroked her neck, soothing and calming her. The hiccupping baby secure in one arm, Faith filled a paper cup with water and gave it to the father, who accepted it in a kind of stunned silence. Taking note of every last thing that was happening, she turned to position the flushed, diaper-clad baby on the examining console.

'The mother couldn't make it today?' Faith asked casually, performing a quick head-to-toe visual inspection of the baby as she pulled on a pair of latex-free gloves.

'No,' he answered.

She waited for him to elaborate. He didn't.

'Let's have a look at you, sweetheart.' She smiled down at the baby, her hands smoothing the agitated arms and chest while the father noisily gulped down the water.

After removing the diaper, one look confirmed Faith's suspicions. 'There's definitely inflammation,' she said in mild understatement, reaching for a swab. The sample secured, she examined the now-compliant baby front and back, top to bottom, listened to her chest sounds, checked her ears and eyes, took a swab of the interior of her mouth, tested her reflexes, then cleaned her genitals carefully with a handful of wipes before gently applying antiseptic ointment to the baby's entire bottom. At last she got a fresh diaper from the cabinet and fastened it on before removing her gloves and tossing them into the trash can. 'Her clothes?' she asked the father, holding out one hand, the other on the baby's belly, keeping her secure. She was certain that the instant she returned Jill to him she'd start screaming again.

There was a brief pause. He gazed blankly at her for a second as if translating the request from a foreign language, then handed over the baby's garments.

'I'm giving you a prescription for some antiseptic ointment,' she told him, writing it up and handing it over to him while Jill lay contentedly on the examining table, trying to get her thumb into her mouth. 'While you're at the drugstore, get some Tylenol infant drops. Given the severity of the rash, she needs to be bathed at least once a day, preferably twice – morning and night.

'I'd like to have another look at her next Monday to see how she's doing.' Fastening Jill's soiled onesie, then fitting her chubby arms into the sleeves of a too-large sweater, she lifted the baby, for a moment allowing herself to savor the feel of her, shunted back in time to a day in a stifling, filthy van when another, somewhat older baby had slept heavily in her arms. Where was that baby now? she wondered as she did so often. Almost thirty-three years later, that baby was a grown woman, perhaps with a husband and child of her own, and no memory of the day she'd spent as a stolen child; no recollection of the small girl who'd been her self-appointed guardian. The sense-memory of baby Gracie had weight and heat, as if Faith had held her only moments before. And again, as she did intermittently, illogically, she longed to see that year-old tot once more. Then she blinked it away. The past was gone; baby Gracie was merely a memory.

'Be sure to apply the ointment after every diaper change, but take a minute to clean the area first with a wipe. Give her the drops every four hours, and make an appointment to come back in on Monday morning. Okay? I want to keep an eye on that rash. We don't want it developing into something more serious.'

Jill's eyes were fluttering closed. She was falling asleep, her head resting on Faith's shoulder. But at her father's touch, she jerked awake and started screaming again. Twisting away from the man, her arms, her entire body strained towards Faith. And it was all Faith could do not to keep hold of her. But it was imperative that she not do that, that she remain surface-calm. She wanted this man, this 'John Brown' back in the office on Monday. Nothing could be allowed to seem the least bit out of the ordinary. It was vital that he return for a second visit. She needed the intervening time to organize a workable plan with the authorities.

Wearily, he said, 'Okay,' picked up the diaper bag with his free hand, and carried the writhing, shrieking baby out to reception to make an appointment.

The instant the door closed behind him, Faith grabbed the phone and spoke to Liz in reception. 'Give Brown whatever time he wants,' she said. 'No matter how many other bookings there are, just give him an appointment.'

Faith put the receiver down and closed her eyes for a few seconds, heart racketing, blood pressure spiking. Then after a few deep calming breaths, she noticed the forgotten baby bottle. She used a tissue to pick up both the bottle and the empty paper cup by their bottoms and deposited them in separate sterile bags. She also salvaged the used diaper from the bin.

Back in her office, she wrote up orders for the swabs and the diaper, and had Fran come in to take care of arranging rush lab service for the samples, before finally putting in a call to Brian – now Chief Kirlane.

It wasn't by any means the first call she'd made to him over the years to report child abuse of one form or another. But this was the most serious instance and therefore the most in need of urgent intervention.

He listened closely, instructed her to send the bottle and cup by courier to the police lab, then asked her to swing by the station after she closed up shop for the day. 'Let's get right on this,' he said. 'I'll order in some Chinese with your favorite mu-shu pork and we can eat while we go over the details.'

It was sometimes hard to believe that so much time had gone by but Faith was reminded of it every time she saw Brian. Now a sixty-two-year-old widower and the grandfather of Lucia's sweet but rowdy nine-year-old twin boys, he was taking retirement at the end of the year. He didn't want to leave the force but after four years of coming to terms with Jan's death – coping with the sorrow, the shocking inner emptiness created by her absence – he'd met Leila, a widow and kindred soul, at his support group. They'd been dating for almost a year and he felt it was time to move the relationship to another level so that he might enjoy whatever time was left to him in

her company. The sudden loss of Jan to a heart attack had
made him hyper-aware of how quickly things could change.

His blond hair had turned completely white, his blue eyes
were still clear, still direct; his symmetrical features had
softened with time but he remained a singularly beautiful man.

'What will I do without you? Who will I call when something like this arises?' Faith asked him that evening.

'Don't you worry about it,' he said. 'I've started grooming
a smart young detective to be your go-to guy. He's better than
smart: he's intuitive and great with kids. You perform an important service, Faith. I'm not about to let that just slip away.'

Reassured, she gave him a rundown on the Browns.

After describing the office visit and the condition of the
baby, she said, 'There's no woman in evidence, and I don't
think this child is related to him, which is why I asked you
to have your lab do fingerprints, DNA and blood-typing from
the samples. I'm positive the baby's oral swab results will
have nothing in common with his. I'm just praying that the
genital swab won't indicate any serious STD but I don't think
that's going to be the case.'

She went silent, looking down at her hands, trying – again,
again, always – to comprehend the sick need grown men had
to force themselves on helpless babies, little toddlers. What
sort of need for power could be satisfied by dominating
someone so small, so utterly defenseless? When she considered
what the evidence indicated had been done to this baby rage
all but overwhelmed her. It was only with concerted effort that
she could battle down her anger and retain control. She needed
to keep her wits about her.

She wanted baby Jill to go forward into the future with no
permanent damage from what had been done to her, and no
memory of the experience – unlike the little girl who'd been
called Humaby, whose nights were occasionally galleries of
horrors that forced her into trembling wakefulness. Unlike the
woman who'd been called Faith, whose body had been emptied
of its diseased reproductive organs, Jill might grow into
womanhood able to give herself freely to someone she found
attractive. She wouldn't wake up the next morning, sick with
self-loathing. She wouldn't waste several years talking to

therapists who couldn't comprehend the experiences that had shaped her, primarily at the hands of a family of psychiatrists who'd infected her with a viral case of shame. Ultimately, she'd abandoned therapy in favor of meditation, and the shame was now at a distance. She had, at last, accepted the reality of her innocence. None of it had been her fault.

'Did you read that piece in the *Times* a couple of months ago?' she asked him. 'It was about the New Jersey state Division of Youth and Family Services searching for eighty children missing from care. The governor has ordered them to search for almost three hundred kids, Brian. *Three hundred!* I just read an article about more kids missing in Florida. We trust the system to look after children taken into care and they *lose* them! All over the country, state agencies have no idea of the whereabouts of kids they've taken into the system. It's scary, but it could work for us.'

'It's bad, and yes it could,' he agreed.

'I have to do what's right for baby Jill. I'm going to rescue her if it's the last thing I do,' she vowed, her eyes on Brian's. 'But putting her into the hands of DCF . . .' She shivered and closed her eyes for a moment.

'I will help you,' Brian promised. 'And we'll make damned good and sure that all the i's are dotted and the t's get crossed. If it's the last thing I do, I will make sure nothing goes wrong. This baby will not wind up in the system.'

'Thank you,' she said softly.

Tally sat on her heels and surveyed the garden, deeply satisfied by its perfection. The weeds vanquished for the moment, the soil dark, rich, and moist around the flowers in the large, irregularly shaped bed that curved from the front porch around to the rear of the house. Her first summer in residence, she'd planted bushes alongside the driveway, with lilies of the valley hiding among the hostas on the near side of the property that came right up to the boxwoods rimming the porch.

Having spent her early years in San Francisco where expansive gardens were all but non-existent, broken by long stretches of time spent with her grandmother in Nevada where plantings consisted primarily of succulents, she loved the wild-seeming arrangement of flowers in the big bed. The outrageous shapes and colors – the bluebells and wild anemones, hollyhocks and trilliums, bleeding heart and jacob's ladder – constituted a glorious riot that cheered her even in dreary wet weather. Keeping her garden weeded, watered and nourished gave her a pleasure so intense it felt slightly illicit.

The vegetable patch at the back of the house provided a different sort of pleasure. It also produced far more food than she could consume. So, from the beginning she'd taken to giving Hay the overages for The Farm. And when he'd become head chef almost twelve years earlier, he began creating dishes that were very well received: lightly steamed, still-crisp green beans mixed with Reggiano parmesan and slivers of red onion in virgin olive oil; sautéed tomatoes, fresh basil leaves and walnuts with a splash of balsamic vinegar; a warm new potato salad with bits of crisp bacon, fresh dill and home-made mayonnaise; grilled coins of zucchini with a hint of garlic, topped with a sprinkling of home-made vinaigrette; leaf salads of different varieties with custom dressings. The food was frequently mentioned as one of the attractions of The Farm, now officially a rehab of renown.

Tally was always the first to taste the recipes he created, and she'd taken to noting the details of their preparation in a notebook she kept solely for that purpose, and taking photographs of the final products. And although Hay couldn't believe it would ever come to fruition, she was more than halfway through the creation of a cookbook that would, when completed, bear his name.

She acquired a digital camera and spent the winter that year he became head chef going to twice-weekly classes on Photoshop and page layout up in Great Barrington. She got into the habit of taking advantage of the long drive to stop on her way home at Guido's for exotic cheeses, out-of-season imported vegetables, and fresh fish or local meat or free-range chicken. A couple of nights a week, Hay would turn The Farm kitchen over to his sous-chefs and head home to Tally's to prepare dinner for the two of them. And on weekends, except for the Saturday night roast-beef commitment, they usually invited Tyler and Mae to join them for a meal and Faith, too, if she was available.

Tyler had been captivated by the elegant redhead on sight, when Tally had taken him to dinner at Chez Mae a few days after they'd flown home together from the west coast. He'd stayed at the bed-and-breakfast for several months while he looked at houses. And with typical wit, Mae had observed over breakfast one morning that winter, 'It's a good thing there's only you and Tally. This could get to be an expensive tradition, family members staying here for months while they shop around for houses and then get them fixed up. Mind you, I do enjoy the company. There's rarely more than a few nights booked in the winter, except for an occasional couple or two visiting someone at The Farm. The rest of the time, I'm rattling around in here thinking it's about time for me to sell up. I'm getting too old to be up at five thirty in the morning to make breakfast for guests and then somehow manage to hold a conversation while it gets eaten. I'm naturally inclined to be on the surly side first thing in the morning.'

'I haven't noticed that. But don't say a word if you don't feel like it,' Tyler had said with a smile. 'I will just enjoy looking at you.'

'You're awfully good for a gal's ego, I must say.'

She had finally sold the big six-bedroom house a few years earlier to an enthusiastic young couple who didn't have a clue about how much work was involved in running a B and B, and she agreed to move with Tyler into the charming little house he'd bought just beyond Kent Falls. They were a fine match, comfortable, conversational and warm. With good-hearted, expansive Mae at his side, Tyler's long-stunted growth accelerated and he caught up with the man Tally believed he'd always been meant to be. She and her father almost never spoke of his deceased wife, but when he did, Tyler always referred to her as 'the late, unlamented Ivory.'

On her knees admiring the garden, Tally realized she was happy. She liked her life. Her father and the wonderful Mae were only a few miles away. There were shopkeepers, people in town who knew her by sight and greeted her warmly. Hay and Faith were fixtures in her life. Via computer she kept in touch with former warden Donna Hughes who'd retired to Las Cruces with her sister and bred Basenjis; with Warren and

Alexis, now living in a villa in Mexico to which they were always inviting her; and sometimes by email with Faith when her schedule had her on the run and prevented her from visiting for a week or two.

Tally's world was far less fraught than it had been when she was young and her primary source of love and consolation had been with her grandmother at the ranch. Shockingly, she was now four years older than Annalise had been when she'd died. Twenty years before, when Warden Hughes had told her not to look back, Tally would never have believed she'd get to be fifty-seven years old and actually content with her life. When she'd left Warren at the airport and got behind the wheel of that Mercedes, nothing seemed to matter – especially not her life. She'd felt as if she were headed to the end of the universe and would simply drive right off the edge when she got to it. Instead, because of an oddly designed highway and dreadful traffic, she drove into Connecticut. And here she still was, with people she loved, whose entrance into her life and ongoing presence had redeemed her.

The telephone rang and with a last admiring look at the garden, she got up to go inside to answer. Mental note: buy a cell phone. She hated the idea of appearing to be one of those people who seemed congenitally unable to be separated from their little phones, but it was absurd to have to drop whatever she was doing and hurry inside to answer every time the telephone rang.

TWENTY

'The house is a furnished rental,' Brian was saying early Monday morning over the remains of breakfast in a restaurant close to Faith's office. 'According to the landlord, who let us in while Brown was out, the guy's only been there a couple of months. Brown said the mother had died in childbirth. So, naturally, the landlord felt sorry for the guy and he didn't check Brown's references the way he normally would have, especially with somebody calling himself *John Brown*. He figured a widower with a baby, why give him a hard time over what was probably his real name? So Mr Brown moved in with the baby and not a whole lot else.

'Four of us exercised the search warrant and discovered that Mr Brown has a little soundproofed "studio" in the basement where he can broadcast his activities to order, live online. I'm not going to go into the details of what we found down there. It'd turn your stomach. Once we take this creep tomorrow, everything's going to be confiscated, and the Feds will keep the Internet connection live while they try to track down the subscribers to Mr Brown's pay-to-view site and any other persons of interest.' Brian rolled his eyes and blew out his breath, then took a swallow of his coffee.

'Not the sharpest knife in the drawer, given all the incriminating stuff we found,' he continued. 'I'm kind of amazed he's managed to get by for as long as he has, because little Jill is not the first baby he's apparently had in his possession. Based on what we found, she's only the most recent of possibly three infants, maybe more. We didn't have much time to go through the place thoroughly but we did come up with more than enough to send this guy away for a minimum of twenty-five years without parole. With multiple counts of crimes against children, he'll probably get a few hundred years, which means life. We don't want to spook him into going on the run, so a lot of stuff was photographed but nothing was moved and nobody's going near him until he brings the baby back in this morning for her appointment. Everything's set.'

'I'm so nervous, Brian. What if he doesn't show?'

'We've got his plate number from the landlord. If Mr Brown doesn't keep his appointment we'll allow him fifteen minutes' leeway before we issue an Amber Alert for the missing baby. If we have to, we've got a judge on standby who'll declare her a ward of the court to legitimize our issuing the alert. Brown won't get far. One way or another, he's going down. Easier and faster if he shows up.'

'What do you think happened to the other babies?' she asked, jittery and chilled.

'We'll try to find out but there's almost nothing to go on. Most of what we found was photos and videotapes. There wasn't much of anything on baby Jill; just a couple of circled names in an address book with arrows pointing to the word "baby" in another circle. One's a woman in West Virginia with a long sheet for drug offenses who's definitely of interest and another one, similar profile, in Pennsylvania. At first glance, it looks as if Mr Brown is in the business of buying babies for cash from addicts, which seems to be the case with Jill. No birth certificate, no records except a recent inoculation card but with a different baby's name, from a doctor in Virginia. Indicators pointing all over the map. We'll be talking to that Virginia doctor this morning, to see if he has anything to provide us with DNA.'

Faith listened, wondering how Brown had come to bring the baby to her. She couldn't help thinking it was purely a random choice but, with luck, if their plan worked, one that would be of significant value to Jill in the long term.

'Every single item of the baby's stuff is pre-used,' Brian was saying. 'The clothes are a mishmash of shapes and sizes. Everything's old and pretty beat-up, quick grabs from the Goodwill or Sally Ann. No crib. She sleeps in an old Pack 'n Play.' He made a face and took another swallow of his coffee. 'He's set up to hit the road on very short notice. We got an ID on his prints right away, but it's going to be a while before we get results on his DNA samples. The good part is there are wants out on him, so the arrest is a sure thing. The bad part is they're mostly for out-of-state traffic violations, the most serious being a charge of reckless driving, doing seventy-seven in a thirty-five residential zone. The rest are a boatload of unpaid parking tickets and two lesser speeding citations. Still, combined, it's enough to bring him in and hold him 'til we get all the results back from the lab.'

Every extra bit of detail he provided, combined with the smell of her uneaten scrambled eggs, added to the cramping in her belly and the headache gathering strength at the back of her neck. She could too easily visualize the squalor in which baby Jill was being kept. And she could feel again the grit of the garbage caking the thin layer of carpet beneath her bare feet, could almost smell the funk of dirty bodies. Her fingers knew every inch of the interior of that van; her nose knew the reek of the mound of unwashed laundry that was her bed. She could hear the tinny music that played night and day on the portable radio taped to the dashboard. And suddenly, arbitrarily, she remembered the time the interior of the van went silent and Wolf looked everywhere but couldn't find any batteries.

Without warning, Toadman's fist shot out and smashed into Wolf's face. A thin whining noise emerged from his mouth as his hands tented over his nose. "GO INTO THAT 7-ELEVEN OVER THERE AND BUY SOME FUCKIN' BATTERIES!" Toadman screamed. Reaching past Wolf, he threw open the passenger door and shoved Wolf out into the road. Scared Toadman might hit her too, Humaby crawled under the pile of laundry at the back of the van and curled into a knot, hoping they'd forget she was there. She concentrated so hard on not making any sound that she fell asleep. When she awakened the radio was playing again and they were driving on a highway, Wolf and Toadman talking as if nothing had happened. A big Band-Aid ran across Wolf's swollen nose; his eyes all red-purple.

Brian had long ago told her that during their interrogations, neither of the men could remember where they were when they snatched the baby they called Humaby. They thought it could've been California, or maybe Louisiana, but it might've been Indiana. And they thought she was maybe two years old when they took her. They'd had her for three years. Both men were consistent on that point, especially Wolf because he'd just turned fourteen when he saw Toadman come running back to the van carrying the baby.

Toadman got sentenced to five hundred and twenty-seven years in prison for a hundred and twenty-one counts of kidnapping, false imprisonment, lewd conduct, sodomy, rape, oral copulation and assault. Wolf hadn't been as crazy and dangerous as Toadman. Sometimes when Toadman wasn't around Wolf had talked to her, told her things, like how to be polite to people and call them Miss and Mister, and the names of things like TV sets or tractor-trailers or food like pizza or burgers, and not to be scared of policemen. Wolf never hurt her the way Toadman did and if Toadman said she was bad and didn't give her any food, Wolf would sometimes sneak some to her when Toadman wasn't looking. If Toadman burned her with cigarettes, Wolf would take an ice cube out of his cup of Coke, wrap it in a napkin and show her how to hold it on the burn. And because Toadman had kidnapped Wolf, too, when he was seven years old, Wolf's original sentence of a hundred and ten years was reduced to twenty-five. He served eleven years before being paroled in 1985. After completing his parole, he vanished.

'The Lazarus parents never stopped bemoaning the fact that I didn't attend the trial,' she said quietly. 'Did I ever tell you that?'

'I'm pretty sure you did.' Brian made a face.

'I was recuperating from surgery,' she reminded him, 'and his parents actually tried to persuade Stefan to take me to court. But Monica said she'd report him to the police for child endangerment if he did that. I never saw her so angry, before or after.'

'She did phone the chief,' Brian told her. 'He promised her he'd arrest every one of them if they brought you anywhere near the courtroom.'

'I didn't know that. She was sweet, Monica.'

'She cared about you.'

'I know.' She was silent for a moment, then said, 'They were furious that I never saw the tapes or photographs so they couldn't get my reactions to any of that.'

'Jesus! What the hell was *wrong* with those people?'

'They were heartless,' she said flatly. 'They never for a moment let me forget a bit of it. They made me feel as if everything that happened to me was my own fault; they made me wish I was dead. And Stefan didn't help me until I staged a scene he couldn't ignore so I could escape from that over-decorated house of horrors. He's come a long way in the past twenty years, once he also got away from his parents. He's recognizably human since he gave up his practice and began teaching. I've audited a couple of his personality study classes and he's actually a great teacher.'

'Good to know that,' Brian said neutrally, never a fan of Stefan Lazarus. 'As for that other stuff, the captain and I made sure no one would ever see any of that evidence. After the case was closed, he and I took all of it down to the basement at the station house and put it into the furnace. Probably broke a dozen laws but we knew there was no chance of an appeal for that Toadman scum. So now,' he said, following the course of her thinking, 'once we take Mr So-called Brown into custody and see to it that he gets put away for a good long time, we'll burn every last bit of media in his possession. We won't be able to do anything about the stuff that's already out there: the Web and hard-core kiddy porn purveyors, but no one will ever know who that baby was. We'll do everything we can to protect little Jill.'

'She has Chlamydia,' she told him. 'Also symptoms of thrush. This baby is in a lot of pain. She needs treatment, and soon.'

'That means Brown is a walking disease factory.'

'At the very least,' Faith said angrily. 'I want him dead.' She vented her feelings and then, as had only happened a few times in her life, she broke into tears. Chagrined at this display of weakness, she pulled a tissue from her pocket and wiped her eyes. 'I'm sorry, Brian.'

'Don't be, honey. There's no shame in tears.'

'I'm a wreck,' she told him. 'My hands won't stop shaking and I've got a headache the size of Rhode Island.'

He chuckled and reached across to place his hand over hers. 'I love you to pieces, kiddo. I loved you the first minute I saw you.'

'I love you too, Brian. You and Jan and Lucia were the first real family I ever knew. Promise me nothing will go wrong, that our plan is solid.'

'I promise.'

Because she knew she'd be too nervous and distracted to pay proper attention to her patients, she asked Liz to cancel and rebook two-thirds of the morning's appointments and space out the others. Faith then told her that Mr Brown and baby Jill, the ten forty-five appointment, weren't to be kept waiting but shown immediately into Room One.

The only member of her staff who had any idea that something was going on was Fran, her pediatric nurse. Faith had told her there was going to be a police presence in Room Three, the biggest of the examining rooms, and that whatever she was doing when the Browns arrived, she was to drop everything and go to Room One.

'Start getting the baby prepped for a typical follow-up exam. I'll be in sooner than usual and if you've left patients waiting, head back to whichever one has priority. And, finally, no matter what happens, keep everyone inside the examining rooms until you get the all clear.'

'Okey-dokey,' Fran said with typical placidity. 'I'll be waiting on tenterhooks to hear what this is all about, although I've got a pretty good idea.'

'Thank you, Franny. We will talk. You have my word,' Faith promised a bit breathlessly, then took a minute in her office to try to calm down before heading out to see her first patient.

Her thoughts were scattered, fraught with scenarios of disaster, and she had to keep dragging herself into the moment to deal with her first appointment – a fortunately routine check-up of a one-year-old. It was hard to focus. Her brain, like a willful toddler, kept darting into mental traffic, forcing her to follow at top speed to retrieve it. By the conclusion of the visit she was overheated, perspiring heavily. And in defiance of the two Excedrin Migraine tablets she'd taken upon arriving at the office, the morning's headache had returned full force. Her vision was intermittently foggy, her ears ached, and nausea kept threatening to overturn her stomach.

Baby Jill's screams announced their arrival. Liz phoned on the intercom just as Faith's second appointment finished, to announce that Mr Brown and his baby were being directed to Room One by Judy, the second receptionist. Faith went to her office and gulped some Pepto-Bismol right from the bottle, wiped her damp hands on her lab coat, then went across the hall to open the door to Room Three and whisper, 'They're here and just heading into Room One.'

Brian gave her a thumbs up and Faith closed the door and started down the hall with shaky legs and knees that felt as if they were going to give out at any moment. She was suddenly a poorly made puppet with tangled strings. Her pulse was in overdrive and she had to pause for a moment, trying to slow her breathing before putting her damp hand on the doorknob.

Baby Jill was on the examining shelf in her diaper and, as arranged, Fran went back to her other patient. Faith had to restrain herself from instantly snatching up the baby. Instead, she placed the flat of her hand on Jill's belly and smiled down at her. 'How is the rash looking?' she asked, glancing briefly over her shoulder at the harried-looking Mr Brown.

'I don't know,' he answered. 'I guess it's a bit better.'

'Well, let's have a look,' Faith said, removing the diaper as the baby's eyes tracked her every move. Time seemed to have shifted into a kind of slow-motion as Faith took in the thick coating of ointment that concealed much of the baby's bottom. She wondered if it was intended to conceal the evidence of his continued abuse or if he was just inept. She carefully phrased a question and opened her mouth to speak when the door was suddenly flung open with force that sent it crashing against the inside wall. The baby was startled into noisy tears as two men in suits, an officer in uniform and Brian all pushed into the room, with Brian closing the door behind him.

All in a matter of seconds, Faith lifted the baby into her arms and held her close, one hand stroking the baby's spine as Brown shot to his feet in instant panic, exclaiming, 'What the fuck?!'

The first of the suited men started reciting a list of charges with the word interstate repeated several times, then the second man followed up with a Miranda warning as the uniformed officer spun the man around and closed a pair of cuffs around his wrists behind his back in one well-practiced move. 'It was you!' he accused Faith, livid. 'You called the fuckin' law on me? You did and I'll kill you.'

'Uttering death threats,' the first suit said. 'That's another charge.'

'*Get fucked!*' Brown raged.

'That's enough of that,' Brian said in a low warning voice. 'You're in a place filled with children.'

'YOU'RE DEAD, BITCH!' Brown shouted. Then, catching everyone off guard, he kicked out and connected brutally with Faith's shin. Faith flinched, gasping with pain, her hold on the baby automatically tightening. A rocket of fire spread up her leg, turning her breathing jagged, causing her eyes to flutter closed for a second or two. The uniformed officer clamped one hand over Brown's mouth, squeezing hard; with the other he gave the cuffs a ferocious twist so that they bit sharply into the flesh beneath. Lifting Brown so that his back bowed, the policeman frogmarched him out of the room. Shamefaced, the two other men followed murmuring almost inaudible apologies, leaving the door open. The baby kept screaming, her body vibrating inside Faith's arms, as if she could feel Faith's pain. The terrified cries, the trembling was almost an exact duplication of baby Gracie's anguish so many years before. Faith's hand curved over the back of Jill's skull, holding her even closer. How was it possible to live through an experience like this twice? She stood, swaying back and forth, working to calm the baby, trying to keep her weight off the injured leg.

Brian watched Faith for several seconds, then said in a low, confidential voice, 'I am so sorry about that. Are you okay?'

Faith nodded, knowing there was going to be a dreadful bruise on her leg.

'We're going to have to take the baby, Doctor,' he then said in a normal tone of voice meant to be overheard. 'Someone from DCF is on the way and should be here any moment. You might want to get the baby dressed.'

Faith went rigid. Baby Jill's cries were subsiding and she was clutching a handful of Faith's hair with her eyes now on

Brian, who picked up a onesie from the visitor's chair and held it out to Faith.

'Get her dressed,' he said quietly.

'*God,*' she whispered, her hands unsteady as she returned Jill to the console and reached for a diaper. She took a moment to wipe off some of the excess ointment, then fastened on the diaper. '*God, God,*' she murmured, her coordination gone, her breathing shallow. She felt small and inadequate, hating the overpowering *déjà vu* sense she had of history repeating itself. Despite knowing in advance what was going to happen, she hadn't expected to feel the way she did.

The onesie on, she grabbed some tissues to wipe the wide smear of ointment from her lab coat, then again lifted the baby into her arms. Her eyes closing automatically, she let her cheek rest against the top of the baby's head. Jill's fingers again wound into Faith's hair. Her heart pushing hard against Faith's breast, she emitted a mournful keening that razored away at Faith's emotions, eliciting a reciprocal sorrow. She couldn't bear to let the baby go but Brian said quietly, 'It's time, Dr Lazarus,' and Faith lifted her head to see a tall, sober-suited, middle-aged woman with skinned-back hair standing just inside the room, her arms outstretched to take Jill. 'Please, just one more minute.' Her hold on the baby tightened. 'One more minute.'

'I'm sorry but I have to take her,' the woman said kindly with a slight smile. 'She'll be well looked after.'

Faith kissed the baby's cheek and forehead, then held her close again as she uttered shushing sounds against her ear. At last, Faith lifted her into the waiting woman's outstretched arms.

Without another word, the woman turned and carried the still crying baby away. Brian quietly closed the door after her.

'Brian, that was terrible.'

'Close up shop for the day, honey, and go home. We'll talk later.' He opened the door again and, nodding dumbly, Faith followed him into the hall where she stopped and watched him go out the door. She stood for what felt like a long time, until she realized the staff were all watching her, waiting for some sort of signal.

Pulling herself together, she said to Liz, 'Cancel the rest of the appointments, please, and rebook them, then send all the patients home. Refer any emergencies to Dr DeCastro and leave an emergency notice on the answering machine. I'm going home. I'll be back in the morning and will explain then what just happened. Thank you all . . .' She couldn't get another word out and went to her office where she dumped her lab coat, grabbed her bag and started for the door, her leg throbbing.

Fran came out from behind the reception desk and went out to the parking lot with Faith, where she stopped in front of her and looked deeply into her eyes. 'I want you to know you're my hero,' Fran said. 'It's an honor to work with you, to know you. What you just did . . .' She shook her head wonderingly. 'As I said, you're my hero.' She hugged Faith, then said, 'Go home, have yourself a drink and get some rest. We'll see you in the morning.'

Faith returned the hug, gave her a watery smile, then went to her car where she sat staring into space for several minutes, her attention divided between the pain pulsing in her leg and what had just occurred. At last, she turned the ignition key, reversed out of the lot and started for home.

JUNE 2003

TWENTY-ONE

F aith was running a little late; her schedule had been thrown off track by a toddler's need for some sutures to a fairly deep cut on the palm of his hand as a result of a playground fall on a piece of broken glass which, all agreed, shouldn't have been there. The mother was on the verge of hysteria, wringing her hands and barely able to sit still, but the boy was composed, watching every step of the procedure with fascination.

'You might just have a future doctor here,' she told the anxious mother as Faith snipped the thread and applied a bandage. 'Keep this covered and try not to get it wet for the next forty-eight hours. Apply antibiotic ointment twice a day, and after the first forty-eight hours, it'll be safe to get it wet. A few days and you can remove the bandage. Bring him back in two weeks and we'll remove the sutures.'

Lifting the child from the examining console, she squatted down to be eye-to-eye with him and said, 'You're a superstar, Cole,' at which the boy beamed. He was one of her regular patients, a lovely child.

'Yeah!' Grinning, he gave her a high five.

'Take good care of your hand, okay, Cole? If your bandage gets dirty, ask mama to change it. Okay?'

''Kay.'

'See you in two weeks,' she said, rising.

'Yeah!' he said again, still beaming as his mother, so distraught she couldn't speak, took hold of his other hand and led him out.

Now, Faith had to concentrate on not speeding. She hated being late for anything. And being late today was unacceptable. Nervous and excited, her hands were slick on the wheel. Luckily, being late meant the traffic flowed well on Route 7 and she made good time up to Kent.

There were a lot of cars parked out front but a spot had been left for her in the driveway. She took a quick appreciative glance at the exquisite garden, checked once again that the documents were in her bag, then hurried out of the car, up the stairs and across the porch. Music and giddy-sounding conversation flowed from the open windows. Utterly elated, Faith pushed open the screen door and gazed at the crowd assembled inside.

Everyone she loved was present: Brian and Lucia, Captain Garvey, Connie and Stefan, Tally and Hay, Tyler and Mae, and Fran from the office.

Catching sight of Faith in the doorway, Tally scooped up the baby from where she'd been sitting on the floor with Hay and Lucia, and came dancing across the room as those gathered went silent with expectation. 'Look,' Tally said to the baby. 'Who's here?'

'Mama!' the baby declared in her surprising low voice, holding her arms out to Faith.

Tally gave Faith a kiss and a one-armed hug as she passed over the baby. 'We were starting to get a bit worried,' she said quietly, touching her hand to Faith's cheek.

'We had a toddler emergency. Sorry.'

'Hush. No need to apologize. We're all just glad you're here.'

'I love you, Tally.' Faith absorbed the woman's beauty, marveling as always that they'd been lucky enough to find each other.

'Love you, too, sweetheart. You've given me back most of what I lost in my life.'

Hay came over to say, 'Food's about ready,' and leaned in to whisper. 'Little Miss ate some solid food today. A bowl of stuff that smelled like a houseful of bad plumbing.'

Faith roared with laughter and stood on tiptoe to plant a kiss on his smooth-shaven cheek. 'Hilarious,' she said, thinking as always how much younger he looked without the beard. 'When did you become so funny?'

'Probably around the same time I had to start finding ways to entertain Little Miss.'

'I love it!'

'How could you not?' he said wryly. And she had to wonder

at the people they'd all become, suddenly filled with a euphoric sense of homecoming. For the first time in her life, she had more answers than questions.

Faith let her bag drop to the floor as she took hold of the baby and swung her up into the air. Then, she lowered her to ride on her hip where the baby immediately began toying with Faith's crystal pendant. She watched the baby for a moment, then looked around at all the smiling faces and said, 'It's official! Thanks to everyone here – especially Uncle Brian, the clever police chief who got the Feds involved to remove the case from our jurisdiction, and Tally, who was brilliant in her performance as a social worker from DCF – as of three weeks ago we welcomed a brand-new family member into the world. She has a social security number and a birth certificate. She also has an extended family right here in this room: aunts and uncles, Granna Tally and Granpa Hay, and Greatgranpa Tyler. And we have all the paperwork to prove her existence, thanks to Aunt Fran's skills with research and creative form-filling to establish the baby's birth.' She drew a deep breath, considering her wonderful good fortune at having such brave and special people in her life. Then she continued.

'Our girl's kind of on the tall side for being not yet a month old, but that'll pass. And soon no one will think anything of her size, because thanks to Wonder Bread and food additives or farm-grown fish, or *something*, children are getting bigger every year. I love you all dearly. Thank you for helping me do this and for being who you are.'

Before anyone could react, Tyler said, 'We all love you, darling girl. And thank you for being who *you* are.'

Spontaneously, everyone applauded.

The baby held very still and looked around, uncertain.

Hay turned down the volume on the stereo and the group began singing 'Happy Birthday.'

'It's okay, Gracie.' Faith smiled down at her. 'It's your birthday party and we're all very happy.'

The baby's hand released the pendant and started waving to the music. Then, she sang, 'Ha-me!' head bobbing, body bouncing up and down. 'Ha-me.'

Acknowledgments

Many thanks to the following librarians in Connecticut: the reference desk in Darien; Judy Riva, Susanna Violino and Vicky Lucarelli in Norwalk, and Anne Killheffer in Stratford. These women were incredibly helpful in tracking down a number of rare articles that pertained to the 1982 kidnapping of a two-year-old – a case that haunted me for years and ultimately inspired the creation of Humaby/Faith.

The second case involved the daughter of a dear friend who spent a number of years in prison for second-degree murder in the death of her six-week-old son. I embellished the tale and altered it but, again, I was haunted by the case which led to the creation of Tally.

My thanks to Randall Toye. His enthusiasm for the early manuscript encouraged me to keep on with it. And finally I am grateful to Duke Fenady and Nina Ring Aamundsen who each read the manuscript in the editing stage and gave much-needed and most welcome feedback.

About the Author

New York Times bestselling author Charlotte Vale-Allen worked (among other things) as a sales person, a waitress, a secretary, an insurance broker, and as an actress and singer before turning to writing full-time with the publication of her first novel *Love Life* in 1976. Born in Toronto, Canada, Vale-Allen moved to the U.S. in 1966. The mother of an adult daughter and grandmother of twins, she has lived in Connecticut since 1970. Her award-winning autobiography (and only non-fiction work) *Daddy's Girl* is in its third edition, after more than thirty printings. Please visit the author's website at: www.charlottevaleallen.com

WHERE IS THE BABY?

A Selection of Recent Titles by Charlotte Vale-Allen

CHASING RAINBOWS
DREAMING IN COLOR
CLAUDIA'S SHADOW
MOOD INDIGO
PARTING GIFTS
GRACE NOTES
FRESH AIR
SUDDEN MOVES

Non-Fiction

DADDY'S GIRL